Dedicated to Morris dancers, Bus drivers & conductors, Police officers, Teachers, Shop owners, Students, Actors, Artists, Gamblers, Couples, Scientists and so on everywhere...

...whether or not they take their traditions, their jobs or themselves seriously.

BLACK JOKE OMNIBUS
Hell's Bells Unleashed!

-o-o-o-

-o-o-o-

BLACK JOKE OMNIBUS
Hell's Bells Unleashed!

Chapter One

Saturday Night

Three pairs of boots tread the hoar-frosted grass that leads them to the eaves of Pockbury woods in the south-western hinterland of Oxfordshire. It's just after midnight, as Sunday takes over its regular shift from Saturday night. The moon is just past the full and throws out eerie shadows fleeing into the trees ahead of the trespassers. Here in early January, under a thin Cotswold night, the interlopers step onto a deep bed of last year's leaves and shuffle their sound beneath the woodland canopy.

"Well, Constable Fielding," declares Detective Chief Inspector Hector Parrott, "so this is what dedication to the force is about."

"What's that, sir? Being called out on a cold winter's night, away from the missus an' all?"

"No, Fielding. Being called out to investigate a report of a mouldy old corpse."

"Right you are, sir. But I'd have thought you'd have brought out Sergeant Bumble tonight, sir. *He's* the one with authority on a case like this."

"Haven't you heard, Fielding?" says Parrott, whispering to prevent the other member of their little trekking party from overhearing. "I should have explained. *Buzzy* Bumble has gone off on extended sick leave. Officially it's a stress related absence, but between you and me I've heard that he's gone off his rocker. *You're* going to be a bit busier for the time being I'm afraid... probably almost as busy as me."

"Oh dear," says P.C. Fielding, more out of surprise at his new apparent responsibilities than in sympathy for Sergeant Bumble.

"Now then, Mr. Stotesbury," says Parrott. "Lead on to the cadaver if you will. How far is it from here?"

"About a half furlong as the dog flies, inspector. You see Twinkle, my Rottweiler, dashed off and made a beeline for a scent he seemed to have picked up. Look ahead, Mr. Parrott. You can see the trail where we disturbed the dead leaves. It's over there... on beyond that hazel brake."

"*D.C.I.* Parrott, if you please, Mr. Stotesbury."

"Sorry, Chief Inspector. Perhaps you'd call me *Professor* Stotesbury then?"

"Sorry, professor. Professor of what?"

"No, nothing, Chief Inspector. Plain Mr. will do. I was joking."

"Hardly the time for joking Mr. Stotesbury. Some poor sod is dead out here, aren't they."

"Sorry."

"And what time did you say you... your dog, that is... found the body?"

"Like I said when I spoke from the phone box to the duty officer at your station in Poxford, it must have been about a quarter-to-ten. I'd left *The Bogtrotters' Arms* at half-past-nine and I was heading across the fields and through the woods for home. I usually take the longer route... into the village, then by the village hall at the far end of Top Street and out to our place just off the Oxford Road. But tonight I took it in my head to take a shortcut. And I'm wishing I hadn't now... it was horrible. When I saw it poking out from the brambles under an oak tree, at first I thought it was a dead sheep, but then I saw the spectacles."

After a hundred yards or so of leaf shuffling, the three of them arrive at the scene.

"Good God! Look at it, chief," says Fielding, shuddering.

"He's right... It's gruesome. Most of the flesh is rotted away... or even eaten away. The specs are just sitting there on the skull."

"I know. But what do you expect? After months lying there

you'd be a bit thin too, wouldn't you? Now… *you've* got the billhook, Fielding. I'd like to see the damage closer up. But take care not to disturb the remains… Nigel Gresley from forensic is on his way over from the station and he doesn't take kindly to the disturbing of a crime scene."

D.C.I. Parrott instructs this ill-advised disturbance of the scene, despite his own advice and Harry Fielding hacks away at the brambles as gingerly as he can with the slashing tool.

"Bloody Hell, chief. Part of the skull's caved in. Whoever it is must have been walloped with something pretty heavy."

"As long as it wasn't with your billhook, Fielding," says Parrott, scrabbling now among the brambles himself. "You *can* at least make out that it's a bloke… I mean look at the size of those rotten shoes. From what I can see, though I could be wrong, there are faint traces of what appears to be dried blood on the remnants of his clothing. We'd better leave it at that for now. *Grisly* Gresley will no doubt soon tell us what *he* thinks. He usually does, though I don't always agree with him. He can be a bit full of his own importance at times."

"Can he, Mr. Parrott?" says Eric Stotesbury.

"*D.C.I.* Parrott, remember, sir."

"Can I go home now, Inspector? I'll need to get back to me dog, if that's alright with you?"

"Yes, shortly, Mr. Stotesbury," says D.C.I. Parrott, "you can get back home in a minute or two, but make sure you're there in the morning. An officer will be round to take a detailed statement from you. Just don't leave the country. It's possible we'll need a blood sample from you to eliminate you from our enquiries. Just routine you understand."

"Will you need a sample from Twinkle as well?"

"Good thinking. We'll get a vet to do that if it's needed, sir. *I* wouldn't go near the dog, mind you. I can't *stand* them."

"Oh, sir," says Harry. "They're lovely, cuddly things. And with a name like Twinkle, Mr. Stotesbury's dog sounds

3

delightful."

"Never judge a book by its cover, Fielding... unless you think it may bite you. I learned that the hard way, before my time as a policeman."

"What did you do before you joined the force then, sir?"

"I was a trainee librarian, Fielding."

"But what's that got to do with dogs, sir? Surely you weren't bitten by a book, were you?"

"Since you ask, Fielding, I *was*, actually. It was a book on how to make your fortune in the literary world. It said its methods were fail-safe and the world of the word is anybody's oyster. Unfortunately, the advice didn't stack up and I *spent* a fortune on attempts to get my own book published, all to no avail. The only one who *made* a fortune was the person who'd written that book I'd read... and *he* was a literary agent in the first place. He had all the contacts, you see."

"So what was your book about, sir?"

"The history of the police force, Fielding. You see, I've always had a passion for the annals of law and order through the ages. In fact one Henry Fielding featured rather prominently in there. I suspect he could well have been one of your ancestors."

"Excuse me, officers," interrupts Eric Stotesbury, reminding the pair that he's still there.

"*D.C.I.*, Mr. Stotesbury, please," says the D.C.I.

"It's just that I'm going to Ibiza in a couple of weeks. It'll be alright, won't it?"

"Actually, I've never been there, so I can't really say."

"No... I mean you shan't need me to stay here in Pockbury that long shall you?"

"I shouldn't think so, Mr. Stotesbury. I can't imagine your statement will take 'til then, will it? And we can turn round blood analysis pretty quickly these days. Bloody quickly, in fact."

Saturday Night

When *Grisly* Gresley turns up, armed with a bright torch, a wealth of experience and a clutch of tweezers and other such delicate instruments, he ascertains that the implement of assault was probably a heavy wooden shaft or club of some kind. Maybe a baseball bat but more likely an old tool handle, he having found evidence of wood-splinters lodged in among the shattered bones of the skull.

"At least six months, I reckon. Say last July," says *Grisly*. "By the look of his clothes he was probably an itinerant. And look here... I believe this is ash."

"You mean he's been burned to death?" says Harry.

"No, constable. The *splinters* are probably ash... Fraxinus excelsior, you know."

"Ah, I see."

"It's unusual," continues *Grisly*, "but there appears to be no obvious identification evidence at all to go on."

"No obvious identification evidence at all to go on?" parrots Hector Parrott, thoughtfully.

"It'll be a hellish job to ascertain who he is," adds *Grisly*. "Evidently no real clues at all. There *is* blood here, but it's old and quite degraded. The science is advancing though and we can find a lot more from this sort of evidence than we could even a few years ago. There could be more we can wheedle out back at the mortuary and in the lab."

Minutes later a police Land Rover arrives, fighting its way through the trees. It's towing a trailer and, after photographs of the scene are taken and other details are recorded, they transport the body in a suitably sealed bag out of the woods, across the frost-rimed grass to the road and on to the morgue.

Rather pointlessly, they cordon off the crime scene with blue and white 'POLICE' tape tied to the adjacent trees, no doubt to keep out all intruders such as badgers, foxes and other animals of the night, though now that the body is gone, so too is the nocturnal wildlife's interest in the scene.

When Eric Stotesbury reaches home, the gentle dog that is Twinkle greets him. The two of them live together, alone.

"There's a good boy," says Eric, patting the animal affectionately. "Don't judge a book by its cover indeed. What does that pompous idiot know?"

The dog barks and, whimpering questioningly, awaits his belated feed.

The next day, the promised officer turns up, pays a cautious regard to the boisterous but benign Twinkle and takes the suggested formal statement. Later the same day, three different officers turn up unannounced, and somewhat needlessly, with a search warrant. They too pay the dog cautious regard. Twinkle is more boisterous and a little less benign, he sensing that one of the policemen, hiding behind the other two, is none too canine-keen.

"Settle down, boy. There's nothing to get excited about," says Eric.

Twinkle obeys and scoots off to his dog basket. The officers search the house from top to bottom, the nervous officer avoiding the kitchen and Twinkle's basket. They find nothing more suspicious than a collection of Beanos. The three of them stand in the spare bedroom, leafing through some of the comics with glee.

"Hey, boys. My favourite's *Dennis the Menace*," says the first officer. "Well, his *dad* actually. I love how Dennis always ends up being thwacked with his dad's slipper. If it were up to me, his dad would have been a policeman and he would have used his truncheon instead of a feeble slipper. That would've taught the delinquent bugger, right enough."

"I prefer *The Bash Street Kids* myself," says the second officer. "They remind me of when I was at Saint Bartholomew's Junior. I'm sure whoever writes it must have gone to our school. There was this kid, Billy Splinger, who wore a pullover just like *Smiffy's*. You could never understand a word he said from under the crew neck, and the neck was always caked with snot. Perhaps it's *him* that writes it. Or it could be Arthur Hodges... he was just like *Plug, he* was. Where are they both now, I wonder?"

"*My* dad had copies from the war years," says officer three. "There was this guy in the comic back in those days called *Ping the Elastic Man*. You should have seen the way he used to bamboozle people. A bit like D.C.I. Parrott... I *don't* think. I can't imagine where me dad's comics went but I bet they'd be worth a fortune today."

"Excuse me, chaps," Eric says with a cough as he enters the room. "Have you quite finished yet? It's just that Twinkle and me need to go down the shops... for Twinkle's dinner you see. He *does* eat such a lot."

"Yes, sir, I do believe we've finished now," says officer two. They each discreetly place the comics back on the pile in the corner. Officer one casts a nostalgic glance at *Minnie the Minx* as he does so.

"Thank you for your time, sir," says officer three.

"That's alright," says Eric, patiently.

"Just one more thing, sir," says officer one. "Why would you call such a butch dog Twinkle?"

"Ah, I thought you'd never ask. Everybody *does*, you know. Well, it's like this... I got him on a Christmas Eve and as far as I'm concerned he's my 'Little Star'. In fact when I went to choose him from the litter up at the kennels, I fell for him before I knew whether it was he or she and I said to him 'How I wonder what you are'... So there it is."

The dog barks enthusiastically as the three wise policemen make their way down the stairs and out through the hall.

Shortly, *Grisly* confirms that there will be no need for a blood sample from the dog, but that two different strains of blood *have* been identified on the body and remnants of clothing.

However, when Eric's blood test results come through, they confirm that there's no match to be had with the secondary traces and Eric is informed that he's at liberty to go to Ibiza anytime he wishes.

Then Eric thinks, *'Hang about? They must have believed I may have been injured in a scuffle with this bloke...unless of course they thought I'd had a nosebleed and bled on the poor sod inadvertently as I clubbed him to death. But why would I go and report our terrible discovery if I'd been the culprit?'* "Ah well, Twinkle," he says to the dog, "It's all double Dutch to me, but that's the police for you I suppose."

Chapter Two

Ida and Albert

The following week a bleak, frost-filled morning finds the eight-twenty a.m. council bus heading into town, crammed full with morning rush hour passengers on their way to work. There had been an unpredicted snowfall but although piled-snow and salted-slush are still clinging to the pavements, at least the nights are drawing out now.

In a seat near the front of the upper deck sits an old boy in his late sixties. He's wearing an ill-fitting, well-worn gabardine mac, which is tied at the waist with a leather belt. He's on the bus most days, despite being retired, and he always wears the mac, come rain come shine, come winter come summer. He's thin bodied and thin featured... a body still showing the impact of wartime food rationing. His grey hair is thin too, and greased back with *Brylcreem*. His skin is sallow and he suffers from recurring *Park Drive* cigarettes that force themselves on him every ten minutes or so.

The bus driver, a miserable rather crabby looking man in his forties, is pelting along like a maniac, screeching to an urgent halt at each stop as if passengers had been standing up to alight rather belatedly or else would-be passengers had been lurking hidden in alleyways or in shop doorways before jumping out at the last moment to ambush the approaching bus.

'Ding' goes the bell. Lurch goes the bus. *Crabby* ratchets the handbrake on. Off and on get passengers.

'Ding-ding' goes the bell. *Crabby* releases the handbrake. Screech goes the bus, unseated passengers swaying and stumbling with this further adrenaline-rush from the driver.

A woman with a small handbag, a large empty shopping basket and a large waist appears at the top of the stairs as if emerging from a surfacing submarine and looking rather apprehensively for enemy vessels. She's all of sixty years old, yet negotiates her way along the aisle like a twenty-year-old and plonks herself down next to *Gabby the Mac*. She sighs wearily as though she's on the *p.m.* bus on the way *back* from an unsuccessful shopping trip when in fact she's on her way *to* the shops. She's all of seven or eight years younger than her seat-partner. Her hair is curled and also grey, tinged with a blue rinse that's seen better days. She seems asthmatic but takes an offered *Park Drive* cigarette gratefully and, aided by a light from her companion, together they do their bit in contributing to the next pea-souper.

"Mornin', Ida."

"Mornin', Bob."

"You made it then?"

"Only just, Bob. Bloody bus was early again, wasn't it."

"Are you sure it's not the one before?"

"The one before what?"

"The one before the one that's early."

"What?"

"Well, maybe it's *late*, Ida. The way the driver's actin', you'd think it's late."

"It can't be late, or it wouldn't be here yet, would it."

"No, listen… if it's the one before the one… oh, never mind. At least you've caught it, haven't you?"

"Yes, I have. You know, Bob… you need to be up before the lark to catch the council out. I'm sure they do it on purpose."

"*What* do they do, Ida?"

"Beats me, Bob."

"Any more fares, please?" calls out the bus conductor chirpily, as he trots nimbly up the winding stairs.

Gabby fends off a coughing bout with a free hand, desperately forcing coughed-up lungs back where they belong. And, thinking absently that the unreasonably cheerful conductor is a ticket inspector, he fights with the pocket of his

10

gabardine with the other hand and finally ferrets out his ticket to wave at him. Ida digs out a large purse from her modest handbag and fishes short-sightedly for coins.

"Good day to *you*, madam," sings the chirpy clippie. "And where are we off to today then?"

"I don't know where *you're* off to. And I don't really care, to be honest. As for me… it's none of your business where I'm off to today… today or any other day come to that."

"Sorry, missus. I meant which stop will you be wanting?" offers *Chirpy*, apologetically. "I only ask so I know how much to charge you for your ticket."

In truth, the clippie knows full well where Ida is usually off to. Both she and *Gabby* are regulars.

"Town centre, if you please," says Ida. "I'm off to see me ol' man in the infirmary. He's gone in with his leg. He's in a right state," she adds, not realising for one moment that she's answered the clippie's questions after all.

"He'd be in a right state if he went in *without* his leg," says the conductor, still effervescent despite Ida's initial rebuttal. "It'll be twenty-four pence to the town centre."

"It was only twenty-two pence last week," protests Ida, handing him the extra coins.

"It's gone up, Ida," says *Gabby*. "New year an' all that."

"My 'ouse keepin' ain't gone up, Bob. In fact, it's gone down what with Bert bein' off work. There's no overtime and the sick pay doesn't cover everything. It's scandalous. *I* blame the Government, *I* do. It's never been the same since we went decimal, you know."

"Ching," goes the bus conductor, and he hands Ida her ticket.

Gabby chuckles at the thought of Ida's Bert without his leg, coughs and lights another fag.

"So, what's wrong with Albert's leg then, Ida?"

"I dunno, Bob. That's why he's in the infirmary… to find out. It went all blowed-up and stiff at the extremities when he was in bed last week."

"Extremities?"

"Well, it's his *foot* really. It flared up after he'd been doin' the *Hokey Cokey* with the widowed landlady up at *The Hat and Beaver* on New Year's Eve. We called the doctor out and he said nothin's broken, but Bert was in such agony, sweatin' with the pain. I had to go across to the phone box the next day to call for an ambulance and it took him to the accident department. They weren't quite sure what the problem is, so they've kept him in for observation. He's been in for a couple of days now."

"I'm surprised he got a bed, Ida. *The National Health Service* is sufferin' a lot of cuts, you know."

"At the rate things are goin', *Bert'll* be sufferin' cuts. They reckon if they can't find out what it is, they're gonna have to open him up. And *I* told him... if he does the *Hokey Cokey* again, I'm leavin' him. I can't cope with all this bringin' the coal in. And I'm havin' to put me hobby to one side altogether now, and I don't have to tell *you* how much application me hobby takes. I mean, I can't get down to the libraries at all just lately."

"You need a simple hobby like mine, Ida. One that you can do from home."

"I *know* how simple your hobby is, Bob... and I couldn't even find time for that at the moment."

Now Ida is the long-suffering wife of Albert Hall and whilst she has something of a scattergun approach to life and seems rather disorganised at times she has her bright side. When she's not embroiled in her daily chores, her inquiring mind is a force to be reckoned with.

"Anyway," she continues, "It seems *The Health Service* can still afford to give out tablets. He's on fifteen a day now. First they gave him three tablets a day to kill the pain and then he had three more a day because the painkillers clogged up his waterworks. Then he had another three because he was weein' too much, another three to thin his blood and another three to stop him bleedin'. It's all bleedin' stupid if you ask me. They've given him a walkin' stick to keep him a bit mobile... to help avoid bedsores, you know... and now he's started rattlin' when he staggers down the corridor to the toilet. I'm gonna have to put them right about him though... he'll swing the lead at every opportunity. I can see him bein' in there for weeks."

The bus conductor is all smiles, untamed mousy moustache and wild mousy eyebrows. His hairy attributes camouflage a kind face, a face that reflects his kind-hearted demeanour. Ever the ebullient optimist, he's the life and soul of the bus route, always ready to share an anecdote with his passengers. His relentless treks around the territory that is his bus, up and down the stairs to and from the upper deck, and his constant ministering to his passengers has kept him slim and agile.

It turns out that this *is* in fact the late early bus and the seemingly maniacal bus driver swerves into the city bus station, on time at last. Now, unlike *Chirpy* the conductor, *Crabby* the driver is overweight, sat in his cab all day, the controls of life at his fingertips and at the soles of his feet. He always struggles to haul himself up into the cab and at the end of his shift he struggles to let himself down again onto terra firma. His pained expression belies his age... He's ten years younger than he looks and at forty-three he's the same age as *Chirpy* in fact. His face is wrinkled with the furrows of anxiety before its time. Yet he loves his bus... after all it's his only companion for most of the day.

Gabby the Mac teases the last remaining cigarette from its packet and attaches it precariously, though expertly, to his well-rehearsed bottom lip. Carefully placing the empty red and white fag packet in his mac pocket he lights up again and he and Ida both get up to alight from the bus.

"Wish 'im all the best from me, Ida. What ward's he on? Tell him I'll try and get to see him before they cut off his leg...

that'll cheer 'im up a bit. Does he like grapes?"

"He's on Ward 13, *Gabby*."

"That figures. Lucky old Albert."

"He *does* like grapes but make sure they're seedless. He's going to seed enough as it is without any help from grapes. I'll tell him you're thinkin' of him, but I shan't tell him about cuttin' his leg off. I've already warned him... if he gets close to that landlady again, *I'll* be cuttin' *somethin'* off... and it won't be his leg."

"Good morning, madam. What name is it?" says the nurse on the Ward 13 reception desk, with a smile. "And who are we visiting today?"

"I'm Mrs. Hall, young lady. I don't know who *you're* visitin', but *I'm* visitin' me husband, Albert... Albert Hall."

"Not *the* Albert Hall?" says the nurse, her smile broadening unable to resist the rather obvious quip. Her comment is made in a well-meant endeavour to bring levity to a miserable ward, to her oftentimes-depressing job and to the depressed visitors.

Ida scowls, unappreciative of the humour... she's heard the wisecrack a thousand times before. The reception nurse takes the hint and tempers her beaming smile.

"He's in the third bed on the right, behind the drawn curtains, Mrs. Hall," the duty nurse at the nurses' station explains. "He's just finished with his bedpan... he says it's too painful to shuffle to the toilet this morning. You can open the curtains now if you wish. The ward's consultant surgeon, Mr. McMorran, will be doing his weekly rounds shortly and I'm sure he'll give you an update on Mr. Hall's condition."

"Thank you, young lady."

"Did you bring me *Sportin' Life*, Ida?" says Albert, irritable after his bedpan ordeal. "I want to look at the racin' tips."

"No, Bert. It's not been delivered yet. I've brought you these grapes though."

"I know *this* week's won't have been delivered yet, Ida. I meant *last* week's."

"And what's the use of that? *I* could tell you who's gonna win *last* week's races without me having the racin' tips you idiot," says Ida, popping a grape into her mouth and unbuttoning her coat. "Look. It's so borin' in here, I wouldn't mind if you brought me last *year's Sportin' Life*."

"It's just turned January, Bert. Last week's *Sportin' Life is* last year's."

"I suppose so, Ida. But you know what I meant."

The consultant sweeps into the ward with an entourage of medical students in his wake. He's a tall, statuesque Scotsman in his early thirties, fresh from Guy's Hospital in London. He has a jaw as sharp as his scalpels and an acerbic tongue to match.

"Here comes Mr. McSporran," says Albert to Ida.

"Shush, Albert. Don't be silly… it's Mr. *McMorran*."

"What? Him as well?"

After visiting the patients in beds one and two, the surgeon reaches the Halls.

"Now who do we have here then? Good morning…" says he, in a broad though cultured Glaswegian accent and, pausing so as to consult Albert's chart hung at the foot of the bed, adds, "…Mr. Hall."

"Mornin' doc," says Albert, grumpily.

"It's not doctor actually. It's Mr., Mr. Hall."

"You mean you're not qualified, Mr.?" replies Albert, rather anxiously.

"Of course I'm qualified, Mr. Hall. It's the way we address consultants, you see."

"Right you are, doc."

"And is this your lovely daughter, Mr. Hall?" says Roderick

McMorran.

"You're stretchin' it a bit, aren't you, doc?" says Ida, in truth flattered by this compliment.

With Ida distracted, Albert nods cautiously in agreement. The medical students chortle with equal discretion.

"Now, Mr. Hall. May I ask you if you're happy for these students to assist me in my chat with you? One day in the future they'll be looking after patients such as yourself, so they need hands-on experience as soon as possible."

"Blimey! I suppose so, but I hope you're gonna sort me out before the day *they're* in charge, aren't you?"

"Of course, we'll do our best. Now, I understand that you suffered some ignominy on Hogmanay?" he asks Albert.

"What?"

"You got your swelling after you'd been cavorting on the smoke room floor at the pub doing the *Hokey Cokey*, did you not?"

"Swelling? Well yes, that's when me foot swelled up good and proper, but it *had* been hurtin' for a month or two before that."

"Yes. So I see from your notes."

The self-absorbed Mr. McMorran turns to his entourage.

"Tell me, Mr. Waterdown... what would *you* say is the problem?"

"Could it be gout, sir?"

"I doubt it. I believe he doesn't drink that much. What about you, Miss Chesterton."

"*I* don't drink that much either, sir," the student replies somewhat bitingly, deliberately misinterpreting the question.

Miss Chesterton is not sure if she likes this man. His manner struck her as somehow arrogant and aloof the first time she came across him.

"No. I mean what do you imagine is causing Mr. Hall's problem?"

"Could it be syphilis, sir?" she replies with covert sarcasm.

"I doubt it. I believe he doesn't… well, *you* know. Looking at his test results, I would say this is a classic case of diabetes. With the right sort of care, we can sort him out quite readily."

"You mean, you won't have to cut him open?" says Ida.

"Not unless you want us to, Mrs. Hall. It's one way we could stop him doin' the *Hokey Cokey*."

"You put your left stump in, your left stump out…" ventures Mr. Waterdown, with rather less aplomb for the oblique comment than Miss Chesterton.

"Are you sure you're in the right profession, Mr. Waterdown?" says Mr. McMorran. "Now then, Mr. Hall. We'll be prescribing a régime of treatment, and you'll be home within a few days and almost as fit as a fiddle."

"As long as he can bring the coal in, then I'll be more than happy," says Ida.

"Will there be any side effects, doc? Will I be able to go up *The Hat and Beaver*?"

Ida coughs a coded warning to Bert.

"I don't see why not, Mr. Hall," the surgeon confirms. "As John Donne nearly said, man cannot live by coal alone."

"Isn't that Jesus?" says Miss Chesterton.

"Where?" says Mr. Waterdown, turning on his heels to look down the ward for the Messiah, wondering for a moment if they're witnessing the second coming.

"Or was it 'No man is an island'?" says the surgeon, scratching his head thoughtfully. I must warn you though, Mr. Hall, that you may suffer some mild long-term effects on your eyesight."

"What about readin' me *Sportin' Life*? I couldn't live without that."

"We'll see about that, Bert," says Ida. "We don't want you straining anything. And as for the sportin' life… I'll be happy as long as you stick to the horses and the greyhounds. The

Hokey Cokey's out for you from now on, my lad."

The consultant and his troupe of would-be medics and nurses move on to the next bed to see how Mr. Perkins is perking up after his hernia operation... an operation necessitated by an injury sustained in the *Argentine Tango* at the local *Palais de Dance.*

"I fear we'll need to open a dedicated ward for the treatment of dancing injuries, Mr. Waterdown. What do *you* say, Miss Chesterton?"

"I've been meaning to tell you, Mr. McMorran... or may I call you Roger?" she asks, in more conciliatory mood.

"Of course you may, Miss Chesterton, though my name's actually Roderick," says the surgeon, for the moment ignoring his hernia patient who is taking in the gossip with interest.

"You see, Roderick. I have a persistent thigh injury. It all started when I was Morris dancing last year... It was after I added a galley in the half-gip."

"I see, Miss Chesterton... or may I call you Imogen?

"If you feel like it, but my name's actually Imelda."

"So, Imelda... your half-gip isn't half giving you gip?"

He laughs at his own joke, with no understanding of what a half-gip might be, and the others in the entourage follow suit ingratiatingly.

"That's right," says Miss Chesterton. "It's my right thigh, above the knee. Thankfully it wasn't a whole-gip."

"Where else would your thigh be, I wonder?" asks the surgeon. "I hesitate to think... perhaps if you were placed with your legs in the air of course? Anyway, I could look at it for you later. We'll have to see what we can do. In the meantime, I should give up Morris dancing if I were you."

"I already have. I decided I don't like it... too many men and not enough women involved for *my* liking."

After a brief hiatus, the surgeon exchanges a few words with Mr. Perkins vis-à-vis his hernia, then a hasty word with other patients on the ward, and they're away like a flock of migrating geese.

"Do you reckon they really know what they're doing, Ida?"

"Of course they do, Bert. It's like prime ministers and headmasters. They don't get where they are unless they're outstanding in their field."

"I thought that was farmers, Ida?"

"Yes, them as well," she says, not quite getting the joke. "Anyway, Bert. I've got to go now. That coal won't get itself in, you know. And *you* get well soon, before the housekeepin' runs out. I want you back at work down the foundry."

"I suppose so, Ida."

She pops another grape, and buttons her coat.

"I'll see you again tomorrow, Bert."

"I suppose so, Ida."

"I've got a bit of shoppin' to do for dinner, before I get the bus."

"Don't forget me *Sportin' Life*," he shouts after her as she disappears beyond the nurses' station.

The next day, *Gabby the Mac* arrives at the infirmary.

"Good morning sir," says the nurse on the Ward 13 reception desk, forcing a smile and wafting away a vaguely visible miasma. "I'm afraid you'll have to put that cigarette out. There's a no smoking policy here in the infirmary."

"Right you are," says *Gabby*, stubbing it out in the amnesty ashtray on the desk. "I'd nearly finished it anyway," he adds, exhaling a cloud of *'Essence of Gallagher'*.

"And what name is it, sir?"

"I'm Bob. Me friends call me *Gabby* sometimes, on account of me mac, you see."

"I *do* see," she acknowledges anxiously, looking down at the leather belt that appears to be holding together the whole package that is Bob. *'Gabby? Shabby more like,'* she thinks.

"And who are we visiting today?"

"I'm visiting Albert Hall. I gather he's on this ward."

"Not *the* Albert Hall?" says the nurse, smiling freely now... she's not tired of the quip and is still attempting some levity.

Bob laughs, "I've not heard that one before, nurse. *The* Albert Hall, eh? I'll have to tell Bert that one. He'll find it *so* funny."

The nurse subtly tempers her smile, not sure if there's sarcasm in the air mingling with the persisting miasma.

"Er, yes, sir," she says. "He *is* on this ward, as you thought. It's through those double doors, then take the first turn right, then straight ahead. You can't miss it."

"Bert, you old sod!" declares *Gabby* as he spies Ida's husband.

He sits himself down on the bedside chair and plonks a brown paper bag of seedless grapes in Bert's lap.

"It's ages since I saw you, you old bugger. It's really good to catch up with you. How're you doin'?"

Albert is more of an acquaintance of *Gabby's* than friend. In fact, *Gabby* sees much more of Ida, largely because he and her regularly catch the same bus.

"Mornin' *Gabby*. It's good to see *you* too. I'm okay. At least they're saying now that they shouldn't need to operate. And thanks for these grapes... I've become quite addicted to 'em in here."

"You'll soon be up and about, mate. It's marvellous what tablets can do these days."

"Don't talk to me about tablets. I reckon they'll be comin' up with pills to do everything soon, a bit like them robots for buildin' cars. They'll just be able to pop a pill in a glass of water, it'll fizz a bit and out'll come a Ford Escort."

"But will it make them any cheaper, Bert?"

"What? Pills?"

"No. Cars?"

"I shouldn't think so, *Gabby*."

"Anyway, Bert, I bet you're itchin' to get back to the foundry, aren't you?"

"I can do without it just lately. To tell the truth, the only time I'm really happy on me feet is when I'm dancin' up *The Hat and Beaver, Gabby.*"

"Hey, steady on. Don't let Ida hear you say that, Bert. By the way... on the way in, when I was tellin' the nurse who I was visiting, she said "not *the* Alb..."

"Albert Hall?"

"Oh, you've heard it then."

"Just once or twice, mate."

The two of them chat for a good while on matters inconsequential, then the bell sounds for the end of visiting time.

"I'd better be off now, Bert. I'll tell Ida you're okay if I see her before *she* sees *you.*"

"Thanks, *Gabby*. And thanks for comin' in. I appreciate it. Oh, and if you *do* see Ida, tell her not to forget me *Sportin' Life*, will you?"

"Will do, pal. See you soon. Don't eat too many grapes."

And with that, *Gabby* heads out of the ward, turning left and through the double doors to the reception. He draws out a *Park Drive*, preparing to light up once he's outside again and as he passes the miserably jocular nurse at the reception desk he calls across to her, "I told him about *The* Albert Hall, but he'd heard it, me dear."

Chapter Three

Speed the Plough

"Wally! The barrel's gone."

"What barrel, Maureen?"

"The *Brewster's Wilt*, Wally. *You* know... the strong bitter. Get down there and change it before that lot arrive."

"What lot?"

"*The A.B.V. Morris Men*. They're like locusts... locusts with tankards. Not that I'm complaining mind. Today should pay for our holiday in Torremolinos next month."

"You didn't tell me *they* were coming, Maureen."

"There's posters all over the pub, Wally. They come here as part of their winter tour *every* January. And you got four extra firkins in... you know you did."

"Oh, yeah. I forgot."

"Give me strength. Am I running this pub on me own, Wally?"

Wally spots two coaches pulling into the car park of their pub, *The Nautical Maureen* in Nether Clampum, and before he can say 'cleanse me pipes', the lounge-bar door swings open to an avalanche of bells and handkerchiefs and sweat. It's the *Aston Barr Village Morris Men* with five guest sides on their Plough Monday outing... or rather their plough *Saturday* outing. Unlike in the old days, Monday is a non-starter, because they're each at their chosen 'artisan' occupations during the week... schoolteachers, doctors, accountants, architects, quantity surveyors and social workers to list but a few. They've already danced in procession to and from two other pubs locally, and are landing here for a well-earned lunch.

"Right, *you* lot. Five-minute warning. Get your drinks in, then we're dancing," shouts George Snaith, the *A.B.V.* Foreman. "*A.B.V.* are on first, then *Bonkinton Morris* followed by *Gaffer Higley's Crotal Bell Molly Dancers*."

The Foreman of a Morris side teaches the dances, and like every other Foreman in the Morris fraternity, and come to that every Forewoman in the Morris sorority, *Snakey* Snaith readily confuses his rôle with that of the Squire... it's the Squire's job to take charge when a Morris side is out and performing.

"We've all six sides to get through before lunch in an hour's time," *Snakey* announces. "One long or two short dances each, so no shirking please, gentlemen. The audience will be expecting a good display."

"But what's the point of bustin' a gut?" complains Crispin Morgan. "There were only three people outside when we came in... and one of *them* was the window cleaner, packing up his ladders, ready to make off for his next pane-full stint, elsewhere."

"Look, Crispin. Pete will want you in the first dance... you actually *know* that one."

"Which one's that then, *Snakey*?"

"I don't actually know... but you'd better find out. Otherwise, you can go round with the collection box. Our travelling expenses don't pay themselves, *Crispy*."

Crispy Morgan, a doctor, has become the habitual sluggard of the side. His lack of will to indulge in mobility coupled with copious beer drinking and the eating of cake has endowed him with more than a few extra pounds. He now weighs in at over fourteen stone and, at only five-feet-five tall his width all but matches his height. There's one of this species in every Morris side... sometimes two... sometimes more. *Crispy* was in fact once an exceedingly good dancer, before the cake took hold, but these days he rarely manages to get both feet off the ground at the same time. And when he does, it's now only ever on his way to the bar after a dance has finished... Otherwise, he shuffles when he walks and he shuffles when he dances.

Pete, is Pete Peverill. *Pervy* Peverill is the side's Squire, and so is allegedly in charge of *A.B.V.'s* dancing when they're out and about... not only the choice of dances for the day but also the choice of who will dance each of them. He weighs as much as *Crispy* but is six-foot-four and a Rugby Union prop forward when he isn't waving handkerchiefs or busy being an architect. In the nicest possible way, he's a bit of a toughie, except when under the over-assertive input of *Snakey*. But then, when you're leading an assignment such as a Morris tour it helps to be a toughie. With the same instinctive and perhaps indispensable of motives *most* architects are toughies, in the nicest possible way, rarely looking to be anything less than a project leader.

Now *A.B.V.* have always considered themselves a sprightly team, so *Crispy Doc* is a bit of an anathema of late. When they'd formed the side a decade-and-a-half ago, their average age was only thirty-one. Now, it's fifty. This is hardly surprising because they've only recruited four new members in all that time and two of *them* are now in their late eighties. Then there's Fred Moulton, the most recent addition and now the youngest member of the team, who's helping to keep down the average age. At only 19, he's an apprentice carpenter and heavy metal fan. Like *Snakey* Snaith, he's slim-built but, more than *Snakey*, is extremely agile and sometimes over-exuberant. The essence of *Snakey's* energies is concentrated in his aim at perfection of the side's public execution of each dance.

"Why call a pub *The Nautical Maureen?*" asks Dan Copley, *A.B.V.'s* Fool, parking his bladder-on-a-stick on the bar and waiting for Wally to surface triumphant from the cellar.

"You know very well why, Dan," says Gerry Newman.

Gerry Newman is *A.B.V.'s* Bagman, and so responsible for much of the planning of events, and communications with other Morris sides and the 'clients'... the one team member that the Squire or the Foreman shouldn't harass... but often do.

"Sorry, Gerry but I really don't know why it's called *The Nautical Maureen. Really*, I don't," Dan protests. "I've not been here before, remember. I've missed out on the January tour for the two years I've been with the side. I'm usually away skiing in the French Alps after the New Year. I'd heard you others mention the name, but I hadn't really given it a thought up to now when I spotted the weird pub sign."

"Well, 'til a few years ago it was called *The Nautical Mooring*," Gerry explains. "Then, after Wally acquired the pub for himself as a free house, he suggested on a drunken whim one night that he'd change the name so as to honour his fine-looking wife. One of his regulars apparently bet him fifty quid that he wouldn't do it. But Wally, never being one to forego an offer of cash, went ahead with it. And more than that, he changed the sign from a three-master resplendent with sails full-billowing in a brisk south-westerly wind to a cartoon of Maureen resplendent with 'sails' full-billowing in a 'double D-cup' bra. It rankles her a bit apparently, but she goes along with the joke. She's a bit of a gal deep down, you know."

The horde of brightly ribboned, loudly belled and pot-bellied revellers files out of the pub onto the forecourt. The gathered audience has passed expectations, swelling to ten, although this includes a pair of red setters and a noisy magpie that perches momentarily on top of the pub sign, only to fluster away inelegantly into the neighbouring trees on the re-emergence of the invading multitude.

"Ladies, gentlemen and red setters," bellows *Snakey*. "We are *The A.B.V. Morris Men* and we're here today with our friends from afar to entertain you on this warm and sunny January day. Our first dance is *The Flowing Bowl* from the village of Adderbury. It's danced, as you might expect, to the tune of *Landlord Fill The Flowing Bowl*."

The announcement brings forth tentative applause, the growing audience not quite sure what to expect.

As if by magic, a motley crew of five rambling drinkers in

Morris kit separates from the throng, joins *Snakey* and metamorphoses into a smart two-line set of dancers with the Foreman leading them. Each man carries a heavy ash stick, held vertical in front of him at arm's length. Prompted by a chord from the accordion of their musician, Barry *Quacker* Duckham who stands before them, they pace in a clockwise circle singing a verse of *Landlord* as they go.

Inside, behind the bar, Wally hears the song strike up and remembers from earlier visits that this is his cue to fill his eighteenth century pewter bowl with the strongest of the beers on tap currently, as a thank you for the men turning up to entertain his customers... another idea, now traditional, spawned of a drunken lock-in at *The Nautical M*. This year it's the *Brewster's Wilt*.

"Foot up!" cries *Snakey* as the dancers complete their walk round. They re-form their two lines and, with a clash of sticks pair to pair, they turn to face front and head up at some speed in unison.

"*Fuck up* more likely, *Snakey* you bastard," complains *Pervy*, as he comes out of the pub. "That's *my* job, and *I* was gonna start things off with *The Queen's Delight*."

Of course, *Snakey* doesn't hear this plaintiff cry, but Kit Harbury hears it loud and clear, having himself just come out from the pub on *Pervy's* heels. Kit is one of the relatively young dancers in the side and is as athletic as any. Dark haired and blue-eyed, he's one of those darlings of the Morris world who can dance every dance and sing every song... reliable and keen.

"But *you* weren't here, were you, *Pervy*," says Kit, "and neither is the Queen, so you *can't* delight her, can you."

"Well, he should have waited for *me*."

"Just be sensible, *Pervy*," says Kit. "Don't get his hackles up, or the rest of the day'll be a pain. Just take over again for the next dance, why don't you?"

"I suppose so. But he'll do that once too often. He'd better watch out," decides *Pervy*.

The dance finishes after much energetic stick clashing and chorus singing. The six troop off and, after a brief excursion for their ration of a pint each of *Brewster's Wilt*, they trundle out to the margins of the forecourt to watch the other sides perform. *Bonkinton Morris* step forward to announce their first dance… *The Flowers of Edinburgh*, a hanky dance from the village of Bledington.

"So, *Pervy*. Who are this lot that are on after *Bonkinton*?" asks Kit. "I mean, *Gaffer Higley Scrotal Bell Molly*? What kind of a name is that?"

"They're over from a tiny village called Diddleton Fenn… in Cambridgeshire," offers *Pervy*. "And, according to *Snakey*, Molly dancing is a sort of unsophisticated Morris dancing from over that way. And it involves men dressed as women."

"Unsophisticated? A bit like *A.B.V.'s* dancing then," says Kit, tongue-in-cheek.

"Blimey, Kit!" says *Crispy*, who's just shuffled up to join them. "Leave it out. Don't let *Snakey* hear you say that. We're one of the best Cotswold Morris sides in the country. I should know. I've been dancing with *A.B.V.* since we started, and folk flock to see us wherever we dance… and we don't need women's clothes to dance in either, thank you very much."

"No, *Crispy*. It's *sheep* that flock to see us, not *folk*," says Fred Moulton.

"And you mean *we* can dance like women without women's clothes on, *Crispy*?" adds Kit.

"All the women *I've* seen dancing have done it *with* their clothes on," says Fred, disappointedly.

"That's because you're too young to have seen the rarer delights of the world, mate," says *Pervy*. "I went to this nightclub in America a few years ago. Oregon it was. And this woman was dancing using a pole. *We* might do stick dances but *she* was doing Pole dancing. *Belle Jangles* her name was. She was so supple that, apart from anything else, it made your eyes water."

"I'm telling you, Kit... leave it out," repeats *Crispy*. "Don't denigrate *A.B.V.'s* dancing or *Snakey* will be on you like a ton of bricks. A heavy ton of bricks at that."

"I suppose so, *Crispy* but what's a scrotal bell anyway? Sounds like a bag o' bollocks to me," says Kit.

"Crotal, you prat... It's *Higley's Crotal*... not *Higley Scrotal*," *Pervy* explains.

"Still sounds like a bag o' bollocks."

And with that, the massed band of *Gaffer Higley's* comes around the corner and into the car park playing *Speed the Plough*. They're followed by a plough pulled by their lallygagged dancers who are sporting a mass of unruly, gaudy ribbons and raddled faces. The dancers park the plough in front of their band and form a ragged set of eight.

"Apparently crotal bells were used on horse-drawn vehicles to warn other approaching vehicles at crossroads," *Pervy* explains, shouting in Kit's ear above the wall of sound blasting from melodeons, trombone, tuba, pipe, drum and fiddle. "They were pretty much the same as the bells *we* use."

"But you wouldn't need them on a plough in a field, would you, *Pervy*?" Kit suggests. "They were hardly likely to collide with another plough unless they were pissed... like you."

"No, they used them on the roads too."

"What? Ploughs?"

"No. The bells, the bells, for God's sake... on horse-drawn vehicles on the roads," says *Pervy*, exasperated.

"Ah, the bells, the bells... I had a hunch that's what you meant. Anyway, they wouldn't be very effective though, would they... when two carts were approaching the same crossroads. It'd be a bit like fire engines today. They wouldn't hear each other for their own bells, would they? And look at that lot. *They're* all wearing them and *still* they're crashing into each other."

"Well *A.B.V.* don't crash into each other do they," insists *Crispy*. "Like I said, *we're* the best."

Kit ignores *Crispy* and continues to question *Pervy's* explanations.

"But why would you need 'em on the roads anyway? You'd just listen for horseshoes on the tarmac."

"Look, Kit. All the roads didn't have tarmac back then, did they?"

"No. That's true."

"So, sometimes it was as if you were still in the field. *Then* you'd have needed them," argues *Pervy*.

"I suppose I can give you that," says Kit.

"And anyway, they used them for decoration too."

"That's probably all they *did* use them for, I reckon," says Kit, still persisting.

So they agree that they're all as confused as when they'd started discussing bells.

"But what's with the red faces?" asks Kit, pensively, not letting the mocking inquisition drop.

"It's raddle, mate. It's like the Border Morris sides... you know...those heathens from the Welsh borders." explains *Pervy*, serious as ever. You know how they *black* up... some say as a disguise and some say to represent coal miners. Well this lot *raddle* up. Red sheep raddle's traditionally daubed on the breast of the tup, the ram that is, so the farmer knows which ewes have been 'seen to'."

"Well, there's plenty of sheep in Wales, ain't there," suggests Kit, tongue in cheek. "They should strut their stuff over there, I reckon."

"I give up," declares *Pervy*, admitting defeat.

All the other sides take their turn to strut their stuff... *The Pockbury Prancers*, *Middlemarch Mayhem Morris*, and *The Old*

Clash and Wave'em Morris Men.
"How come there aren't any sword dancing sides out today then?" asks Kit. "I like a bit of sword dancing. Rapper Sword, Long Sword... I don't care which."

"I *did* ask one or two sword sides along, but they said they're a bit rusty this year," chips in Gerry, the Bagman.

"What? The dancers or the swords?" quips Kit.

"Ha, bloody ha," says Gerry.

Then all the dancers and musicians leave the audience, now grown to a dozen or more and *three* red setters, to their own devices stuck at the back of a queue of over fifty Morris devotees all keen to replenish their tankers whilst anticipating a well-earned lunch. And believe it or believe it not... *Crispy* is first to the bar.

"*Crispy!* Thirty pints of *Fartin' Ferret* and twenty-two pints of *Mother Cruddlington's Best*," comes a cry from somewhere in the swarm and up goes a cheer, but *Crispy* ignores the call as he dips into his purse for loose change to pay for his own pint.

"Is the hotpot on its way yet, Maureen?" asks *A.B.V.* Morris man Robin Watts, as she brushes by him in the corridor that leads to the kitchen.

"It's about ready," she tells him. "Maggie's keeping an eye on it but it can simmer for another ten minutes, no bother," she adds, fluttering her eyelashes. "Come and see me now if you're hungry, sexy boy. I'm sure I can find you a little something to nibble as an appetizer. Wally's behind the bar up to his eyeballs with tankards. And *my* behind could do with some attention too."

So, the hotpot that is Robbie Watts follows Maureen discreetly up the stairs to her private quarters.

"Right, everyone," shouts *Figgy* Figgis over the discord of noise in the lounge-bar.

…The noise subsides.

"The hotpot that Maureen has so kindly prepared for you all will be along in a minute or two."

… Loud cheers and thumping of cutlery on tables.

"It's two pounds per man and the same price for hangers-on."

… Loud boos.

"I'll be coming round to collect the cash while you're eating, so please have the right change ready if possible. Enjoy."

…More cheers rise to the beams as the hubbub returns, and *Figgy* turns to hunt down Maureen to see if the meal is coming.

Terry Figgis is the side's Chancellor… charged with accounting for the 'vast' quantities of petty cash generated by street collections and the occasionally generous gig fees at special events such as weddings and other extravagant celebrations. Then again, he's required to expend the side's amassed alms on replacement corporate elements of worn-out kit such as hats, baldricks, bell-pads and ribbons and to cover mileage expenses for the men. Maureen's hotpot and other such indulgencies might occasionally be funded by the side too.

Now, *Figgy* has a tendency to collect women like he collects petty cash, and similarly can't always fully account for them. But at least he regards them as his equals, unlike Robbie who is more likely to regard them as casual conveniences. In his search for Maureen, *Figgy* makes for the kitchen corridor and catches her voice echoing faintly from the top of the adjoining stairs. Making his way on tiptoes to the top, he can see that the bedroom door is slightly ajar, and hearing subdued giggles from within, gingerly nudges it open a little further. There he spies Robbie and Maureen, she sitting on a wicker chair, he standing facing her with his back to the door and his bells tinkling gently. *Figgy* coughs deliberately and knocks on the door.

"*Figgy!*" exclaims Robbie, half turning as he fumbles with his shirt tails and re-adjusts his baldricks. "It's Maureen. She's got something in her eye. I'm trying to get it out with one of my hankies."

"Well, get whatever it is out of her eye and make sure its back where it belongs, you bloody idiot, before Wally puts something in *your* eye."

"Right. Okay, *Figgy*. I hope it's better now, Maureen," says Robbie lamely as he squeezes by his fellow dancer and retreats to the top of the stairs.

"Much better thanks, Robin," calls Maureen demurely, whilst regaining her composure ready for attendance on the other hotpot.

Figgy follows his fellow dancer, turning briefly as he goes.

"I'll see you later with the money for the food, Maureen," he says, with a wry smile.

"Right you are. I'm on my way," she offers.

The meal goes well. Then the massed Morris crowd sings a few finger-in-the-ear songs and thumbs-in-the-belt-loops songs. *Figgy* thanks Wally and Maureen and pays for the meals. Then the whole caboodle is on its way to the next pub. Robbie tips Maureen a wink as he slips away to his next conquest.

The rest of the day goes successfully and, with sore feet and in some cases sore knuckles, the dancers prepare to head off each to their homes and well-earned baths.

"Panto practice on Wednesday, lads," shouts *Snakey* before *A.B.V.* can disperse. "It's the dress rehearsal, so I want everybody there. We still haven't mastered the stick clashing in that finale dance."

"For fudge sake!" protests Fred Moulton to *Quacker* Duckham who's busy squeezing his squeezebox into its case. "*Snakey's* a real glutton for other people's punishment isn't he.

I'll be glad when it's all over, then we can get back to some normality."

"You know, you could have ducked out of it like I did back in early November when we first started rehearsals," butts in *Crispy Doc*, gloatingly.

"So... it's behind you then, *Crispy*," quips Dan Copley, swatting the doc playfully with his bladder.

"Oh, no it isn't," says *Snakey*, who's overheard *Crispy's* comment. "Gerry's sprained his ankle... at the last spot."

"What... in *Bobbing Around*? That's the gentlest dance we do," complains *Crispy*.

"All the dances *you* do are gentle, *Crispy*... even when they're not. Anyway, you saw Gerry go over on that dodgy paving slab in the sidestepping. He won't be bobbing around for quite a while, so we need *you* for the panto and you'll have to catch up and learn things a bit faster than you usually don't."

"But, I'm washing me hair on Wednesday night."

"I bet you say that to all the boys, *Crispy*," laughs Dan.

"No excuses, Crispin. Be there, right?"

"I suppose so, George. But you owe me one."

Now, the *A.B.V.* Morris men have been practising for *The Old Board-walkers'* pantomime production with the theatre group in Poxford once a week for two whole months. This preoccupation has taken over from normal practice sessions, much to the chagrin of some of the purists in the side. *Crispy*, being no purist but pure lazy had given up on it after one session until this enforced re-immersion. The producer-cum-choreographer had persuaded them that it was 'a perfect marriage, darlings... panto and Morris dancing... what sublime fun.'

The panto in question is *Goody Two-Shoes*. The production, as now devised by *Whispering Willie*, the inspired producer, has three Morris dances inserted seemingly seamlessly into the plot. These dances include a boisterous stick dance finale, *The*

Black Joke from Bledington, adapted to suit the theme of the production and aimed at rousing the inevitably enthralled audience to a crescendo of applause as the curtain comes down. In truth, Willie had been short of men for the chorus scenes, where they were to play brigands. He'd craftily worked on inveigling the Morris men to take part, aided greatly by *Snakey's* enthusiasm to promote the public profile of *A.B.V.* He'd finally secured their agreeing to perform with the promise of a female chorus surpassing all others in voice and beauty... there *are* a couple of corkers in the company, one being the Principal Boy but the rest are at best frumpy and at worst downright ugly, much to the disappointment of Robbie Watts. But overall, the rehearsals have turned out to be great fun and everyone in the side, except for *Crispy*, is looking forward to the theatre performances.

Chapter Four

Janet and John

"After you, mi dear," says a lively young chap standing at the stop as Ida's bus pulls in.

"Thank you, young man," she replies from under her clear plastic rain hood. "I'm glad to see the age of celery's not dead."

"I believe you mean the age of chi..."

But before he can correct her, she's up the stairs, sat down and lighting a *Woodbine*. It's four-twenty in the afternoon and winter gloom is pervading the town. The upper deck of the bus is smoke-fogged and nearly full.

She wipes the condensation from her window and sees that rain is setting in. In the street, people scurry under hastily hoisted gamps from buses into shops or from shops onto buses, the urgency of the weather upon them. The overcoated man selling evening newspapers on the corner, faced with a fast-fleeing audience, turns up his collar and gives up his holler.

Ida is returning from another trip to see Bert in the infirmary. He's now been scheduled for surgery on his foot after all. Mr. McMorran has decided Bert has *Tarsal Tunnel Syndrome* and *will* need an operation.

"According to Mr. McSporran it's a sort of hand pain in me foot," Bert had explained to Ida, "He says that it's a relatively straightforward procedure that should relieve the pain, but I'll need an exploratory operation first to confirm that his diagnosis is right," Bert had added.

And today had been the day for the exploration, so Ida had set out prepared for a long stay in the waiting room that's attached to the operating suite. And she hadn't been disappointed... she'd been there for about six hours, but she'd prepared herself corned beef and mustard sandwiches and a large flask of tea. And the day before, at long last, she'd managed to get to the central library and borrow two books

35

that she needs to digest in pursuit of her long-neglected hobby. She'd invested in a new spiral-bound reporter's notebook and splashed out on a pack of three biros... one black, one blue and one red to note the rather complicated tips she was expecting to find in the books. She knew that Bert was bound to be away from the ward for ages while the operating team went through all their rigmarole of procedures, first the pre-operative checks and preparation, then the operation itself, then the post-operative checks, not mention all the inefficiencies in between. So, she'd resolved to make good use of all that time whist she'd be waiting for Bert to be wheeled back to his bed on ward 13.

But for the moment, Ida's attention is drawn to the couple seated in front of her on the bus. She listens intently, unable to ignore their intriguing conversation...

"No, Janet. I can't see that I'll secure the Headship for many an age. I've only been at the school for two years and it's probably a case of dead man's shoes. I must be at *least* tenth in the queue. The last headmaster at the school was seventy-eight when he got promoted and about a hundred and ten when he retired last year... *I'm* only twenty-seven. And the new headmistress is a lively, sixty-one-year-old woman who does yoga in her lunch breaks."

"Perhaps you mean a case of dead *woman's* shoes then, John?"

"Not really. All the others in the queue are men. For a start, there's old Humphrey Harrison, the deputy head, and a half dozen or more looking over his shoulder."

"Maybe *you* should take up yoga. With any luck, you could master yogic flying and rise above them all."

"Don't be silly, Janet. I'll only achieve my ambitions with hard work and application. I'll concentrate on teaching geography for now. Anyway, what about you? I can't see much future in opening a coffee shop."

"I wouldn't say that. I've got a great idea. It's going to be a coffee shop that has a little area for reading books. That way people will stay longer and buy more coffee."

"If you say so, but it'll probably have to wait 'til the baby's old enough to go to school," John says, gently patting Janet's swollen belly. "Anyway, the next stop's ours."

They stand up and shuffle into the aisle, swaying with the bus as it negotiates a series of bends.

'Well, this John doesn't seem to be outstanding in his field for a start... he'll never make a headmaster or a Prime Minister as far as I can see. And certainly far too young for now', Ida thinks, disappointed as the conversation recedes to the back of the bus and down the stairs. She wipes the condensation from her window again. It's almost stopped raining, but everything is even more depressingly cheerless outside in the streets now as they leave the well-lit roads behind and reach the poorly lit suburbs. Ida watches as Janet and John alight and head down a side street, arm in arm, John's chivalrous umbrella held more to shield Janet than himself.

"Here we are, Janet," says John, as he turns his key in the *Yale* cylinder on the front door of their rented Victorian flat.

Instinctive in the darkness, he deposits his disengaged, dripping umbrella in the hallstand, switches his briefcase to his left hand and switches on the hall light. The bleak, bare sixty-watt bulb reveals a depressing landscape of cream emulsion-painted walls and brown gloss-painted skirtings. He removes his overcoat briskly and helps the swelling Janet to remove her raincoat. He hangs both coats on a single peg and they make their way into the lounge, which is so much more inviting with its paper-lantern pastel-shaded lampshade, its understated summer-flowered wallpaper and its warm sheepskin rug.

The removal of John's overcoat reveals him to be of slight build, bulked out only by his heavy, drab-coloured tweed jacket. The jacket has regulation leathern elbows and is infused with chalk dust. He removes the jacket too, placing it on the back of a sit-up-and-beg chair. Beneath the jacket, he's wearing a trademark bottle green geography-teacher tank top, a white shirt and an orange tie. His trousers are grey, with turn-ups hinting at charity shop demob-wear. His shoes are brown brogues that have seen better days. His hair is mousy, profuse and wiry and needs taming after his day's ordeal with all the chalk dust and the inclement weather.

Janet, raincoat dispensed with, is dressed immaculately in white blouse, black skirt and practical black shoes... all rather more librarianesque than coffee-cum-bookshop style. Her hair is between brown and blonde. It's neatly cut to shoulder length and with a fringe it frames her timid face well. Her figure cuts neatly too, except for the bulge that is their imminent baby. The blouse and skirt have been purchased recently in larger sizes than her normal so as to accommodate the growing bump.

John switches on the two-bar electric fire and, looking down at the intimacy of their rug, ponders the imminent arrival of the baby. Janet goes into the tiny kitchen, fills the kettle and lights the gas ring.

"Coffee?" she calls to him. "I can find you a book to read with it if you'd like one. There's that pile of Charles Dickens in the corner. Then I'll set about cooking dinner after our coffees."

"Fine, as long as it's not *Bleak House*," says John, submitting to the warmth of the electric fire and his young wife's twin offer of both literary and culinary sustenance.

"We need to decide on names for the baby, John," she declares, as she brings in the coffees.

"How about Ebenezer?" suggests John, with light-bulb enthusiasm inspired by the invocation of Dickens.

"I don't *think* so, John."

"Anyway, we don't know yet if it's a boy or a girl, Jan."

"It might even be one of each, John."

"What? Triplets?"

"Twins, you idiot. Men!"

"If we call it *Sprog,*" says John, "it won't matter whether it's a *he* or a *she,* will it. And it had better not be twins. If it *is,* we're selling that rug. Even *one* child's more than we can really afford for the time being. If it's a boy, we'll have to train him as a chimney sweep as soon as possible."

"And if it's a girl?"

"Scullery maid."

They settle on the small sofa and bathe in the heat of the electric fire, content with their coffees and each other. John's book is *Great Expectations,* but he doesn't get past page two. His expectations are already great enough, what with contemplating *Sprog* and yogic flying.

They wake three hours later in pitch darkness with the fire fled. They ferret in the dark for a ten-pence piece, feed the meter then feed themselves. Dinner turns out to be supper and supper turns out to be bread and strong cheddar cheese. Janet eats nine of the twelve pickled onions in the jar… fortunately they have no coal. The surfeit of cheese gives them both nightmares.

Janet sees a vision of three babies in their matching cots labelled variously, *Sprog, Sprogetta* and *Sprogit.* They're all crying out for pickled onions.

John is in the classroom, teaching his ten-year-olds the fundamental mechanics of rain shadows. Suddenly, he's sitting in the lotus position wearing a toga over his everyday trousers and tank top. He drifts ethereally out of a sash window that opens of its own accord as he approaches and, floating with the clouds, he draws near to what look to be the Rocky Mountains. As he rises to transcend the peaks, he pees himself copiously and as he descends into the plain beyond, his trousers mercifully become arid in an instant. In the blink of an eye he's drifting over the school and back in through the window. After three reluctant circuits of the room, he floats down to his place in front of his pupils, calmly removes his yoga-toga and retrieves his leathern-elbowed tweed coat from the back of his chair.

"I must give up eating pickled onions, John. I had an awful nightmare last night," says Janet the next morning.

"Tell me about it, Janet."

"It was like this…"

"On second thoughts, *don't* tell me about it. *I* had a nightmare too. I suspect it must have been the cheese… not my three pickled onions."

"Then *you* tell *me*, John. What was *your* dream about?"

"You don't want to know, Janet. Anyway, I'll be late for school. *You* look after yourself and *Sprog* now. I'll be home at the usual time tonight."

"Please don't call the baby *Sprog*, John. I've developed quite an aversion to it."

"What? The baby?"

"No. The name."

Later in the week, at Saint Jude's Primary School tucked away in the warren of Oxford's back streets, John is addressing the ten-year-olds of class 3C.

"Right, class. I was going to tell you today about rain shadows, but that can wait for now. Instead, we'll concentrate on revising the capital cities of the world… I mean, not actually changing them… just ensuring they're instilled into your pea-like brains. We only did them just before Christmas, so you should be able to remember them all. Now, who can tell me the capital of France?"

"Please, sir," calls out Mickey Jackson, stretching to raise his hand higher than anyone else.

"Yes, Michael?"

"F, sir."

"I beg your pardon, Michael. Report to me after, boy... Oh, I see... F."

"Yes sir. F... F is the capital of France. It's obvious."

John's not sure if Mickey is a thicky or just having a laugh.

"Right then, Michael. So what's the capital of Finland? I suppose you think that's F too... we'll, I certainly don't think it's *Funny*, is it?"

"No, sir. Sorry, sir."

"You know, there must be something missing in your genes."

The boy looks down at the fly of his short trousers.

"Your *genes*, Michael... *g-e-n-e-s*. How your father manages to hold down a job as bus depot manager if he's anything like you, I really don't know."

"Yes, sir. Sorry, sir. But I haven't got any jeans, sir."

"Exactly, Jackson. I imagine you may be right, boy. Now then, class... you all should know by now that the capital of France is Paris... not F. Can someone else tell me... what's the capital of Spain?"

More arms go up, less bashful now, all confident that no one could be as stupid as Mickey.

"Yes, Molly Flanders," says the geography teacher, in renewed hope.

"Europe, sir."

"So the capital of Spain is Europe. Right, Molly... I mean *wrong*, Molly. The capital of Spain is Madrid. Look, We'd better go back and cast some light on rain shadows after all."

'God, give me strength,' thinks John. 'Saint Jude's? Don't they say he was the patron saint of lost causes? I'm sure headmasters don't have all this trouble.'

Then, just as John is about to confront his dreamed incontinence, the school secretary bursts in, fit to burst like a rain cloud.

"Mr. Barrington! Mr. Barrington! Your wife's been taken in to the maternity unit at the General Hospital. Her waters have broken. She's having the baby."

"Oh, my word! Oh, my God!" calls out John, running around like a headless chicken, while the school kids all start cheering and raising and dropping the hinged lids of their desks in unison with a rhythmic clatter.

"You get away immediately, Mr. Barrington. I've called on Humphrey Harrison to take over here. He's on his way *now*."

And off dashes John Barrington, leaving his capital cities, his rain shadows and his briefcase behind him. He reaches the bus stop and, after what seems like a two-hour wait for a Number 9 bus that's actually less than two minutes, it arrives. A little calmer now, he sits on the bus for what seems like a fifteen-minute ride that actually *is* fifteen minutes. Alighting at the bus stop outside the hospital, he dashes through the crowded car park, anxiety building once more, and runs into maternity reception.

"Mrs. Baby's having a Barrington. Which ward is she on?"

"I presume you mean Mrs. Barrington's having a baby don't you, sir?"

"That's right. How did you know?"

"They *do* tell me these things, sir. It does seem to help somehow. Apparently she's in theatre. There were some minor complications, but everything is okay and she should be back on the ward shortly. Mother and baby are both fine. If you make your way to Ward 7, they'll see to you there."

"Thank you. Thank you, doctor... nurse..." says John, absently.

"Just plain Mrs. Smykolowszyczovski will do. It's that way, sir... down the corridor."

"Thank you, Mrs. Sm... Mrs. Smyk... Mrs...." he burbles, as he fades from earshot down the long corridor to the ward, still not knowing if it's a boy or a girl, but at least relieved that it's not both.

"We're *not* calling him *Sprog*," insists Janet, after she's wheeled back into the ward with the baby safely in her arms.

"Of course not, Jan. I shan't mention it again. Is it a boy or a girl? What *shall* we call her... him... it?"

"I did just say *'him'*, John. I rather like *Oxford*," says Janet.

"So do I. We should go there again in the spring. We can take in the Ashmolean."

"No, John. We *live* in Oxford. I mean Oxford for the *baby's* name."

"Oxford Barrington, Jan? It sounds like the name of a car."

"Now *I'd* say it sounds distinguished. Anyway, my dad and his forefathers came from Oxford... and the Barringtons aren't far from Oxford either remember. Lovely villages, the Barringtons."

"Four fathers, Janet? Your grandma was a bit of a girl, wasn't she?"

"John! Don't be so childish."

"I suppose you're right. *I* quite like Oxford too. And it's far nicer than naming him after your father. That *would* be a mouthful."

"And what would be wrong with Bartholomew Barrington, might I ask?"

"He'd need extra-long cheque books for a start."

"Oxford it is then."

"Right, Jan. Oxford it is."

Chapter Five

Algernon and Romulus

'Oxford Barrington. I really do like it,' thinks John, as he mounts the bus back to their flat. *'We must take him to see the Barringtons sometime soon... seat of his heritage, I suppose. And we can take in Burford too. Lovely place, Burford.'*

The bus is heaving and, with standing room only, John inches his way along the lower deck, nudging up to a tall but muscular, spotty young fellow who is sporting a goatee beard with an accompanying Jason King moustache. He's wearing a lilac and blue university scarf. At the next stop, a fat clean-shaven fellow of about the same age as the spotty youth, with tortoiseshell-rimmed, milk-bottle-bottom spectacles and a yellow, blue and black university scarf, jumps aboard and stands next to John.

"Algernon Merryweather! How the devil are you?" declares the tall, spotty youth to the fat, bespectacled youth, with an affectation suited to a Noel Coward play, projecting his voice with such gusto that John's hair wafts in the wind of words.

"Romulus Goodbody! Well met," says fatty to spotty, with less camp but equal zest, not even noticing John's interposition. "What in crikey are *you* doing in this neck of the woods?"

"I'm collecting a few books and things from mater and pater's pile out in the sticks, then I'm back to Magdalene in a day or two for the new term."

"I didn't know you were at Oxford, Romy. *I'm* at Wadham. We do have to meet up, you old rascal."

"I'm *not* at Oxford, Algy. I'm at Cambridge... it's Magdalene with an E. Look at the scarf... lilac and blue, not black and white."

"Of course, you scoundrel. And so you're a light-blue to boot, eh?" says Algernon.

"Yes, and if you have the bottle I'll see off you and your dark-blues in the boat race next year," declares Romulus.

"No fear. I can't *stand* rowing, chap. I hate water after that jellyfish thing. And water's bad for the complexion you know," shudders Algernon.

John cringes, thinking, *'is this the product of our education system? Thank god we've called the boy Oxford and not Romulus or Algernon. Oxford seems almost common after all.'*

The three of them cling to the leather straps overhead and sway to and fro in unison as the bus tackles every bend in the road at unforgiving, unpredictable speeds.

"We must catch up in the summer hols, Romy. I'll show you the delights of the magnificent Oxford and you can show me your piddling Cambridge."

"If you insist, Algy. I'd quite *like* to see a recently founded college. The dust of ages in Magdalene must be inches thicker than the dust at Wadham, what, what!"

"I'm sure you're right, Romy, but I'd imagine that the dust is even worse for the complexion than water, isn't it?" says Algy, avoiding direct mention of Romy's acne.

"I've never found it a problem myself, Algy. And as for water? How can you believe that's a promoter of skin conditions? It's the purest cleanser there is. God's nectar, my son."

"We can agree to disagree there, I think," Algy retorts, adding. "Personally, I find aqua-aversion quite the reason for my beautiful visage. It could knock spots off yours, don't you know."

Algy couldn't resist this acne related comment after all, but Romy takes the gentle gibe in good humour, if he actually notices it at all.

"Are you sure you haven't got hydrophobia, dear chap? *You* know… rabies…. fear of water," Romy replies, in a matter of fact tone.

'Dear Jesus,' thinks John. *'Thank the Lord that my stop's next.'*

-o-o-o-

Back at the depot, *Crabby* parks the bus for the night. *Chirpy* extricates himself from his ticket machine and places it carefully in the allotted space in its metal box alongside a fresh supply of brightly coloured rolls of tickets ready for topping up the machine the following day. *Crabby* jumps down awkwardly from the cab and joins his conductor. They walk over to the changing rooms, *Chirpy* sauntering, *Crabby* shuffling.

"How was the afternoon for you then, *Crabbs*, me old mucker?" asks the clippie, knowing that his driver gets pretty dejected at times and tonight he's showing every sign of dejection.

"I'm alright, I suppose," *Crabby* replies. "At least I am except when we're stuck in those infernal roadworks. Temporary lights never take account of the directional rush-hour traffic, do they. I was really having to motor on every run after four o'clock this afternoon to make up for all the long stoppages on the outbound trips."

"Don't go imagining I didn't notice, *Crabby*. One poor young chap got up to get off and he nearly *got off* with the old girl whose lap he landed in. Knocked her specs clean off he did. She didn't seem to mind though... he *was* rather good-looking."

"This is it, *Chirpy*," says *Crabby* I never get to see any of that sort of action... sat up in the cab all day."

"That's what *she* said to *him*... well not the cab bit."

"Did she really? I'm glad my driving did someone a favour then. I just *hate* it when we're in heavy traffic."

"Just remember, mate. You're not *in* traffic... you *are* traffic."

"Comments like that don't help, *Chirpy*. Look, do you fancy a drink in *The Eagle and Child* before heading for home, mate?"

"Oh, *The Bird and Baby*, you mean. I suppose so. We'll have a swift half. I'll get them… you deserve it, *Crabbs*."

"What'll you have then, *Crabbs*?" offers *Chirpy* as they approach the pub bar.

"Pint o' mild, thanks."

"I did say a swift *half*."

"Sorry."

"Seein' as how generous *I* am and how cheesed-off *you* are, I'll make it a pint. Just this once mind."

"You know, that bloke Tolkien used to drink in here," says *Crabby*, with an air of literary knowledge.

"Didn't he write that thing about *hobnobs*, *Crabbs*?"

"They were *hobbits*, mate… not *hobnobs*. He used to come in with his mates to discuss what they were writing. That there Lewis chap was one of 'em. My dad used to drink in here sometimes, on his way back home from the cattle market and he bumped into Tolkien and Lewis a couple of times. Apparently Tolkien used to call him Farmer Giles."

"Was Lewis a farmer then?"

"No, not *Lewis*. Me *dad*."

"Got it."

"And Lewis wrote something about a Lion and a Witch and a Wardrobe. They used to talk about elves and fairies and that sort of stuff. Me dad says they didn't have an inkling about real life."

"Knowin' your dad, he was probably right."

So *Chirpy* and *Crabby* spend an hour and a couple of pints each discussing the merits and demerits of the willing suspension of disbelief, though they don't realize they're doing it.

-o-o-o-

That evening, Romulus Goodbody is with his parents in the

picturesque little village of Much Rompington on the skirts of Oxford. They live in one of four obligatory, rather insubstantial council houses up on the hill in Allotment Close, away from the posh thatched cottages in the heart of the hamlet. Romy had achieved good A level results at the nearby grammar after passing the 'Eleven Plus' at the junior school. He'd been encouraged at an early age to embrace all things 'posh' despite his working-class upbringing. The books he's collecting are largely on Ancient Greek history, the principal subject he's covering at university and, for many years before, a particular passion of his. He's also assembling a small selection of his favourite L.P.s; Verdi, Puccini and Flanders and Swann to name but a few, for his entertainment back at college.

"Tell me, young Romulus. Have you settled in now?" asks his father. "How are the studies going, my lad?"

"Fine, dad. Would you believe, I bumped into that chap, Algy."

"Algy? Who's Algy?"

"*You* remember... Algernon, in Devon, three years ago."

"Was he the boy with the hang glider?"

"What? I don't know anyone with a hang glider."

"Sorry, lad. I meant surfboard."

"Yes, that's him. He's at Oxford."

"Is he really? Do they have surfing in Oxford then? I thought it was just punts."

"No, dad. The surfing was a holiday passion of his but he had a nasty experience with a jellyfish and he seems to hate water now. He's put on a lot of weight too. He certainly couldn't consider competing for a place in the rowing eights."

"A nasty experience with a jellyfish, eh? Has anyone ever had a *nice* experience with a jellyfish then?"

"I doubt it, dad. But you get my meaning."

"I hope you're eating well, Romulus," says mum. "I've made you one of my cakes. You know... the jam and cream sponge."

"But, mum. I won't have room in my suitcase, will I."

"So, you don't like my cakes anymore?"

"Of course I do. I'll just have to eat some before I go."

"Oh, I suppose so. The thing is, your father doesn't like jam. He won't eat it."

"But *you* don't like jam either mum, can't you give what's left to the dog?"

"Of course not, darling. I'll have to take it round to the neighbours tomorrow, while it's still fresh."

"What... the dog?"

"No. The *cake*, Romulus. The *cake*," she says, somewhat hurt by her son's reticence to embrace her inspired baking... a rare foray into serious deployment of the oven now that he's flown the nest.

Romy's acquaintance Algy had also travelled to visit his own parents at *Merryweather Towers*. *They* live on the edge of the attractive village of Nether Bedding, just five miles from Leamington Spa, in an eighteenth century stone edifice of a building with its own two acre Lancelot Brown lake set in a landscape created by the prolific garden architect himself. Algy had flunked all but one of his A levels and hadn't done too well at Winchester at all. Always on the lookout for females, he's continuing that tradition at Wadham. There are no obligatory council houses in 'Feather Bedding' as some of the more self-conscious bourgeois residents call it. And if there had have been council houses in the village, Algy probably would've been protected from them. However, over the latter years of his growing up, he'd become rather wayward, despite the 'posh' proclivities and encouragements of his parents. On his current visit, the prodigal son had been at the 'Towers' to pick up a selection of *his* old books, like Romy, for company at college. They were in fact mainly magazines rather than books, mostly exposing the sometimes controversial, even sordid, lives of exotic models such as Bridgette Bardot, Jean Shrimpton, Veruschca von Lehndorff and latterly Gia Carangi and Patti Hansen. He too had retrieved some of his L.P.s; Deep Purple, Frank Zappa, ZZ Top, The Clash and more.

"What are you doing these days, Algernon?" his father had asked. "Are you still surfing?"

"No dad, I sold the surfboard remember, after that jellyfish thing. I've told you more than once that I don't like water anymore, but it just seems to wash over you."

"Oh, I see. I'll try to not to forget in future."

"Anyway, dad, would you believe it... I bumped into that chap Romy."

"Romy? Who's Romy?"

"You just think... Romulus, in Devon, three years back."

"Was he the boy with the hang glider?"

"What? No. That was someone I knew at Winchester... If you remember, he apparently used to practise the controls hanging from the joists in his parents' garage, much to the consternation of the neighbours. After the surfboard I had roller-skates. Surely you remember *them*, don't you?"

"I do, lad, now you come to mention them. I imagine they're up in the attic. Do they have roller-skating in Oxford?"

"They probably do, dad... but *I* don't. And the skates can *stay* in the attic too."

"I hope you're eating well, Algernon," his mum had said.

"Of course I am mum, but have you baked me anything?"

"Don't be silly, lad. You know I can hardly boil an egg. I've got some fresh ones though, if you want to take them with you?"

"There's no room in my bags, mum."

"So, you don't care about my eggs, then?"

"Of course I do. I'll have a couple poached, before I go."

"Poached? That could be a bit tricky. Will boiled do?"

"Okay, mum. That'll be fine."

"Soldiers?"

"Of course, mum."

Some days later, Romulus alights from his coach in the centre of Cambridge, stepping into the wild wetness of a January squall. He sets down his heavy suitcase of books and stuff and grappling with his briefcase, he endeavours to deploy his ageing black umbrella. The world-weary contraption springs to life and bat-like it flips itself inside out, flip-flapping violently and dancing to the tune of the capricious wind. Reluctantly placing his briefcase on top of his suitcase, Romy tears at the wings of the umbrella, awkwardly clipping their flight, and wrestles the fractured piece of equipment back into a poor semblance of its original shape. At the last, he gives up on it, closes it as best he can and stuffs it into an adjacent litterbin as his briefcase is blown from its perch on the suitcase into an adjacent puddle. As he stoops to retrieve it, a speeding MG Midget throws a bigger puddle at *him*. He throws his arms up in despair exclaiming, "Bloody midgets!" then picks up his cases and makes a dash up Bridge Street. On he goes to Magdalene Street, over the deserted Cam and into the shelter of the porters' lodge.

"Good day to you, Mr. Goodbody. I trust you are well?" offers Percy Pottinshead, the head porter, peering dubiously over his *pince-nez* spectacles.

"I'm well enough, but I cannot agree that it is a good day, *Potty*," proclaims Romy breathlessly while shaking himself down like a bedraggled whippet.

"I understand your sentiments, sir," says the porter. "The rain has poured almost non-stop for three days now. It's less than characteristic for Cambridge and I fear the end of days is nigh."

"I trust you've been carrying your heads to safety, two by two, *Potty*?"

"I beg your pardon, sir?"

"Heads, *Potty*... head *porter*, don't you see?"

"Oh, yes. I do see, sir. Very amusing, sir," says *Potty*, disguising a sour smile.

"Mind you, *Potty*, I *do* declare that I've just spied Noah's dove settling on the roof of the college."

"I *am* surprised, Mr. Goodbody. Would that mean the waters of the Cam may be subsiding then? Are you sure it wasn't one of the pigeons?"

"I have to say that I saw no olive leaf, my dear *Potty*. But if it *is* the dove returned, and if she *did* have a leaf, then what shall we do with the ark?"

"Which ark would that be then, sir?"

"Like I said, *Potty*... 'Noah's dove'... she'd return to *Noah's* Ark. What else? I mean, I don't know of any other arks, do you?"

"Well, there *is* the *Ark Royal*, Mr. Goodbody."

"Have they launched the new one yet, *Potty*?"

"I had in mind the one that was material to the defeat of the Spanish Armada, sir. Elizabeth I, you know."

"Of course, *Potty*. I see. Are there any letters for me?"

"No, sir. 'Not a sausage', as I believe the young folk might say."

"In that case I'll get across to my room and wring myself dry."

"Very well, sir. But before you go, sir. I've been meaning to ask you."

"Yes, *Potty*. What is it, dear chap?"

"I just wondered. Your name... Romulus. It's an intriguing name, sir. How in the world did you acquire it?"

"Oddly enough, *Potty*, my parents gave it to me. Or perhaps in truth, our good Lord and Saviour gave it to me... when I was baptized."

"No. Sorry, sir. I know *how* you got it. Perhaps I meant... *why* did you get it?"

"Ah, I see. That's a different kettle of caviar, *Potty*. You see, many generations ago, in the early eighteenth century my forebears were very rich, hobbing and nobbing with royalty they were. And these ancestors went on *The Grand Tour* in Europe. They took in all the sights of Turin, Milan, Verona, Padua, Venice, Florence, Rome, Naples and even Mount Vesuvius. Now, our family history has it that this particular pair of ancestors, Cornelius and Christabella Goodbody, named their first son Romulus on the strength of him being conceived whist they were staying in Rome. Had it been twin boys, there may have been a Remus too. So *I* was named after that son in keeping with our family tradition. You see we've lost the wealth but kept the quirky name."

"That's very interesting, sir. My ancestors came from Rottingdean, east of Brighton and if *my* family had maintained a similar tradition, I could easily have been named *Rotting* Pottinshead, instead of *Percy* Pottinshead. Or worse, people may have called me '*Rotting-shed*' of all things. I mean, I like my gardening, but that would have been awful, sir."

"I don't know, *Potty*. It has a certain caché, wouldn't you say? However, to persevere with the answer to your question… When my ancestors visited Mount Vesuvius that year, there was an almighty explosion and it's said that the pair of them had been *in flagrante* in an olive grove on the lower slopes of the blazing beast when the volcano had erupted… and so that son could quite easily have been conceived *there*, rather than in Rome. Not many people know that. And to think… I could have been named Vesuvius Goodbody. Now there's a name to conjure with, don't you know?"

"I do indeed, sir… to be named after a mountain, what?"

"A mounting, did you say, *Rotty*?… err, *Potty*?"

"No, a mountain, sir," says *Potty*, impervious to this Vesuvius copulation joke.

Romy's room is well appointed, yet rather bleak. There's a view of the Cam, and the ready access to it is of good use to him, as he rows on the river at every opportunity. He hangs up his wet mackintosh and briskly dries his face and hands. He turns on the electric fire and boils a teacupful of water in a saucepan on the single gas ring. The room feels damp from the interregnum of the Christmas. He sinks back into his worn-out old burgundy leather armchair gleaned from the local Oxfam charity shop thinking, *'Surely it should be called Camfam.'* He sips thoughtfully at his Earl Grey, so much better than the *Tesco's* budget brand served up at Allotment Close, and contemplates the new term.

In Oxford, on the very same day, Algernon Merryweather steps down from his bus under a bright and breezy sunny sky. He prances along the Broad as lightly as his broad frame and his holdall of magazines and stuff will allow and turning into Parks Road makes his way to Wadham.

'Oxford is so bracing,' he smiles to himself as he half-skips, vaguely resembling a poster for Skegness. Breathless, he thinks *'I must embark upon some fitness régime now that the festive season has drawn to a close'*... He thinks this every year.

"Good day to you, Mr. Merryweather. How does the world find you, sir?" offers Victor Crapper, the head porter, peering at Algy from behind the ponderous oak reception counter in his lodge.

"It is a fine day indeed, *Poo*," declares Algy, lifting his Panama hat in mock deference to the porter.

"I do agree, sir," says the porter, with an excuse for a smile and doffing his bowler hat to the student in reciprocation of the deference he'd been shown, with an equal degree of mock. "But I hear that Cambridge has had a poor time of it with the weather these past few days. I believe the Cam is in full spate."

"Good thing too, *Poo*," says Algy. "My dear friend Romy Goodbody will be encouraged to train even harder in his battle to make the Cambridge eight. Good luck to him I say. In the meantime, *I* shall repair to my room and prepare for the battle of the new term."

"Don't forget to take your post with you, sir. It's in your pigeonhole as always."

"Thank you, *Poo*. It looks quite a handful. I'll open it in my room."

"Very well. But before you go, sir. I've been meaning to ask."

"Yes, *Poo*. What is it, my fine fellow?"

"I just wondered. Your name... Algernon. It's an unusual name, sir. How on Earth were you bequeathed it?"

"Now strangely enough, *Poo*, it was my parents who gave it to me. Or more precisely, our dear Jesus gave it to me when I was christened."

"No. Sorry, sir. It's quite clear to me *how* you got it. What I really meant was ... *why* did you get it?"

"Ah, well that's a different kettle of pish. You see, many generations ago, in the latter half of the eleventh century my forebears were very poor, though they knew royalty back then, for they came over from France with William the Conqueror. Now when I say they *knew* royalty they were common foot-soldiers, but they saw William ride by on his horse. Now, the name Algernon stems from the Norman-French... apparently it has something to do with moustaches, so I imagine my ancestors were of the hairy-lip brigade, and it's become a family tradition to name the first born Algernon."

"Really, sir. Even if it's a girl?"

"No *Poo*, not the girls. The first of *them* is always named after William's supposed eldest daughter, Adeliza. You see we've gained the wealth but kept the eccentric names."

"You won't be growing a moustache though, sir?"

"Definitely not, *Poo*. Bad for the complexion, you know."

"That's all very interesting, sir. *My* ancestors came from Yorkshire and they moved down to Chelsea where they became plumbers."

"Of course, *Poo*. Didn't they invent the flushing loo?"

"No, sir. That's a bit of a misconception, though they did do a lot to revolutionize toilets... they invented the ballcock, I believe. So if *my* family had maintained a similar tradition to your family, I may well have been named *Ballcock* Crapper. I flush every time I consider it, sir."

"Good God! That certainly would be a retrograde step from Percy, wouldn't it, *Poo*?"

"Yes it would, sir, thought I can't see that it would be any worse than *Poo* Crapper, can you?"

"I suppose not, *Poo*. You don't mind being called *Poo*, do you, *Poo*?"

"No, sir. I've become quite used to it really... it's become rather de facto."

"Or even *defacato, poo*?"

"Yes, very good, sir," says *Poo*, seeing the shitty joke for what it is. "And just imagine if they'd have come from Wells... there's a place near there called Wookey Hole. The mind boggles, sir."

"I have to agree, *Poo*. *My* mind is certainly boggled. Oh, talking of names, *Poo*... a friend of a neighbour of a cousin of mind has her two kids here in college at Oxford... Willy and Fanny. Perhaps you know them?"

"What are their surnames, sir?"

"No idea, *Poo*."

"We've got any number of Willies and a few Fannys at the college, Mr. Merryweather, sir. It could be any of them, I suppose," says Victor.

"I can imagine," says Algy. "After all, Willy is very popular, and Fanny probably comes a close second."

Algernon's room is generally well appointed and not at all bleak. It's some distance from the Isis, where is situate the rowing club boathouse. He's grateful for its remoteness, for even watching rowers on the water sets him thinking anxiously about his complexion. He hangs his Panama hat on a hook on the door. The gas ring provides him with a cup of tea brewed with a *Tesco's* budget brand teabag, and an opened oven door provides some immediate warmth for the room. He sips his tea, so much better than the Earl Grey served up back home at *Merryweather Towers,* and ponders the prospects for the new term.

Chapter Six

The Black Joke

The theatre changing rooms are alive with half-dressed chorus girls and half made-up *A.B.V.* brigands preparing for the dress rehearsal. The chorus girls' costumes comprise extravagantly frilled skirts, white blouses and bright, primary-coloured embroidered waistcoats... they somehow resemble an ensemble of respectable *Can-can* girls. The brigands wear white full-length socks, black knee breeches, gold brocaded epauletted jackets and less than authentic plastic daggers. The head brigand has an unconvincing plastic flintlock pistol. The merry band resembles an ensemble of less than respectable brigands. The greasepaint is heavy and colourful to ensure that the remote rows of the audience can make out facial features. All is mirth.

"Ah... the roar of the greasepaint, the smell of the crowd," pronounces Dan Copley, for once performing bladderless.

"Our Fool doth think he is wise, but the wise man knows himself to be a Tool," calls out *Pervy* Peverill. He'd studied Shakespeare's *As You Like It* a long time ago for O level English literature... and failed the exam.

"I come to bury Copley, not to praise him," adds Fred Moulton. He'd studied Shakespeare's *Julius Caesar* more recently for O level English literature... and failed the exam.

"A horse! A horse! A pantomime horse for my kingdom," suggests Kit Harbury. *He'd* studied Shakespeare's *Richard III* awhile back for A level English literature... and *passed* the exam with an 'A plus' grade, much to the surprise of his teacher, Ben Johnson.

"No, no, no!" calls out *Whispering Willie*, in a fit of desperation. "How many times do I have to remind you all?"

Miss Pilkington's fortissimo piano performance shrinks to a

whimper and dies.

"Pantomime is about positioning and timing, boys," *Willie* rants. "When the music for this brigands' ambush scene strikes up, you come on *immediately*... and it should be from stage *left*, not stage *right*. Master Crispin is the only one among you with any sense of anything at times."

"It must be the costumes that are confusing me," protests young Fred. "Now we're doing it for dress rehearsal, it seems all different somehow."

"Look, darlings. This is our last chance to get it right before Saturday. Please, please... follow Crispin's lead, or the whole thing will turn out to be a disaster. Now, take up your correct positions. Miss Pilkington... give the brigands a few moments to re-assemble in the wings, then strike up again from the top if you will."

"I'm sure it was stage *right* last week," complains Fred to Kit as they troop off to the wings stage left.

"You're probably right," Fred, "but just humour him, or we'll be here all night."

"And how come *Crispy's* so brilliant all of a sudden?" says Fred. "He's been running around the set like a ferret all night, nudging his way in here and pushing in there."

"I know. I think he must be on drugs, Fred. Anyway, I'll be glad when Saturday comes. Let's get first night out of the way, then we can see the beginning of an end to all this."

"I suppose so, Kit. It's all a bit bonkers if you ask me. Mind you, Robbie and *Figgy* seem keener than usual tonight too. What's got into 'em all?"

"I reckon I can tell you what it is, Fred," says Kit, as Geraldine, the Principal Boy, takes her place again downstage centre.

"What's that then, Kit?"

"Look out there in front. It's that Geraldine. Robbie had the hots for her the first time he saw her. I mean she *is* a bit voluptuous isn't she? And her voice... siren material isn't it, mate?"

"I suppose she *is* voluminous... yeah. Especially now she's in her costume," says Fred.

"Voluptuous, Fred."

"Yeah. That too."

"Robbie's in there as well as *Crispy* as soon as we run onstage, drooling away, like *Baron Hardup*," says Kit, as he and Fred shuffle into position in the wings, ready to pounce on cue.

"Wasn't *Baron Hardup Cinderella's* dad, Kit?"

"Was he? I'm just thinking Robbie... hard up by nature if not by name? Anyway, he's certainly unprincipled with the Principal Boy. It must explain *Crispy's* new lease of life too. I mean, didn't you notice just now?... in this cave scene, when we were all stood at the back, directly behind her, the spotlight shone right through her costume... 'Diaphanous' is what *Willie* called it, but *he* wasn't standing behind her. *I'd* call it down right erotic, myself. I bet she doesn't realize... or possibly she does. Either way, you can see almost everything. Those silky knickers wouldn't fit a *Barbie* doll... and I'd know... my little sister had a *Barbie* for Christmas."

"I didn't notice actually, Kit. I was carried away with Miss Pilkington's piano playing. She was doin' an incredible three-chord riff. *Status Quo* would be proud."

The company is ready again and *Whispering Willie* shouts action. As Geraldine floats a few steps forward into position the lighting technician hits the spotlight. Cue brigands and on they dash headed by *Crispy* who nudges Robbie and *Figgy* out of his way.

Fred and Kit park themselves next to Robbie.

Fred coughs, "She's not wearing a bra, Kit."

"Where? Let me see."

First night comes around and the brigand scene runs to plan, except that *Crispy* is taken by a fit of breathlessness near the end. *Snakey*, consummate showman that he is helps *Crispy* off the set stage right without fuss. Unlike the others, poor *Crispy* hadn't quite been up to another dose of those skimpy silk knickers exhibited in sultry splendour before him.

Fortunately for *A.B.V. Crispy* makes a full recovery, Geraldine by now wearing a heavy cloak for the finale that includes the modified *Black Joke* dance.

The public performances go well. *Snakey* is particularly pleased with the standard of dancing throughout, reinforcing his arguably justifiable belief that Morris dancing can be at the same time very dignified *and* great fun. *Whispering Willie* and *The Old Board-walkers* are all appreciative of the effort the lads have put into supporting their venture and invite them along to their after show party as a big thank you. Geraldine has dispensed with her cloak and the diaphanous Principal Boy gives *Crispy* a full frontal kiss much to the envy of Robbie... and *Crispy* sits down, breathless once again.

"It really *is* behind us now," declares Kit, with some relief.

Morris dancing has for many generations been overtly a bastion of misogyny, despite its salvation in the hands of the women of the early twentieth century literally picking up the cudgels and dancing whilst many of their men-folk danced their own way to oblivion in the First World War. And certainly as late as the nineteen-seventies this misogyny had still been prevalent.

Thankfully, women's sides have now blossomed again and sit on a par with, often surpassing, the men in many aspects of the dark art; in the skill of dancing, in discipline of execution, and in all things aesthetic... and they tend to drink less beer. 'Mixed' sides of men and women also now proliferate... a sad trend, some would say. 'They seem to jar,' or 'a disparity in physical style,' or 'neither one thing nor the other,' can come the plaintiff cries.

The misogyny trait persists in many walks of life, of course, but the 'liberation women' are also in danger of being hoist with their own petard... perhaps overreacting to history and applying the old perspective to an improving place at the table. Soon they may become as heathen and insular as the men, wishing dominance rather than equality... and what modern woman would wish to be domineering... surely, not one? Yet who in their right mind would want equality with Morris men in any case, for heaven's sake? Vive la différence! Or of course, as some Morris *men* would still insist, Vive *le* difference!

Now *A.B.V. Morris Men* might be regarded as collectively misogynist but individually one or two of them *love* women with a passion... one of them is Robin Watts, though love is perhaps the wrong word. Robbie is such a consummate rake, he can simultaneously clear a lawn of autumn leaves using a garden rake in one hand and seduce a girl in the contiguous shrubbery using the other hand... an ambidextrous rake, in fact.

-o-o-o-

At home, Ida sits herself down at the dining room table and carefully places her latest library books to one side. Then she unrolls an impressively large scroll of paper and weights the corners down neatly with four small, lead-filled linen pads that she's made... modelled on the ones in the reference library. She lifts down a heavy tin box from a high shelf and unlocks it with a key that's hanging hidden on pink ribbon around her neck. Lifting the lid, she takes out her spiral-bound reporter's notebook and her three biros... one black, one blue and one red. She shuffles the remaining contents of the box around and produces a small electronic calculator.

"What the heck is it that you find in those books, Ida?" asks

Bert, who's now home from the infirmary and showing more interest than his usual *no* interest. "And that chart, with all those moons and planets and things? Is it astrology? Can you tell me fortune then?"

"You may well ask, Bert Hall. But I don't need astrology to tell you your fortune. I already know that you're destined for a shock if you don't soon get your big lazy bum into gear."

"I'm doin' me best, Ida. It was a serious operation. I mean Mr. McSporran said it was textbook, so it must have been a serious one."

"You know, Albert. I sit next to *Gabby* on the bus most times when I go to the shops in town but I've no idea why he's on the bus so much... he hardly ever brings back any shoppin' because his daughter brings his groceries for him. But, whatever his reasons, I swear he covers more mileage in a week than you do in a year. Come to that, he does more mileage than most of your racing tips do in a year. So, never you mind about my little pastime here. *Gabby* shows more interest than *you* ever do and I've half a mind to run off with him. And if I do, I'll take me tin with me. Got it?"

"Yes, Ida. I'll do me best... I *will* start trying harder... tomorrow."

"Good!"

-o-o-o-

When Algy Merryweather had settled in for the new Hilary term at Wadham in Oxford, he'd been more than a little apprehensive. With poor A level results, he'd felt a bit of a fraud at obtaining his place in the first place. And with his aversion to rowing and all things aqueous, he'd felt even more of an impostor. And when he'd considered his equal aversion to the disciplines of study, all he seemed to have left as a salvation of his sanity was the prospect of conjoining with the perceived plentiful supply of female students. And so the journey through his degree course is destined to be a rough ride if not an absolute failure.

Now, already in February, he's still failed to hook-up with a member of the fairer sex. He wonders if it's because he's so overweight and so embarks upon a fitness régime. Firstly, this involves making do with a modest beef-burger and *no* fries rather than a double cheeseburger with *extra* fries and a king sized sugary drink on his nightly visit to *Burger Heaven* on the high street. Secondly, it involves jogging instead of walking whenever and wherever possible. Thirdly, it relies on the drinking of sparkling tonic water instead of full-bodied Shiraz. Sadly, just a week after he's activated his efforts at fitness, he undertakes all three disciplines within a half-an-hour of each other and pukes gloriously in *Potty's* hallowed porters' lodge on his way back into college. And so, giving up his régime, he remains as full-bodied as the Shiraz he's reverted to and his totty-tackling has to proceed unaided by fitness or indeed finesse.

January had brought Romy Goodbody the new Lent term at Magdalene in Cambridge. He'd been zestful and ebullient.

Now, in February, just a week or so into term he's reconnected with the rowing club. However, with the dearth of serious female company, harassed only by the inevitable frivolous rowing groupies, and with an over-abundance of testosterone, he's decided to get embroiled in the *Footlights Dramatic Club*. Unfortunately he'd missed the *Smoker Auditions* last term and now finds it to be a bit of a closed shop for the coming year. And anyway, for the large part, the in-crowd seems to be plagued with chronic affectations of one kind or another. They're pursuing a performance of loosely slung together sketches involving papier mâché circus animal heads, two dozen umbrellas and a mad lion tamer dressed as half man and half woman... with the pretext of what they regarded as sophisticated satire. So he thanks his stars that he'd missed the boat on this particular river... and anyway, his mother has always told him that opening umbrellas indoors is bad luck. However his brief enquiries have brought him *some* apparently good luck, for he's bumped into a very attractive Amazon of a girl called Angela, who appears to take rather a shine to him. *Her* particular affectation is that, at six-foot-two, she habitually swans around imitating Virginia Woolf on plant growth hormone. But with her accompanying air of aggressive authority and a tendency to get physically very, very close to Romy at every opportunity, she's less virgin and more wolf. And he soaks it all in with relish. He can live without the *Footlights* and still hook up with Angela.

Chapter Seven

Roderick and Imelda

Early April comes along and medical life goes on apace at the infirmary.

"Well, hello! Imogen, isn't it? Imogen Chesterton?" calls Roderick McMorran as he approaches the student doctor in a ward corridor. "It's seems an age since I saw you last. So, how's your thigh now, Imogen?"

"I'm at the General Hospital most of the time. And it's Imelda, *not* Imogen. I wish you could recall my name as easily as you remember my thigh, Mr. McMorran. Anyway, the thigh is quite a lot easier, thanks."

"Sorry about that, Imelda. It's just that my grandmother was named Imogen."

"I remind you of your grandmother, do I, Roderick? Thanks a bunch." she says, indignantly.

"No, not really. I'm sure your thighs are nicer than hers. So, how long is it?"

"How long is what?"

"Since your thigh eased up."

"It's about three months. It improved soon after I started taking those tablets you recommended."

"Good. Good. So you can dance again now?"

"I suppose I could, but I don't. Remember, I told you I'd given it up, didn't I? I gave it up there and then after the injury. I don't want to become permanently crippled at *my* time of life."

"Really. At what age *would* you like to become permanent crippled then?"

"You know what I mean."

Despite the banter, the surgeon admits to himself that he's drawn to the student inexplicably. Her abrasive temperament strikes him as being rather defensive. He doesn't perceive that

66

this apparent distrust is largely because *she* finds *him* somewhat less than attractive. He interprets her cautious glances as coyly suggestive when in fact they sit on the edge of dismissive. She's in her mid-twenties and her build is slight. Her white lab-coat fits her snugly, barely disguising petite, yet pert breasts and with her short-bobbed auburn hair and scintillating green eyes, she presents a rather androgynous figure. Yet she carries herself with an element of exotic allure that he finds quite intoxicating, his pulse racing in her presence. She puts him in mind of a soft-focussed French dream, but then he realizes that his specs are steaming up.

"Anyway, Imogen... Imelda," he says, correcting himself. "I've been meaning to ask you if you'd like to come out for a drink with me sometime."

"But you're not going to?"

"Er, oh... would you like to come out for a drink with me sometime? And a meal perhaps?"

"I thought you'd never ask. Anyway, I'd better not. What would my husband say?"

"Sorry. I didn't realize that you're married," replies the surgeon with a clearly disingenuous air of chivalry, a hint of horseplay in his expression.

"I'm *not*, actually," says the student, a look of mischief spreading on her face. "I just wanted to know what your reaction might be... and since your response appears to be honourable then, yes, I'd like very much to come out with you. But what about *your* family situation, Roderick? Do *you* have a wife?"

"I did have, but she left me last year for a bloke who owns a pig farm in South Africa."

"Any children?"

"No. Just pigs. He couldn't make children farming pay."

" I meant do *you* have any children?"

"No. None. It's probably rather a good thing, under the

circumstances."

"Oh dear. A bit of a come down isn't it... surgeon to pig farmer?"

"Not really... he's worth around two million Rand."

"Blimey! Two million!"

"Don't get carried away. That's not even a million quid."

"Still... it's hardly a pig-in-a-poke," says Imelda.

"I know, but money isn't everything."

"Maybe not, but it helps, Roderick."

"Anyway, have *you* any children, Imelda?"

"Yes... seven. They're aged between four and nine. Thank God five of them are at school age now."

"Sorry. I didn't realize," says Roderick, sheepishly, wondering what the Hell he might be getting into, but with a hint of inquisitiveness showing on his face. "Surely, you must only be in your early twenties? Are they all twins and triplets?"

"I haven't *any* children actually," she replies, giggling almost cruelly. "I just wanted to know what your reaction might be."

Roderick McMorran is now unsure as to whether he is titillated by this vision of loveliness or frightened to death by her. Is she angel or harpy? She's certainly capricious. But despite being so apprehensive he's egotistical enough, or more specifically foolish enough, to pursue his quest.

"How would tomorrow night suit? We can go to a lovely country pub I know. It's called The Upper Thigh... I mean *The Upton Tithe*... it's over at Watery Bottom, the other side of Water Upton. I can collect you at yours if you tell me where you live."

"Sounds good," she says rather unexpectedly, persuaded against her instincts or perhaps embarking on a little more mischief, "but you can collect me at Carfax in the town. That'll be easier."

"Right... say seven-thirty?"

"Fine."

Now Roderick is rather disappointed that Imelda has suggested he meet her at Carfax. He doesn't yet know where she lives and he's keen now to develop their merely professional relationship beyond the medical. He lives alone since his wife upped sticks and, having established that Imelda isn't married and that she's free of the undesirable baggage of children, his hesitating ardour is rekindled.

Imelda, on the other hand, is perfectly happy to keep him at arm's length. Despite her life independent of family ties, she has in the past been treated appallingly by more than one man and so is hesitant to get involved too readily. She's regarding this encounter more as an experiment... an experiment she feels precarious embarking upon.

Roderick arrives at the Carfax Tower at seven-thirty precisely. Many women would find him attractive and almost as many wouldn't. He has a gymnasium physique, a freshly after-shaved angular jaw and freshly gelled hair. He's dressed in light khaki American style casual trousers, a white linen shirt that's too thin for the April evening and a navy-blue blazer. He'd considered a cravat but, displaying a modicum of good judgement, had thought better of it. He looks as sharp as the creases in his chinos. He wears rimless, rectangular designer specs and through them he casts a dubious eye at a bank of storm clouds gathering overhead. The brooding, boiling mass is bringing on an early twilight and there's no sign of his medical student. On the pavement lie two tramps in a spilled cocktail of vomit and strong cider. They're moaning as if in the throes of dying, but this is their nightly demeanour. Roderick, ignoring his oath to Hippocrates, steps gingerly around the drunks and places himself upwind elevating his nose as he goes to best avoid the pungent odour of vagabond. He resumes his surveillance of the streetscape, looking for his expected companion. Before long a police car turns up to deal with the human flotsam and jetsam. Imelda arrives, looking radiant in a plain white, long-sleeved blouse under a *Levi* denim jacket, boot-cut ice-blue jeans and tan ankle-boots.

The heavens open and the surgeon produces a telescopic umbrella from a blazer pocket, unfurling it with a flourish... he's come prepared.

"Quick, Imelda. My car's parked just around the corner in Market Street. Where have you parked?"

"So you think medical students can afford cars do you, Roderick? I'm afraid we're in penury, supporting the vast salaries of you surgeons, she taunts. I've come on the bus, actually."

"Then I suppose I'd better offer you some redress by paying for the meals."

"I thought you already were, Roderick. Drinks too, I should hope?"

"Of course."

The evening exceeds Roderick's expectations. The meal is a triumph. Imelda warms to him and agrees to his offer to drive her back home. She'd intended to keep her place of abode from him, but aided by that old faithful tongue-loosener, alcohol, she reneges and invites him in for coffee. She turns the key to her front door. He follows her into the hallway.

"Go through to the lounge Roderick, while I put the kettle on," she smiles. "You can introduce yourself to Emma, Gemma and Celina, my flat mates."

"Bugger," mouths Roderick, quietly to himself, crestfallen.

Imelda catches his curse and chuckles to herself impishly.

"Evening gorgeous," calls out Emma, as he enters the lounge.

"Hi, handsome," declares Celina.

"Hello there," says Gemma.

"Hi all, I'm Roderick," responds the slick surgeon, mustering a smile amid his confusion and utter dejection.

"We're all trainee nurses. Not quite aspiring doctors like

Imelda," says Emma.

"I haven't seen any of you three at the infirmary?"

"No. We're based at the General Hospital, the same as Imelda... when we're not in college, that is. Unlike the rest of us, Imi gets to escape to the infirmary sometimes though, her being a trainee doctor," explains Gemma.

"Oh, right," says Roderick, dejectedly.

"It's really good at the General, darling," adds Celina.

"Yes... of course," says the surgeon, resignedly. "Like you say, Imelda's there most of the time then, isn't she?"

"She is," says Gemma. "When *she's* not in college, that is."

"Sugar, Roderick?" calls Imelda from the kitchenette.

"Err... yes... two spoons, please."

Of her three friends, Imelda is closest to Gemma. Unlike Imi herself, Gem presents a more feminine persona... she is shapelier and so a little heavier than Imi without being on the plump side. She wears her chestnut hair longer and in a more formal style. When out and about, she more often than not wears the sort of slinky dresses and accessories that might attract the likes of Roderick McMorran, were he not smitten with her good friend Imelda. Emma and Selina are like two peas in a pod, if being respectively ginger and blonde can allow them to co-exist in one pod. They're both bubbly to the point of being scatty and are forever flirting with the men. Their flirting always seems to result in the men running a mile and this, in its turn, necessitates more flirting with more men.

Roderick grits his teeth, now finding himself in the company of four young women instead of the one girl who is the focus of his expectations. Despite his being a surgeon, he has always found great difficulty in multi-tasking and sinks into the sofa sat between a barrage of attention from Emma and Selina. Gemma sits in the only comfortable chair in the room.

Imi comes in from the kitchen with the tray of coffees and places it on the coffee table. Persisting with the teasing of her date, she parks herself lightly on Gemma's knee.

Chapter Eight

Old Tom of Oxford

With April had come the start of the summer Morris season. In the winter months, *A.B.V. Morris* normally have little to occupy them in the way of dance venues, so they fall to practising newly proposed dances to be added to their repertoire, or else reminding themselves where they've been going wrong with the ones danced in the preceding summer season. However, of course, during this winter just passed they'd indulged much of their practice time in rehearsing and performing their part in the pantomime.

Now, the public at large often regards Morris dancing as the epitome of pointless and effeminate prancing or else associates it with extreme madness. They expect to see it danced on a balmy summer's evening outside a pub where it is a tolerable minor distraction from the fishing of wasps out of their lager, or perhaps to wake them from their obsessive conversations on the weather or on the apparently inappropriate selection of players for a forthcoming England international football game.

There is though a subliminal association linking the two pastimes, football and Morris dancing, represented by the emblematic Saint George flag. And there is in truth a stronger link... the unfailing tendency in the two sports to knock the shit out of their opponents whenever the opportunity presents itself, hence the continuing necessity for shin pads in the one sport, and the popular preference for stick dances over handkerchief dances in the other.

The Morris tradition has many branches and *A.B.V.* have a dance list that covers several of the individual Cotswold village traditions; Bampton (in-the-Bush), Bledington, Bucknell, Headington, to name but a few. Particular favourites of theirs are the stick dances from the Adderbury tradition. These stick

73

dances employ alternating rather than concurrent striking of the sticks with the facing dancer, and the slightest error of judgement can result in the heavy rapping of stick on knuckle… this is an effective spur to learning the dances well, or else to endow the less able and the less attentive with a condition known widely as *Adderbury Knuckle*.

"Are you all on board?" calls out *Pervy* Peverill, standing at the side of the impatient coach driver. *Pervy* is in charge of the coach and the three Morris sides represented on it.

"*I'm* not," calls a plaintiff voice from the nether reaches. It's vaguely recognisable as that of young Fred Moulton.

Pervy strains his eyes, endeavouring to count numbers, but to no avail. The whole coach is a heaving mass of baldricks, bells and beer-swilling dancers, so he takes the death-defying decision to walk the length of the aisle to make his count in-situ.

"It's okay, *Pervy*. I'm on board now," calls out the same plaintiff voice before the Squire reaches the back of the coach. And after three attempts at counting, *Pervy* decides everyone *is* on board.

"Off we go then, driver," he confirms. "*Oxford Union* here we come."

A.B.V. are on their first proper outing of the new season, guests of *Old Clash and Wave'em Morris* who they'd last seen in January. The tour is a big one, involving twelve sides on four coaches. This morning, each coach has already covered its own selected itinerary of several villages around Oxford, stopping to allow fulsome, largely liquid, lunches and they're all now converging on 'The City of Dreaming Spires' for a massed afternoon show in the courtyard of *The Oxford Union*. Trestled barrels are laid on in the debating chamber… Hear, hear! The rabble assemble some two hundred yards from *The Union* and make their way in procession to the venue under a beautiful blue sky… a gaudy show of ribbon and hankies, a maelstrom of stick waving alcohol fuelled revellers driven on enthusiastically by the massed bands of twelve Morris sides. The Scots would have won every battle if this band had been deployed as an alternative to an intimidation of bagpipes.

"Right, lads," calls out *Snakey* Snaith. "*We're* on next. We'll do *The Roast Beef of Old England*, Adderbury."

"No we shan't, you prick," says *Pervy*. "I've told you before. It's *my* choice. We're doing *The Postman's Knock*. At least you got the right tradition."

Four sides had danced already and had worked the crowd into a frenzy of indifference. A dapple of white clouds had appeared overhead on a stiffening breeze.

A.B.V.'s musicians strike up the tune. Eight men in two files of four stand facing front, bellowing a discordant chorus of the song. To the shout of 'rounds' they dance around clockwise and back to place, do a double 'foot up' and back to place again then commence stick bashing with great vigour. As they do, the white clouds turn to gunmetal, the breeze whips up a devilish howl and a crack of thunder breaks on the idyllic scene. Then it pisses it down.

"Remember, lads," calls out *Pervy*. "*We* don't stop for anything… rain, sleet, snow, gunfire, plague… anything."

Kit Harbury is dancing opposite *Crispy* Morgan.

"Ow! You nutcase, Harbury. That bloody well hurt. You could kill someone!"

"You shouldn't put your fingers in the way, *Crispy*. And stop complaining, why don't you? Smile for the nice audience."

"What audience? They've all dissolved. They're inside the hall."

"Well, smile for *me* then."

"You did it on purpose, didn't you, you tit."

"No, I didn't. It's about time you woke up and kept up. You

could do with some fitness training, you could."

"Don't be stupid. I always watch the athletics on the telly, so I must be fit."

"Oi! Argue *off* the field of play, if you must argue," says *Pervy* as he passes them in the hey.

The eight aspiring postmen finish the dance and dash inside, too late now, as the rain flees as quickly as it had arrived. The blue sky fights off the fiendish clouds and sunlight slants down onto the paving flags, steam rising.

"I told you our timing is crap," says Dan Copley, Fool that he is.

"Anyway," says Kit to *Crispy*. "Can I get you a pint? You know I didn't really mean it."

"I never refuse a pint, Harbury," the doc concedes, nursing a swelling knuckle. "I'll believe this once that you didn't mean it."

-o-o-o-

Now John Barrington is out in Oxford today too, on an expedition. He's accompanying his colleague Joseph Jobbings the history teacher who's arranged to bring a class of ten-year-olds on an innovative lightning outing to visit some of the historic sights of the city. The tour venues are as new to Joe as they are to the pupils and, true to his usual expedient manner, he's a little ill-prepared for the subject. For a dusty old sixty-four-year-old, Mr. Jobbings is a sprightly fellow and John, let alone the party of fifteen school kids, is struggling to keep up with him and his list of venues. Old Joe talks ten to the dozen in class *normally*, but *today* he's in overdrive... a good thing really because otherwise they would never cover the schedule.

By arrangement, they're at the Sheldonian Theatre and Joe has explained to the kids that it was built in the 1660s and how the upper structure of Christopher Wren's building had to be strengthened latterly because of the weight of books and documents being stored there.

"Did anybody get killed, sir?" asks little Molly Flanders timidly.

"I don't know, Molly."

"What books did they store here, sir?" asks young Mickey Jackson, boldly.

"I don't know, Michael. But I believe you mean *which* books."

"Which books then, sir."

"I don't know, Michael."

"You don't know *much*, do you sir?" says Molly, less timidly now.

"No time for that now, young Molly. We're off to the Bodleian Library. We've arranged to be there by a quarter-past. Must dash... best foot forward."

John smiles to himself as he follows at the rear of the human crocodile.

As they arrive, Joe explains to the kids that the old Bodleian was opened in 1602 and that the library has about ten million books and other documents.

"Did *this* roof need strengthening, sir?"

"I don't believe so, Michael. Though I couldn't be sure."

"What books and other thingys do they store *here*, sir?"

"*Which* books, Michael."

"Well *I* don't know if *you* don't, do I sir?"

"Yes, well... I *don't* really know, Michael. But if there are ten million of them it's probably pretty much everything that you or I could imagine."

"Did anyone get killed, sir?"

"I wouldn't think so, Molly, my dear, or I would probably have heard about it."

"Well, if you don't know if anybody was killed in the theatre, you might not have heard about it here either, sir."

"No time for that now, Molly. We're off to the Radcliffe

Camera across the way. We've arranged to be there by a quarter-to. Must dash... best foot forward."

John tags onto the back of the human crocodile again and away they weave.

And this time, Joe explains to them that the Camera was built later than the others, in the mid-eighteenth century, and that it's actually now associated with the Bodleian Library.

"I *can* tell you children that, as far as I'm aware, the roof didn't need strengthening and no one was killed."

This is sufficient to silence young Molly, but Mickey is rather more intrepid.

"So why is it called a camera, sir?"

"Ah. Now that's something I *do* know Michael. The word camera in Latin can be translated into English as chamber or room... a bit like chambre in French."

"Does it take pictures, sir?"

"I wouldn't imagine so, Michael, but there's no time for that now. We're off to the Ashmolean Museum straightaway. We've arranged to be there by a quarter-past and it's nearly half-a-mile away. Must dash... best foot forward."

John silently mouths this last sentence discreetly, having decided not to speak out to the kids on the trip, knowing how testing they can be. It's Joe's outing after all. *'I reckon with all this traipsing around the streets of Oxford, they've learned more geography than history anyway, and that can't be a bad thing,'* he decides.

And, as the crocodile forms anew, old Joe starts to explain about the museum, to save wasting preciously vanishing time for when they arrive.

"You see, children," he calls from the head of the chain, "the Ashmolean was constructed in the later seventeenth century. One particular item of interest is the *Alfred Jewel*, made in the time of Alfred the Great over a thousand years ago."

"I've heard of him, sir," calls out Mickey, who's at the head of the crocodile. "My dad says that he burnt some cakes. He had a big fireplace... that's why he was called Alfred the Grate."

Joe doesn't catch the comment as he speeds along towards their final venue. John, unable to contain himself longer, dashes for the head of the sprinting reptile intending to correct Mickey as they trot along.

But they don't make it to the Ashmolean... they take an unscheduled detour. Thunderclouds are gathering overhead. Joe is now dashing along way ahead of them, oblivious to his charges, with the crocodile chasing him up Cornmarket Street. Then Mickey turns suddenly sharp left into Saint Michael's Street. The body of the crocodile follows the head on autopilot as if the Pied Piper of Hamelin is charming the kids. This is not far from the truth, because Mickey has heard the excited, if not exciting, sound of Morris musicians. There's a lightning flash and a simultaneous crash of thunder overhead before they can reach the *Oxford Union* courtyard. The heavens open, the girls are crying, the boys are crying... all except for Molly and Mickey who are in awe of the lightning. John is almost crying, but is relieved that apart from old Joe, they're all still together. The heavy skies relent as quickly as they'd shed their watery load and into the beer-fest the crocodile heads rather too late for shelter, hot on the heels of *The A.B.V. Morris Men* who've just finished their wet version of *The Postman's Knock*.

Old Joe at last realizes they've all turned off from his intended route and hurries back after them, soaked to the bone.

The rain-sodden throng inside *The Union* comprises three main elements. First there are juvenile Morris men, both young and old, of every shape and hue, many of them steaming after their exertions out in the rain like a rotting muckheap on a frosty day. Then there are students and other so-called adults of every shape and size, as interested in the many trestled beers as in the primary reason for the event... the steaming Morris men, that is. And finally, there are the so-called children of virtually only one size who are probably as grown up as the other elements of the gathered host. Little Mickey Jackson, with Molly Flanders in tow, has broken away from the huddle of pupils that John is trying to maintain intact. John is wondering how in God's name you can dry fifteen bedraggled kids in a place like this, whilst Joe Jobbings is off explaining the history of brewing to indifferent Morris men who know more on the subject than *he* ever will.

"Michael! Molly! Where on Earth did you find those glasses of beer?" shouts John across the crowded hall, spying them through a temporary parting in the heaving mass, and then losing sight of them as the parting closes as if Moses has signalled again with his staff. Unable then to fight his way to the wayward pair, and fearful too that the other thirteen might break off like charged particles from the nucleus of an unstable atom of Plutonium, he begins to panic.

"Where's that damned Joe Jobbings?" he mutters to himself.

"You'd better put those glasses down, children, don't you think?" suggests a fat bloke in a Panama hat and a houndstooth check jacket. He's standing at the trestle where Mickey and Molly have found two almost full glasses of beer left unattended for a moment by *Snakey* Snaith and Gerry Newman.

The kids obey sheepishly and Algernon Merryweather ushers them in the direction of their Mr. Barrington.

"Thank you, kind sir," waves the geography teacher across the ebb and flow of heaving bodies as the two agile little escapees reach him.

"You're welcome, my dear man," shouts Algy, with a reciprocal wave.

"I hope you didn't drink any of that beer, did you?" asks John.

"*I* tasted it, sir, but it was horrible. All bitter and warm. I really would prefer a lemonade," says little Mickey, angling for his teacher to acquire one for him.

"*I* quite liked it, sir," says Molly, "though it *did* make me think of cooled-down tea with cat pee in it."

"How do you know what cat pee tastes like?" asks Mickey, quite reasonably.

"I just *do*, that's all," she replies.

"Now don't go wandering again. Either of you. Understand?"

"Yes, sir," the two of them say in unison.

John casts his eyes to the ceiling muttering, "Where the Hell is that Joe Jobbings? He's a bigger liability than the kids. Who'd be a teacher?"

-o-o-o-

"I trust everything's under control here, Constable Fielding? It looks pretty packed," says D.C.I. Hector Parrott who's dropped by to check up on his junior officer.

"Yes, sir. Everything's just about under control. Trouble looked like flaring up at one point though, sir… I thought I was going to have to take in a couple of kids for drinking best bitter. But luckily some fat bloke in a Panama hat and a check jacket relieved them of their pint glasses. I asked him if he's the father. 'Heavens no! They're with that chap over there,' he says as they scoot off. It turns out they're with their geography teacher."

"That *is* a relief, Fielding. I always find that when we have to deal with kids, either their parents or their teachers can get quite unreasonable. Give me a seasoned criminal any day."

"Yes sir. Anyway, this fella had a really nice jacket, so I asked him where he got it. 'It's just a routine check, officer…' he said, 'from *Marks and Spencer*.' I'll probably take a look in there myself later on, sir."

"*After* your shift, I trust, Fielding."

"Of course, sir. When I'm off duty."

"Good man."

"You know, sir, *The Union* was pretty busy even before that downpour, but the storm seems to have brought in the whole of Oxfordshire and his dog."

"Eric Stotesbury's not here with Twinkle is he, Fielding?" asks Parrott nervously, casting his eye around the courtyard. "Did I tell you?... I can't *stand* dogs."

"You *did* sir. When we were in the woods with Mr. Stotesbury. But dogs are adorable, sir. Apparently even Twinkle the Rottweiler was really friendly."

"I told you before Fielding. If you want to get on in the force, never judge a book by its cover."

"I agree with you there, sir. I've bought loads of books that have turned out to be a disappointment, even though the covers were beautiful. I blame the publishers, you know. They'll push anything if there's money in it and I'm sure a lot of the good stuff gets rejected because of it. In fact, I've got a friend who wrote a book about a mysterious killing that baffled the police. Funnily enough, there was some Morris dancing in it. The publishers wouldn't touch it though, apparently. Mind you, it may be that it's just sour grapes on his part. I read bits of his manuscript and it wasn't that good really. It portrayed the police as idiots and Morris men as fools."

"Well, they are, aren't they?"

"You shouldn't talk about the police like that, sir. You never know when you might need them."

"I meant the Morris men actually, Fielding."

"No, sir. *They're* not fools either... except one of them... look... that one with the balloon thing on a stick over there. You see, I find them invigorating and commend them for their upholding of an important tradition. I was talking to one of them just before you arrived... Mr. Snaith I believe he said his name is. Apparently a lot of the dancing that they do comes from the villages of the Cotswolds. Each village had its own tradition and their particular dance steps and arm movements are distinctive to each village, except when they're not. The tunes and the 'figures' and 'choruses' I understand they're called, all come from each individual village too, except when they don't. It's really very complicated and accomplished. I might even try it myself, but you have to be very fit and dedicated, apparently."

"Very interesting, Fielding, but don't get carried away. You have to be fit and dedicated in the police too, especially if you want that promotion. And I'm sure there're ways to get fit that are saner than Morris dancing."

"Of course, sir. But as my author friend says, 'there's not much difference between policemen and Morris men'."

"Yes, Fielding. You told me. Now, on with the job. I'm off back to Poxford to follow up a few possibilities on that *'Caved-in Skull'* investigation," declares Parrott. "You know... there's an awful smell of beer and sweat around here."

"That's law and odour for you, sir," quips Harry Fielding, prompting a critical sideways glance from Parrott as he turns to beat his retreat.

The storm having passed, the crowd magically re-emerges to watch the Squire of *Old Clash and Wave'em* dance a solo jig... *Old Tom of Oxford* from the Bampton tradition.

"He looks more like *Old Mother Oxford,*" says *Snakey,* rather disingenuously.

"Don't be such a nit-picker, George," says Gerry.

"Well. What do you expect? They're never up to *our* standard."

"Possibly not. But the worse they dance, the better we'll look."

"That's as maybe. But dancing like that will lower the esteem of the Morris."

"What esteem is that then?" asks Dan. "There's more esteem rising from the pavement than from the whole of the Morris put together."

"Don't let Cecil Sharp hear you say that or he'll set Maud Karpeles on you," says Gerry.

"Maud *who*?" says Dan.

"Maud Karpeles. She lived with him and his family for a while. She used to dance for him," Gerry replies.

"Sounds a bit dubious to me. I bet she was a burlesque dancer."

"Probably more of a Burl Ives dancer, Dan," says Gerry.

"Foggy, Foggy Dew?"

"I suspect she was more Jewish than dewish?"

Once *A.B.V.'s* dancing is finished for the day, they make their way to the coach for their return journey, bedraggled but now dry on the outside and befuddled and wet on the inside.

-o-o-o-

This summer for *Aston Barr Village Morris Men* proves to be a busy one... busier than usual and accompanied by an ambivalent mix of glorious sunny days and depressingly grey, drizzly days.

To start with, they're busy on their round of regular midweek pub-spots that cater to an odd mix of exotic, rural Oxfordshire life...

There are the *pretty* villages, now commandeered by residents of questionable discernment... largely bourgeois imports from conurbations to the south, not least from London. These colonisers have not only swamped the indigenous artisan population but have nudged 'old money' into a reclusive existence... an existence all too often saved only by the essential involvement of such bodies as *The National Trust*. A good few of the novel interlopers populate their glorious sandstone homes only at weekends... properties bought ahead of the price boom of the early seventies and afforded largely by the hyperbolic rise in salaries that City commerce has offered. These pretty villages would be better called upon by the Morris at weekends when more of the commuters are up from '*The Smoke*' to enjoy their country seats and prepared to tolerate with a smile the eccentricities of mad Morris men.

Then there are those disappearing, less attractive, *utility* villages still populated by the aboriginal folk who rarely find themselves separated from the harsh seat of an old *Massey Ferguson* tractor, except to sit on the harsh seat of a bar stool and pontificate on the benefits or otherwise of membership of the *Common Market*. They tolerate the chocolate-box village interlopers for providing them the opportunity of labour in maintaining pristine lawns and producing hay and straw for daughters' ponies.

And beyond the mid-week, the weekends provide the opportunity for *A.B.V.* to arrange displays with the effect of terrorising the very institutions that hold the fabric of the county together... *The National Trust* themselves, *The Women's Institute, The Round Table*, the country fêtes and many more... a sort of whirling symbiotic nostalgia trip to be enjoyed by sundry, if not by all.

And so the summer will glide by through May and June and July... the commuters commuting, the aborigines aboriginising, the institutes instituting and the fêtes fêting. And the dancers drift through the months whirling hankies and twirling sticks and so intimidating anyone or anything prepared to, or unwitting enough to, submit.

Chapter Nine

Chirpy and Crabby

It's five-thirty, Monday morning, dank and foggy. In the gloom of the council bus depot it's all headlights and diesel fumes as *Chirpy* clocks on.

Now, *Chirpy* has worked for the council since he left school some twenty-five or more years since. He'd started with the council selling tickets for concerts at their official booking office in the high street. But after five years he'd been bored to the eyeballs and so determined to move from nadir to zenith in his career. He'd angled for a job selling tickets on the double-deckers and, securing it, he was looking to go up in the world. In the sales kiosk he'd felt as if he was a mere fish in a tank, to be ogled briefly by people offering no more real interest in him than they would a piece of artificial seaweed waving in the ebb and flow of the water. He's so much happier now, sparkling of eye and ruddy of cheek, sprinting up and down the stairs of the bus all day making small talk with his passengers. And into the bargain he's become fitter and leaner, losing a stone or so and now weighing in at around eleven-stone-seven. He inhabits an end-of-terrace house, where he's lived for over thirty-five years, only a mile or so from the depot. He inherited the house about five years ago from his elderly aunt Nettie, who'd brought him up there with her husband after *Chirpy* had lost his parents when he was only seven. He's almost part of the fabric of the house now and, although he has an element of adventure in him, he's never seen himself living anywhere else really. The terraced house is well appointed, furnished largely in the late Victorian style by his aunt's parents. Most of his happier memories are there; delicious ice cream in the summers on humble holidays at the seaside always travelling by motorcycle and sidecar, hot toast and cosy Christmases in the winters at home, birthday treats at the cinema.

Now, he's in his element on his regular bus route to and fro in Oxford. In the warmth of the summers he wears his regulation issue short-sleeved shirt under the leather harness of his ticket machine. In the winters he wears his council-blue serge jacket and fingerless gloves. Today, he's braving the short sleeves for the first time since the autumn.

"Good mornin', *Crabbs*," say *Chirpy*, as bright as ever as he straps on his ticket machine.

"What's good about it, *Chips*?"

"Everythin'. The winter's behind us, the birds are all singin' and we're off on another adventurous day with all our wonderful passengers... there's *Gabby the Mac* and Ida *The Rinse*. Then there's *Caffeine* Jan and *Geog-in'* John and loads more. And then, when college is in, we've even got *Wadham* Algy. So I'll say it again... '*Good* mornin', *Crabbs*."

"It's alright for you, *Chips*. You get to talk to 'em all. I just sit in me cab all day with nothing to occupy me but handbrakes, gear sticks and traffic lights. And then there's you dingin' that infernal bell at me all the while."

"I dunno, *Crabbs*. You must've got out of bed the wrong side this morning. You're usually bright and smiling on a Monday," says *Chirpy*, sarcastically.

"You may well laugh, but I've just about had enough of this job. It's lonely up front. I've even developed a close relationship with the traffic lights at the bottom of the high street. I dreamed the other night I was walkin' them down the aisle. They were dressed in white... with a veil and all."

"Blimey *Crabbs*. It's really gettin' to you isn't it. If you *are* actually thinkin' of askin' them out, then take heed of the *Highway Code*... a green light doesn't mean 'go', it means 'proceed with caution'... just the same as proceeding with women."

They both don their regulation caps and *Crabby* resigns

himself to another day of grind while *Chirpy* looks forward to his regular chats with his regulars on their regular itineraries.

Crabby, unlike his mate *Chirpy*, doesn't live alone and doesn't live in the confines of the town or indeed of the terraces. He'd been born on a farm, out beyond the Oxford suburbs, and still lives there with his ageing, though energetic mother and his arthritis-ridden, though persisting father. Despite their progressing incapacities, his parents still do the work of three people between them. *Crabby*, like *Chirpy*, is ruddy of face and, thanks to the over-generous portions of his mother's farmhouse cooking, he's as chubby as can be. And chubby is unfortunate since he spends much of his spare time under agricultural machinery on the farm. Dependant on the relative progression of disintegration, he's to be found variously servicing, mending, attempting to renovate or resurrecting the many items of plant. You could fry a breakfast on his oil-ingrained hands... the *Swarfega* has given up its battle and even when he's spruced up they betray his workshop propensities. He carries a deeply resigned attitude to life, engendered by his parents' dogged determination but now, behind the wheel of his bus, he's bored and would rather be underneath it.

The bleaker, winter nights seem a distant memory now and here in April, spring is doing its best to get into full swing. Yet *Crabby* is as dismal and down as ever, despite the lengthening days and the relative warming of the weather. He's still perversely besotted with the traffic lights, though he's had several affairs with the stop sign at the opposite end of the high street too. There's no evidence of a ring except for *Chirpy's* incessant ringing of the stop and start bells.

"I've been thinking, *Crabbs*," says *Chirpy* on their lunchtime trek to the works canteen back at the depot one bright blue Monday. "I don't like to see my best mate down in the doldrums."

"What do you mean?" *Crabby* protests. "I'm as bright as ever."

"Exactly," says *Chirpy*. "And that ain't bright enough is it?"

"S'pose not," says *Crabby*, despondently, as he shuffles across the oily tarmac.

"Well, do you remember I mentioned my cousin Jim?"

"What, Little Jim?"

"No. *Big* Jim. *Little* Jim's my *uncle*... Big Jim's dad."

"I didn't imagine it was his *mum*, did I?"

"No... that's Big Joan."

"Why do you call her *Big* Joan?"

"If you saw her, you wouldn't need to ask. Anyway, listen. Big Jim's been doin' up an old Bedford coach. It's a cracker... just your sort of thing. Cream and red he's paintin' it. Only thing is, he can't drive it at the minute... he has a habit of ignoring traffic lights and he's been banned for six months for driving his car without due care and attention."

"I wish *I* could."

"Why would you want to drive his car?"

"No... I mean ignore traff... no matter."

"The good news is, he says we can take the coach out anytime we like, once he's finished working on it... well *you* can... *I* haven't got a bus driving licence. So I thought why don't we take it on an excursion for a short holiday later in the summer? He says we can do that as long as we look after it. Surely that'd cheer you up, wouldn't it?"

"S'pose so," says *Crabby*, half-heartedly. "But *you'd* miss all your customers, wouldn't you?"

"Look, you miserable sod. They're *our* customers aren't they?"

"S'pose so," says *Crabby*, three-quarters-heartedly.

"Besides, I have a plan. We can invite some of our regulars on the excursion with us... It'd be maybe just for two or three days. We charge them a reasonable amount and that way we can pay for fuel and for ice creams too."

"I don't like ice cream. I've got a morbid fear of it."

"What? Everybody likes ice cream!"

"*I* don't. I reckon ice creams don't like *me* either. I once dropped a cornet on its head when I was young."

"Well, fish and chips then."

"I *do* like fish and chips."

"There you are then. Let's go for it. Forty pence worth of chips and an enormous portion of cod... every night."

"And a pickled egg?"

"And a pickled egg."

"Right then," says *Crabby*, now full-heartedly.

"So," says *Chirpy*, "I'll set about the arrangements. Big Jim's sister, Little Joan, don't ask, is married to Frank..."

"What size is Frank then?" asks *Crabby*.

"He's sort of medium-sized."

"I suppose someone has to be."

"Don't interrupt my flow, *Crabbs* you idiot."

"What size is Flo, then?"

"Leave it out, *Crabbs*. Look, Frank works at a printing firm and I'm sure he could do us some really classy tickets."

"You'd better get the punters to pay for the tickets up front, don't you think?"

"Possibly. But I reckon at least Frank can get them printed for free. Posh tickets at the right price are bound to persuade them to sign up and we can tentatively earmark bed and breakfast venues for a couple of nights without commitment 'til a bit later."

Chapter Ten

Morning Star

Back in September the previous year, Kit Harbury wakes before the proverbial lark. Venus, the morning star peers down on the snoozing village of Pockbury as the merest hint of dawn pokes through the inadequate curtains of the village hall.

'Where am I?' he thinks. *'I'm bloody freezing.'*

He raises himself gingerly onto his left elbow, head throbbing from the night of massed dancing, drinking and feasting, hosted by *The Pockbury Prancers*.

'I reckon the volume of alcohol in the A.B.V. men must be about the highest in the Cotswolds after last night. I think I had nine pints myself... or was it ten? I'm not used to it. And all that curried chicken... Gordon Bennett.'

He can recall a whole chorus of snoring and farting as he'd drifted into an alcohol-fuelled sleep around an hour after midnight and congratulates himself on sleeping through 'til now. He shivers as he comes to his senses and drags himself from his sleeping bag. The farting has stopped, but it seems the whole world is snoring around him in a discordant symphony.

'That's it.' he decides, *'The entire Morris population of the world has arrived in Pockbury for the world beer-swilling, curry-eating, farting and snoring championships, and descended on the village hall.'* "I need air, and a pee," he says quietly to himself."

He gingerly removes the bell-pads that are still clinging to his shins, stands up, wobbles, takes a step towards the vague outline of the doors, wobbles again, then plays slow-motion hopscotch as he negotiates the abundance of heaving bodies littered about the floor. He ignores the toilets in the lobby, having decided to take the air and to pee at the same time outside in the fresh, dewy morning. Reaching the outer doors, he stumbles over a massive lump of Morris man. It's *Crispy Doc. Crispy* groans, then farts... a last remnant of the gases that seem to have departed the rest of the assembled host... then continues to snore, deep in conference with Morpheus, probably asking if Orpheus has found his wife, Eurydice.

Kit makes his way to the nether reaches of the car park, where the formal margin of mown grass gives way to the woods. He vaguely remembers venturing there to pee in the middle of last night's proceedings because of the queue inside the hall.

Finding the beech tree that he'd generously watered not much more than four hours before, he takes a deep breath as he unzips his fly and contemplates the world as the steam rises before him.

"What a relief," he sighs.

Then, finishing with a shake and fumbling for his zip, he notices the hankies that are still lodged in his belt loops are stained with blood.

'What the F... Oh, I remember. That weedy bloke who came on his own from somewhere over Midwinter Regis way... I gave him a right clout when we were dancing Happy Man. He just couldn't get the hang of the Adderbury sticking. Serves him bloody right, I say... unhappy man that he was.'

It turns out that the bloke's gone home and nobody really knows exactly where he'd come from. Perhaps he didn't exist at all?

Chapter Eleven

Just the Ticket

Back in April of the new year, *Chirpy* and *Crabby* had continued their discussions about taking Big Jim's coach on a short holiday trip later in the summer.

"Shall we go to the seaside?" *Chirpy* had said, enthusiastically.

"Like I said, I don't like ice cream," had been *Crabby's* dour insistence.

"But the fish and chips by the sea are great," *Chirpy* had said, adamantly. "The fish is so fresh you can taste Neptune's trident."

"That's as maybe, but the sand gets everywhere at the seaside."

"How about Wales then?" *Chirpy* had offered. "The fish and chips aren't so good, but the scenery's beautiful there."

"I don't fancy driving an old coach up and down all those mountains and valleys," had been *Crabby's* terse answer. "And besides, it's full of foreigners."

"But the Welsh are *British*, like us. In fact they're *more* British than we are," *Chirpy* had protested.

"Well, they shouldn't be. If they *will* insist on speaking Welsh, then we should build the Great Wall of England on the Welsh border to keep them out."

"The Cotswolds would be good," had suggested *Chirpy*, desperate to persuade his mate. "There's some lovely chocolate-box villages and they're on the doorstep. My aunt Gertie says there's loads of places that do bed and breakfast... at reasonable rates too."

"Now you're talking, mate. I love chocolate... especially if it comes in boxes."

And so it had been settled. By the end of June, *Chirpy* has thirty tickets from Frank, hoping for a good take-up. They've decided on September for their little jaunt because much of the desirable accommodation is already booked up for high summer, or else carrying quite a premium. But at least this has given *Chirpy*, and the prospective customers, plenty of time to plan.

At the first opportunity, *Chirpy* is touting the tickets. He knows a fair few of their passengers by name, so he starts with *them*.

"Ida! It's lovely to see you on such a bright morning. Off anywhere nice today?"

"Well, if you can call goin' to the chiropodist *nice*, then yes. But seein' as I'm gettin' me in-growin' toenail seen to, then no."

"Is it really painful then?"

"It flares up in wet weather, but generally it's not too bad. I just want to nip it in the bud before it stops me gettin' about me business. It's bad enough in the house with just one bad foot."

"How *is* your Bert these days? Is that problem with his leg getting any better?"

"No, he's still not a lot better. At least he *says* he's not. He seems to be laid up good and proper, but I reckon he's swingin' the lead now. The surgeon, Mr. McMorran, says the operation went perfectly... a '*textbook* operation' he said. Bert seems to think it was more of a *newspaper* example 'cause all he does all day is sit on his arse readin' his *Sportin' Life* and watchin' the horse racin' on the telly. He *is* goin' for another appointment at the infirmary though, so I'm hopin' they shake him up a bit before the autumn... all that coal. And the sick pay from the foundry's run out too, so we're dibbin' into our savin's. I tell you, it's makin' my life a misery."

"I don't suppose you've booked any holidays then?"

"No. 'fraid not. We were gonna go somewhere exotic this year... to Barrow-in-Furness in the Lake District. Albert's got a cousin who lives in Workington."

"Lucky old cousin," says *Chirpy*, smiling broadly, seeing an opportunity for his first sale here. "Well, how about you gettin' away for a bit of a break and comin' on our little local excursion to the Cotswolds with Albert?"

"If you think I'd go away with *him*, after all this nonsense, then you're wrong. Even if he's better by then, I won't be holidaying with *him* for a while… lazy bugger."

"You know, you could always get away *without* him, if that'd make you feel better. You're one of our best customers and we only want you to be happy, Ida. Tickets are only ten quid each, and for that you even get to travel back again, unless you'd rather not. It's two nights away… first week in September. We've got B & B lined up too… you'll have to pay for that on top, mind you. Look, take a ticket for yourself, and if your Bert's better before then and you've made it up with him, I can let you have another. Or take two in any case and I'll refund you for one ticket in full if you decide to come on your own. And I'm sure the bed and breakfast arrangements could be juggled as well, if you don't leave it too late."

"Don't tempt me. I'd do anything for a break from Bert how he is at the minute, but it seems he still can't look after himself for a day at a time, let alone three. He even forgets to take his tablets if I don't remind him."

"You could get the district nurse to keep an eye on him couldn't you? And surely you've got neighbours who'd see that he's fed and watered?"

"Maybe. There *is* Mabel next door. Mind you, after all the fuss with that landlady at *The Hat and Beaver*, I don't know if I can trust him."

"How old is this Mabel, then?"

"Ninety-three this coming autumn."

"I guess you're probably safe there. I imagine Mabel's given up on the *Hokey Cokey* by now, don't you think?"

"She *is* quite sprightly still… she still brings her own coal in. But you're probably right. Let me sleep on it. I'll let you know on Friday... I'm goin' into town again then."

With this, *Chirpy* turns his attentions to *Gabby the Mac* who's sitting next to Ida, staring out of the window at the passing world, hoping to avoid the attentions of the overly cheery mercenary bus conductor.

"Bob! I didn't see you sitting there. How are things with you?"

"Much the same as ever," he says, turning reluctantly to acknowledge the bright ray of sunshine that is *Chirpy*.

"And what do *you* reckon to a few days away in the Cotswolds, *Gabby*?"

"Mmh. What do you mean?" he mumbles, endeavouring to give the impression that he's paid no attention to *Chirpy's* conversation with Ida.

So the resolute bus conductor runs through the details of the wonderful excursion again for the benefit of *Gabby*. And *Gabby* too is rather non-committal.

"Look, I tell you what, Bob," says *Chirpy*, undaunted. You take this ticket now and let me have it back if you decide not to join us... but you'll regret it if you don't."

"What if I decide not to go but *don't* let you have the ticket back?" says the reluctant *Gabby*.

Ida takes hold of the ticket impulsively and asks *Chirpy* for another.

"I've got a little money put away in me secret biscuit tin. I'll pay you for both tickets later in the week, thank you," she says. "If Bert can't go, or if I don't want him to, then I'll come with Bob instead," she declares, rather adventurously.

Bob coughs on his cigarette, but says nothing.

"There you go, Ida. You won't regret it. You buying those tickets has just put the 'ida' in holiday," declares *Chirpy* as he turns to make his way further along the aisle. "Any more fares please?"

Now sitting at the front of the upper deck, a couple of seats in front of Ida and Bob, is Algernon Merryweather. Wearing his tortoiseshell spectacles, he's still sporting the cherished university scarf.

"Town centre please, my good man," says Algy, tendering his fare.

'Ching' goes the bus conductor and he hands the student his ticket.

"Thank you, kind sir," says the ebullient student. "I couldn't help but overhear your conversation with those two rather reticent passengers back there, and I wonder, are you offering student discount for your excursion tickets? You see, college will still be out come early September and I'm intending to invite my good friend Romy up to stay for the last week of the hols, so I'd be interested in buying two of your esteemed tickets… at the right price, of course."

"To be honest, Algy my friend, there *has* been a high demand for them, and numbers *are* limited," says *Chirpy*, with an element of wishful thinking. "I suppose I *could* let you have a couple with a ten percent discount… That would be twenty-eight pounds to you, sir."

"I believe you said 'ten quid' each to those others did you not, *Chirpy* my man? I make that eighteen pounds for the pair, not twenty-eight. I *am* studying *Economics* with elements of *Accountancy* at university, you know and so I'm well equipped for the calculating of discounts."

"Sorry, your heminence," says *Chirpy*, in parody of the young man's apparently snobby stance. "A heasy mistake for one to make when one is collecting bus fares on a busy morning run. I do hapologize."

"That's quite alright, my man," says Algy, oblivious to the mirrored caricature being presented to him.

And *Chirpy* dispenses two discounted tickets in exchange for his first cash of the project.

"Don't *I* get discount then, *Chirpy*?" calls out Ida.

97

"Well, it is *student* discount, Ida," calls back *Chirpy*. "If I give *you* a discount, everyone will want one."

But, I *am* a student. You should see my library books and my reporter's notebook, and my biros."

"Alright, Ida. Eighteen quid it is then."

"Thank you very much, me dear."

Truth be known, Algy is not the calculating genius he's suggesting. His *'Economics* with elements of *Accountancy'* is not progressing at all well and his eighteen pounds calculation has just taken him to new heights of achievement in the field of mathematics.

-o-o-o-

It's past midnight and pitch dark at the Barringtons' house. The baby boy is wailing.

"Janet?" says John, with a question in his voice. "I know you love me and all that, and I love you too, but I'm still having these nightmares... about rain shadows and yoga and things. They seem more frequent now. I'd say it's all the restless nights with the boy waking us. I'm not sure I can cope with it, Jan."

"I know what you mean, John. Oxford is so demanding," Janet agrees, sympathising with the love of her life.

"Well, yes. The school really *is* a headache at the moment, but I think a school anywhere in the country would be a bit heavy going."

"Actually, I meant *our* Oxford, John. Not the *city* of Oxford."

"Oh, I see," says John apologetically as he reaches for the bedside table lamp. "Sorry, Jan."

"Now, John. What are we going to do about you and these nightmares?"

"I dunno, Jan."

"You know, a friend of mine had a lot of sleepless nights last year. She'd felt depressed over the fact that she's getting old."

"Is she nearing retirement then?" asks John.

"No. She's twenty-two, John. Anyway, she heard about some yoga classes in town and after her first few sessions she felt so much better... Something to do with re-balancing her chakras, as I recall."

"Sounds painful, Jan."

"There was something about connecting with her energy vortices too."

"I don't think that would help, Jan. My dreams have enough yogic connotations as it is. I want to get out of them... not deeper into them."

"It's just a thought. It might be a sort of aversion therapy."

"I'm contemplating something a little more conventional actually. You see, on the bus to school yesterday, the conductor was selling tickets for a short coach holiday that he and his driver are arranging. It's an outing to the Cotswolds with two nights away. It sounded a good idea... relaxing and touring the hidden hamlets of Oxfordshire. It's not 'til September though, but I thought if I could persevere with the sleepless nights 'til then, we could go on the outing. It'd be just the thing."

"I really don't think that's for me, John. I know it's a while away, but I'd rather be at home during Oxford's first summer. I'd feel more secure here, in the place I know. But a break away from him would benefit *you*, don't you think? I'm sure you get enough of unruly kids at school. Look, get yourself a ticket and go without us, regardless. But I'd still consider that yoga seriously in the meantime."

"You're so understanding, Jan."

"Oxford may have settled down a bit by then, John, but it would do you good to go on your own. Re-assert you free spirit. It'll be something to look forward to... if they'll let you have time off at the start of a new term. After all, you'll have had about six weeks off by then... six solid weeks of the boy."

"Don't I know it. Anyway, they take stress very seriously at the school. They'd just have to get a supply teacher in for a few days...like with *any* sickness."

"Well look, get a ticket while they're still available, then you could always reconsider come the day."

"Thanks, Jan. And I *will* look into the yoga thing too in the meantime."

-o-o-o-

By the end of the week, *Chirpy* has signed up a total of eleven takers including the two tickets sold to Ida for her and *Gabby*, the two tickets for Algy Merryweather and Romy Goodbody and a single ticket for John Barrington. This has now enabled *Chirpy* to pay a general deposit for bed and breakfast reservations.

"I guess eleven tickets is a bit disappointing, *Crabbs*," says *Chirpy*, "but I'm sure we can sell a few more yet. There's plenty of time. And if we don't, it'll still be worth it, even if we make a bit of a loss. I reckon the passengers who've bought them so far are a great bunch... *The Magnificent Eleven*."

"Some of 'em sound a bit bonkers to me, *Chips*," says *Crabby*.

"Yeah, a bit bonkers," agrees *Chirpy*, "but great too."

o-o-o-

When John arrives at *The Poxford Working Men's Club*, situated next door to the police station, he explains to the steward on the door that he's here for the yoga classes.

"Sorry, mate. You can't come in unless you're a member," says the steward, rather officiously.

"But I'm only here to sample the yoga classes upstairs. I may not like them."

"Sorry. Rules is rules, I'm afraid," insists the steward rather confrontationally, wafting beer-breath into John's face.

"Oh, dear," says John, dejectedly.

"*I* could sign you in as a guest if you like. It'll cost you thirty pence and a pint though. Don't worry, the beer's quite cheap here."

"Fine," says John, handing him the appropriate loose change and glancing with suspicion at the three pints already lined up on the shelf behind the steward's desk.

"Right you are. Sign here, just under *my* signature. That's it. Now, it's up those stairs and first door on the left."

"Thanks," says John as he turns to scale the staircase, a vision of Kathmandu before him and a queasy reminder of mountains and of rain shadows in his mind's eye.

He knocks and enters, finding a rather formal gathering... a mix of yoga aficionados and yoga hopefuls, all sitting crossed-legged and paying undivided attention to their tutor, a Miss Abigail Nightingale. They're all women. Half of them appear to be unfit masses of flesh who perhaps need the attentions of a *Sumo* wrestling instructor before they graduate to the supple requirements of meditative yoga. The other half are lithe and slim in the extreme, perhaps needing to consider the attentions of a Charles Atlas instructional before proceeding to the gentle art of contortion that is yoga. Nonetheless, they've all invested in the appropriate accoutrements for their efforts... snug fitting but comfortable stretch garments in every pastel shade imaginable. Some are wearing casual pumps whilst others are barefoot. As they go through a pre-ordained series of exercises, all of them, both large and small alike, now seem more supple than John can imagine.

A lazy Sanskrit mantra pervades the air, drifting serenely from the stereo speakers placed at the nether end of the room. The calm is interrupted only by the faint leeching of bingo calls from the room below and by a couple of police cars sounding off as they dash from the police station next door.

John has no kit at all, his yoga-toga existing only in the

subliminal chaos of his nightmares. He introduces himself shyly, explaining the tentative nature of his interest. He takes off his jacket and shoes and, realising that he has a hole in his left sock through which his big toe is protruding vulnerably, he removes his socks too.

"Now then, class. When it comes to inner peace and bodily harmony, achieving an advanced state of calm through yoga is the *Holy Grail*," Abigail Nightingale says.

'Or possibly even achieving calm by filling the Grail with ale, Abigail Nightingale,' thinks John.

And Abigail, as slim as the slimmest slim member of her audience, breaks off her instruction of the class to take John through a few loosening up exercises, she turning herself inside out like plaited liquorice, he ricking his neck just watching her perform.

"Right, John. I'd say that's loosened you up enough," suggests Abigail. "Now, sit yourself on that mat and gently try these exercises that the class is performing."

They start with the *Extended Triangle* pose, and John makes a passable attempt at the manoeuvre. Then they move on to the rather more ambitious *Half Lord of the Fishes* pose. John fails miserably after locking his right foot behind his left knee, and requiring the rather firm attentions of Abigail to extricate him. Next they try the *One-Legged King Pigeon* pose. At this point John decides to throw in the towel.

"I'll take an enrolment form, please, Abigail," he says as he puts his socks and shoes back on. "I'll bring it in next week, all being well."

"Okay, John. We look forward to seeing you *then*."

John puts on his jacket and heads back down the stairs, hobbling awkwardly and with his head painfully twisted to one side.

"Come back next week? Who am I kidding?" he mutters to himself as he makes his way swiftly by the steward, who appears to have cleared three of his four pints already.

"Oi!" shouts the steward after him. "You forgot to sign out, mate."

Chapter Twelve

Ladies' Pleasure

Hector Parrott sits imperious in his office. A tray with a pot of tea, two china cups and saucers, a sugar bowl and spoon is perched to one side on his desk. He pours the tea and, as he reaches for the milk, calls out in response to a knock on the door.

"Come in, Fielding," he commands and, as the P.C. enters, adds. "Sit yourself down. Help yourself to a cigarette."

"Er, I don't smoke them, sir, thank you."

"Neither do I, Harry. Actually, I'm afraid I've run out of cigarettes anyway. And cigars too. It's the budget situation, you know. First cigarettes, then cigars... it'll be the biscuits next."

"That's alright, sir. I don't smoke cigars either."

"Neither do I. Anyway, it's Hector, Harry. Please, call me Hector."

"Oh, very well, sir... Hector."

"Just plain Hector will fit the bill today, Harry. My knighthood hasn't come through yet, though people in the know tell me I can expect it any time soon."

With the hint of an embittered smile, Parrott casts a glance at the portrait of Her Majesty on the wall behind him. She returns the glance with an enigmatic Mona Lisa smile... oh, so inscrutable.

"I *would* rather like a biscuit, Hector."

"Don't push it, Fielding," says Parrott, suddenly stern.

"Wah...?"

"Only joking, Harry. I'd give you a biscuit, but I haven't any of those either... not to spare anyway. You see, I usually keep cigarettes for when I'm interviewing villains and the cigars are for the bigger rogues. Offering a smoke works wonders you know, but now I'm reduced to a few biscuits and that's why I can't even offer you one of *those*. With the budget the way it is, the few I have left are the only persuaders in my constant fight against crime... and we're only just into the new financial year. How do they expect me to keep up my excellent crime resolution rate? I'll soon have to shell out for biscuits from my own pocket, if I want to keep my knighthood on track."

"I see, sir... Hector."

"Just Hector, Harry. Like I said, I'm going to have to keep the *Sir* locked here in my desk drawer for now, along with the few remaining biscuits. But you'll be sure to hear as soon as I can unlock it."

"Right you are, Hector. I suppose we *could* have a whip round or even organize a fund raiser for some more biscuits, couldn't we?"

"Nice thought, Harry... but I'll manage. Right now... I called you in for an important word. I spoke just now about fitting the bill. Well, the old bill has fitted *you* up with that promotion. I heard it just now, Detective Inspector Fielding. Nothing about that bloody knighthood though.

"No? Really, Hector?" says Harry, sympathetically but in truth fairly bursting with excitement at hearing his own new title.

Parrott is already beginning to regret putting the two of them on first name terms.

"The thing is, Harry, with this promotion comes more responsibility. I'll be putting you in total charge of the '*Caved-in Skull*' case from now on. Our efforts need to be stepped up and *you're* the man to do it. So, if you find any new suspects I'll see what I can do about biscuits. We might even stretch to a pack of Benson and Hedges."

"But I don't smoke, Hector."

"Neither do I, Harry. Neither do I."

-o-o-o-

With a feeling of déjà vu, Roderick McMorran arrives again at the Carfax Tower, Imi's continuing preference, at seven-thirty precisely. To his relief, on this fine July evening, there's no sign of storm clouds or vomit-laden tramps. He ponders on whether the arms of the law have gathered up the pair of vagabonds and dispatched them to a more congenial life, or perhaps they've been detained somewhere less than pleasant.

Imi appears and draws him from his thoughts. She looks radiant and, as ever, is wearing only a hint of makeup... lashes lightly tinted with mascara and the blusher on her cheeks almost imperceptible.

They're off to Watery Bottom once more. Imi likes it there. It's a quiet place with no boisterous, intimidating crowds and it seems it might become their favourite watering hole. Imi has started to feel quite enamoured of her newfound companion.

They head for Market Street to his prized Alfa Romeo, and away they fly in the summer evening haze.

"Roderick," she says, as they sip at their Pinot, waiting for their meals to arrive. "I've bought two tickets for a holiday outing. It's quite weird really... I don't often catch the bus in to work because I prefer to walk, but the other day I caught it and the conductor was selling the tickets. Apparently, he and his driver had this mad adventurous idea to offer a place to their bus passengers. It's set for early September... I know you'll be able to arrange the time off, won't you."

"Imelda! How *could* you? You of all people should know how far in advance my work diary is committed. And anyway, who wants to go on a bus trip of all things?"

"It's not a *bus* trip Roderick. It's a *coach* trip."

"I wouldn't be seen dead on a bus *or* a coach, even if I had the remotest possibility of arranging the time off. Whatever were you thinking of?"

"Fuck *you* then, Roderick bloody McMorran. You can drive off into oblivion in your poncey sports car for all I care. And don't bother following me, you prat."

And with that, she stands up, throws her table napkin in his face and heads for the exit. Roderick, mortified at her unexpected reaction to his rebuttal, stares after her vanishing form, incredulous and unable to follow. Recovering from his trance, he pays for the wine and cancels their food and by the time he makes it to the car park, there's no sign of her. He makes out the faint sound of a car retreating into the distance, gears changing as it negotiates the steep hill out of Watery Bottom, and he can only deduce that she's cadged a lift back into town from a departing customer. Deflated, knowing that he's blown his chances with his newfound love, he slinks over to his Alfa and climbs in dejectedly, his alpha-male ego seemingly dented beyond repair.

"Bastard, bastard, bastard," complains Imi, as she slams the door of the flat behind her. "How could he? The pompous, ungrateful bastard!"

"Had a good evening then, Imi?" says Gemma, from the comfort of their sofa.

"Oh, Gem. I didn't see you there," says Imi, in her fit of rage, bordering on tears. "It's nothing, really."

"Sounds like a pretty *something* nothing to me. You were meeting that surgeon bloke, weren't you?"

"Not any more, I'm not. If I see him in theatre, I'll cut off his balls with a scalpel, I swear."

"I didn't know you could get that on the *N.H.S.*," says Gemma, trying to make light of it. "Don't you have to go private for privates?"

"Very funny, Gem. I tell you, he's worse than that bloke I ditched last year."

"Who? Sid?"

"Don't mention his name, Gem. His name is enough to make me cringe. The way *he* treated me, the fat slob."

"So you don't see him around nowadays?"

"No, thank God. I'm told he lost his job and moved away sometime after I gave him the push... the further, the better."

"Yeah. Good riddance, eh."

"Anyway," says Imi, calming a little, "where are Emma and Celina?"

"Oh, they're out with a couple of blokes they met in the *Feisty Fandango* bar last week."

"Good luck to them is all I can say. Bloody blokes. You can have 'em."

"No thanks, Imi. I feel more and more like sticking with women myself these days."

"Join the club."

"Yep, I'll drink to that. I'll get the vodka."

They snuggle up on the sofa, consoling each other in an unwitting shadow of reciprocal chauvinism, two ladies in pleasure.

"Gem? Do you fancy coming on a coach trip with me? It only involves two nights away... in the Cotswolds."

"Eh, hold on. When I said I'll stick with women..."

"No. I didn't mean like that. It's just... well, I bought a couple of tickets from a bus conductor. I was hoping to go with *Alfa-pants*, but that isn't gonna happen... not now. And you don't have to pay, because I want to treat you. The trip's set for the first week in September."

"Seeing as it's you, and college holidays won't quite have finished then, I'm sure I can make time, so let's do it. I bet it'll be a real pleasure of a trip."

Imi may not have meant 'like that', but deep down Gem wishes she had.

"Thanks Gem. I'm sure it'll be good fun."

-o-o-o-

"So, Imi's out with Gem then, Emm?" says Celina. "They're seeing an awful lot more of each other lately... ever since Imi gave the heave-ho to *Slasher*."

"*Slasher?*"

"Yeah. You know, Emm. That surgeon bloke, Roderick."

"Oh, him. I'm not sure he heaved enough to be hoed, did he?"

"Anyway, Emm. You'd almost think Imi and Gem are a couple. They've been a bit close ever since we all moved in here and in all that time I've not heard them mention many blokes. To *my* knowledge *Slasher* is the only guy Imi had got pally with since that Sid last summer. She's always gone kind of crazy if you mention Sid... and *Slasher* too now come to that. You know, *I* reckon Imi and Gem must bat in the other belfry?"

"Celina! Come *on*. I can't imagine that. I think Imi's on the rebound and Gem probably just feels protective of her after Imi escaped from *Rod the Scalpel*."

"Maybe, Emm, but they *are* going on that coach outing together. They're out now buying bits and pieces for it."

"Sure... probably sun cream and stuff?"

"Not likely... they're hardly going to the tropics. Travel sickness pills, more like. I know *I* wouldn't fancy traipsing round the Cotswolds on a coach. Would you?"

"S'pose not."

-o-o-o-

It's Wednesday night and *A.B.V. Morris Men* are out on one of their regular summer pub spots. Tonight, having danced at the imaginatively named *Fordlington Arms*... at Fordlington, they've just arrived at *The Bottom and Barnacle* at the other end of the village with bells jingling, sticks clattering and with hankies akimbo. The unsuspecting customers are caught off guard because the landlord has forgotten to put up the warning posters. Half the regulars, the unadventurous ones, make a beeline for the car park and for *The Fordlington Arms*. The adventurous ones and the uninitiated ones sit tight, despite the chaotic profusion of baldricks and tankards, expecting to be entertained in good old English traditional mayhem.

After dancing a blend of sedate hanky dances, a rather more sedate hand-clapping dance and a couple of downright dangerous stick dances in which several sticks are shattered and several skulls narrowly escape the same fate, *Pervy* Peverill announces that the troupe will troop into the pub for a *tea* break.

"That's T for tipple," *Pervy* bellows above the applause of the audience.

Crispy Morgan, reluctant as ever to over-dance, has been shaking the collection box whenever he can at the bemused audience who, having largely capitulated to the dancers' hypnotic gyrations, are not ungenerous with their cash. Even so, *Crispy* laments the early escape of the *Fordlington Arms* crowd.

"Not a bad spot this," he suggests to Dan Copley the Fool, as he hobbles up and plonks down his replenished tankard on a table occupied by Dan, by Gerry the Bagman and by *Snakey* the Foreman.

"Not bad at all," says Dan, moving his bladder off the bench seat to make room for *Crispy*. "It *must* be a good spot if we can get a pint and a seat before you, mate."

"Well, it's *Pervy's* fault. He insisted I got up for the stick dance we just did. I tried to explain to him that I'd got a twisted ankle, but he wouldn't listen."

"Right, you lot," calls out Gerry to the gathering cloud of Morris men. "Get your drinks in and come over here, away from that T.V. I can hardly hear myself think. We need a quick business meeting before we do our second stint."

"What is it with him?" says Fred Moulton to Kit Harbury as

Kit pays the barmaid. "Business, business, always business."

They pick up their filled tankards from the bar and head over to the beckoning Bagman. Kit manoeuvres his way through the crowd and glances at the T.V. as he passes it on the way to the business meeting. He recognizes the introductory theme tune to the *Cotswolds Evening News*, dramatic as it is… if anything in the Cotswolds *can* be dramatic… as it fades out to make way for the newsreader announcing the headlining stories of the day.

"Right," says *Snakey*, muscling in as he often does as spokesman for Gerry. "As you know it's fifteen years this autumn since *A.B.V.* rose from the ashes to resurrect the Morris tradition in Aston Barr. Now then… Somebody get the landlord to turn down that T.V. a bit, will you… Thank you. Now then lads, the committee has decided it would be good to arrange a *Fifteen Pub Tour* for September. It'll be on the first weekend of the month, spread over two days, if everyone's in agreement. We're looking to invite two or three guest sides to join us."

"Which two days?" says *Crispy*.

"I *did* say weekend, Crispin. Last time I looked that involved a Saturday and a Sunday."

"What? In that order?"

"Stop buggering about, Crispin. All those in favour, raise a hand?" requests *Snakey*.

There's a unanimous show of hands, but as *Snakey* knows of old, this is a vote for the idea… not necessarily for a commitment to it, *'If only hands were raised so enthusiastically in the hanky dances,'* he thinks.

"Right," says Gerry, seizing back the initiative since he's the only one with a notebook. "I'll take names from those who can commit. George, Pete and myself are already on the list, of course. Now…Kit… Kit?"

"Yep, sure," Kit confirms inattentively, one eye and a strained ear on the T.V. screen.

"Dan?"

"Hopefully. I'll have to check with the wife though."

"Make sure you let me know before next Wednesday then. What about you, *Quacker*?"

"I'm not sure. I might be going on a narrowboat holiday that week."

"Give me strength. We need you for music."

"Right, I'll arrange my boat trip around it. For the greater good of the side, you understand."

"*Crispy*. Are *you* available?"

"Maybe."

"For heaven's sake!"

"Put me down as a definite maybe, then."

"Why did I ever sign up as Bagman? Fred, what about you?"

"I'm a definite probable."

And so on it goes. Gerry now has a list of four yeses, two nos, three definite maybes, four definite probables and three wives.

"Aghhhh! I give up. Look, I need to know by next Wednesday, latest. If there aren't enough of you committed by then we'll start arranging a *sixteen* pub tour for next year instead."

Kit is still distracted by the T.V...

"Police are making an appeal to the public..." the T.V. presenter announces, barely loud enough for anyone in the pub to hear, "to come forward with any information that might help them in their search for the killer of the man whose badly decayed body was found in Pockbury woods in January this year. It's believed that the crime was committed in July *last* year. Hector Parrott of the Oxfordshire Constabulary says that, despite their best efforts at resolving the crime, there's been no trail to follow but they are now redoubling their efforts to solve this baffling crime. Over to our reporter, Benjamin Scibbler, in Pockbury."

"Well, Detective Inspector Parrott..." says Ben Scribbler.

"It's Detective *Chief* Inspector, actually," interrupts the D.C.I.

"Sorry... Detective *Chief* Inspector Parrott. What line of enquiry are you following?"

"It's too early to say, Ben. All I can confirm is that I've now put my best man, D.I. Harry Fielding, fully in charge of the case and he'll be keen to receive information from anyone who believes they may have seen suspicious activity last July in the vicinity of Pockbury woods, We made fruitless door-to-door enquiries in January, after a gentleman and his dog, Twinkle, found the body and contacted us. It's hardly surprising we drew a blank. After all, Pockbury is a bit of a backwater... off the beaten track as you might say."

"I suppose you *could* say that the victim was beaten off the track," says Ben Scribbler, rather inappropriately, "but do we know who the poor unfortunate is... or rather *was?*"

"Well, no... it's too early to say really, Ben. He's definitely male and in his thirties according to our pathologist, Nigel Grisley."

"*Grisly?*"

"No, sorry, I mean Gresley. Unfortunately, there was nothing to pin a name on him... the victim that is, not the pathologist. And he, the victim, had perfect teeth so we've been unable to match him with any dental records. His glasses turned out to be off-the-peg readers and even his rotten shoes were as common as you could buy. The best we might hope for is a blood match... there *were* bloodstains found on our victim that we're sure belong to the perpetrator. No one in the area has been reported missing, so we feel the dead man must have been a bit of a loner who may have fallen off the radar. He could have come from anywhere."

Kit is straining to hear all this, but picks out much of what is said. Fred is earwigging too.

"I can assure you," continues the D.C.I., "that anyone calling us will be taken seriously and anything they do say will be written down and used in confidence. Anyone can call on the following number..."

As the T.V. detective turns to camera to give out the details, *Snakey* stands up and shouts his fervent instructions to the disassembled Morris men, oblivious to the screen and it's dramatic though whispering outpourings.

"Come on, you bunch of reprobates. You're all needed outside. We'll start the set with *Monck's March*."

"There he goes again," mutters *Pervy*. "He might as well call himself the Squire. I was gonna call *Room for the Cuckolds*. Let's face it, I'm cuckolded at every turn. He takes all my dances from me. I'm giving this job up at the end of the dancing season. It's all too much to bear."

So the meeting breaks up in relative limbo and out they jangle into the deepening twilight for their second dance spot... all but Kit and Fred that is.

"Blimey, Kit," says Fred. "Pockbury woods, eh? *A.B.V.* were over that way last year, weren't they? In the village hall with *The Pockbury Prancers?*"

"I know, Fred," answers Kit, absently.

And Kit's thoughts are carried back vividly to the Morris gathering; his hung-over pee in the woods, the bloodstains on his hankies, the weedy bloke from Midwinter Regis way who'd mysteriously left the gathering. If this crime had been in the news back in January, Kit hadn't caught it. Now, he breaks into a cold sweat, his mind racing... *'We were in Pockbury, but that was in September. What if their dates are wrong and this bloke was killed then instead of in the summer? What if the weedy bloke was the victim? What if I killed him?'*

He regains his composure as best he can, deciding not to mention his anxiety, but with growing panic nonetheless.

"Kit?" says Fred. "Are *you* listening? I said *A.B.V.* were over that way last year, weren't they?"

"What?... oh, yeah, Pockbury woods. Terrible affair, but *we* were there in September," he says absently, swigging at his tankard to hide his emotions. "Look, Fred. I need some fresher air. It's a bit stale down this end of the room."

And so they pick up their tankards and Fred follows Kit as they weave their way through to the far end of the bar where there's a quiet corner. Kit, deeply lost in thought now, is not the life and soul of the party.

"What's up Kit? You look like you've seen a ghost."

"Maybe I *have* mate. Maybe I have," he mutters, contemplating the ghost in his mind's eye.

"What do you mean?"

"Oh... nothing. It's nothing. Lets get outside and back to the dancing. I feel like thwacking a few sticks."

Fred shrugs his shoulders and follows him out to the car park.

-o-o-o-

Now Hector Parrott really *does* mean that Fielding is his best man. Not that he means it in a *wedding-y* sort of way, because Parrott has been married since before Harry Fielding was out of nappies. It's simply that Parrott has precious few officers that come up to the mark. Fielding's only rival at the station is a young woman police constable, but she's been with the force for only a short time. If anyone had been up for promotion, it was Harry Fielding. At thirty-three years of age, he's already served in three different constabularies... in Birmingham, Nottingham and Lincoln. He secured a transfer back to the Oxford suburb of Poxford, his birthplace, after solving a case involving two outlandish theatrical clowns and a Madame Roquefort at a renowned cheesy brothel in Lincoln.

"We know there've been some very funny goings-on in that brothel recently," Fielding had said when he'd arrested the fat man with the long-nosed mask and his thin sidekick with the baggy trousers, "and there's a strong smell of something much older in the place."

When the police had raided the bawdy house, the two Italian clowns had made a dash for it in their bright yellow Fiat 128, but the wheels and one of the doors had fallen off at the traffic lights on the high street, thwarting their escape. Fielding and his driver had jumped from the police *Panda* car and had given chase on foot as the clowns had legged it down a side street. The thin clown had then tripped over his over-long baggy trousers and the fat clown had obligingly tripped over the thin clown, his forward vision hampered by his mask.

"You are not obliged to say anything... etc.," Harry had said to them as he and the driver had handcuffed the two of them, "but your names would be useful."

The zany pair had a basic understanding of English and answered with a strong Italian accent, each in his turn.

"I ham thee world famous Pantalone from Turin," said the outlandish thin man with the extravagant loon pants.

"And me... I ham thee renowned Capitano from Padua," said the weird and wonderful fat masquerader.

"The Commedia Dell'arte, she leeves," added Pantalone.

In all the confusion, Madame Roquefort had escaped, but was found later with the aid of a scent-trained tracker dog.

Chapter Thirteen

Bobbing Around

"*Crabby!* Big Jim says the coach restoration is finished," *Chirpy* enthuses. "We can go and look at it tomorrow in the workshop, on our day off. Let's ride out to his place in the morning on the motorbike."

Chirpy is very proud of his motorbike combination. He inherited it from his aunt Nettie along with the house. The bike had belonged to Gregory, her husband, who'd died ten years before she did. It had lain for those ten years under tarpaulin in the small impromptu timber garage that uncle Gregory had tacked onto the side of the terrace. He'd bought the '*Norton Big 4*' bike and sidecar outfit brand new back in 1937, a couple of years before the outbreak of war and it had been his pride and joy for over thirty years. By co-incidence it was bought the same year that *Chirpy* was born... he remembers being whizzed around wartime Oxfordshire from the age of four by his uncle, with aunt Nettie riding pillion and with him in the sidecar. Gregory had worked in heavy engineering, which was a reserved occupation, so he'd joined the local *Home Guard* to do his bit. There were very few vehicles on the roads back then due to petrol rationing but uncle Gregory knew a man who knew a spiv who had access to 'spare' petrol coupon books, so the country roads were almost their very own. There seemed to be endless sunny-day picnics with occasional thunderstorm dashes back home. Then when *Chirpy* was seven, his parents were killed in a dreadful fire at home, when the boy had been with Nettie and Gregory. It was then that he'd moved in with them.

As Gregory had gradually become infirm in his sixties, he'd de-commissioned his pride and joy, mothballing it in the shed. And when he'd died, the bike was left there pristine in deference to aunt Nettie's wishes. But as *she* became ill herself, she asked *Chirpy* to look after it and to relive some of those halcyon days in memory of his adoptive parents. And so now, it gets an airing whenever *Chirpy* has the time, especial on sunny days.

"What time then, *Chirpy*?"

"We can have a lie in, so say about six-thirty? It'll only take about half-an-hour to get to Jim's, but he's always up before the lark."

When they arrive, Big Jim is still in bed, but his dad, Little Jim greets the pair brightly.

"Big Jim's not up yet. He never gets up before the lark, *Chirpy*."

"I thought he did?"

"No. That's me. Maybe *I* can help you, and meanwhile I'll get Big Joan to give him a nudge."

"He said to come over to see the coach," says *Chirpy*.

"That's alright. I know where he keeps the keys to the workshop. I've got some coffee on the stove. I'll get you a couple of mugs."

"Two sugars each, Jim, thanks," calls out *Chirpy*, as off Little Jim scoots. "We'll wait for you over near the workshop."

In a trice, Little Jim returns with the workshop keys, hotly followed by Big Joan who's balancing two mugs of tea and a couple of huge buns on a tiny tray.

"Thanks Jim," says *Chirpy*, grasping the keys.

"Thanks Joan," says *Crabby*, taking hold of a mug of tea and grasping one of Joan's deliciously enticing buns.

"Didn't you say *coffee*, Little Jim?" says *Chirpy*. "Not that it matters."

"You don't want his stewed coffee, boys," says Big Joan. "Even when it's fresh, *his* coffee tastes like tea, so I thought you may as well have the real thing."

Joan puts down the tray on a nearby 45-gallon oil drum.

"How about that then, *Crabbs*. Almost as good as the personal service we get from our Agnes in the depot canteen."

Crabby, face stuffed with cake replies, "I *do* prefer Joan's buns though."

Chirpy tackles the heavy security locks and the hasps and staples on the workshop doors with the bunch of keys that Little Jim has handed him and in they go to an Aladdin's cave of motor maintenance. The workshop is essentially an old brick barn, but it has all the kit anyone could imagine. The wall-benches and the shelves behind them are decked out neatly with vices, spanners and screwdrivers, micrometers and callipers, sparkplugs, red-lead oxide paint, cellulose paint sprayers and a hundred exotic pieces of kit even *Crabby* doesn't recognize, all collected through the ages by Big Jim and his forebears. The smells of engine oil, *Redex* and fibreglass resin mingle on the air. And there before them is the much-vaunted coach.

"Just look at that, will you, *Crabbs*. That cream... and the red... and the chrome. The colours are so fresh, aren't they? And with the seats all reupholstered, it's gorgeous."

"It does look good, mate. Big Jim's a craftsman, no doubt about that."

"All it needs now is the chequered go-fast tape for when you get stuck at the roadworks."

"Leave it out, *Chirpy*."

"Sorry, pal. I was only joking."

"It's not funny."

"I know. I just can't help it, can I. We can forget the tape though... there won't be any roadworks on the itinerary for our trip. In fact we'll be drifting along like a dream in the peacefulness of the country lanes, stopping off at leisure to enjoy all those quiet rural pubs."

"We can't thank you enough, Big Jim," declares *Chirpy* when the man himself turns up. "She's a beauty."

"Sure is," agrees *Crabby*.

"And she goes like a dream, lads," says Big Jim, proudly. "Now that I've done the re-bore and all the other tweaks to the engine and gearbox, you'll think that you're driving a Bentley."

"Can we give her a tryout before September then, Jim?"

"Of course you can *Crabby*. The sooner the better, and I'll be grateful for you taking her out. I'll come with you of course... you know, I really can't wait to get me licence back."

Chirpy and *Crabby* finish their tea and buns, thank both Jims and Joan, and off they go, motorbike and sidecar droning along back to town.

On their next free shift, *Chirpy* and *Crabby* are off to Jim's again to take the dream coach out for that test drive. It's mid-morning. The sun is proud in his heaven and has beaten away early morning wisps of cirrus cloud. The skies are blue as blue. A heat haze is rising on the tarmac ahead as the three of them hit the back lanes.

Crabby is transformed... in his bus-driving element, but free from the shackles of the urban streets.

Big Jim stands proudly next to *Crabby*, oily rag in hand... his emergency kit for all eventualities on this maiden voyage. He sways to and fro with the rhythm of the winding lanes. Eyes half-closed and taking in the smoothness of the gear changes, he's purring with pride in concord with the sweet note of the engine.

Chirpy sits in the front passenger seat sporting a beaming smile from ear to ear and thinking ahead to the planned outing.

After a country mile that's a lot longer than a mile they take a turn and encounter a railway bridge running over the road ahead. It's a low arched bridge and *Crabby* hesitates, apprehensively changing down right through the gears. He slips the coach expertly through the shadow of the arch and then accelerates away.

"Phew, I thought for a minute I was driving the double-decker. That bridge put me in mind of Rogues' Lane back in town. The bridge there wouldn't take a bus, but the coach... brilliant... no frontiers, eh lads?"

Big Jim smiles, oily rag in hand. "Too right, *Crabby*. I'm feeling the urge to wrest the wheel from you and take over. I'll drive us to the nearest pub, shall I?"

"Best not, Jim," advises *Chirpy*. "That'd be like breaking out of prison just before you were due for release."

"I know, but there won't be any police cars out here in the sticks. I can't resist the urge. Look, *Crabby*, pull into that lay-by ahead. I'll take her from here."

Crabby pulls in, acknowledging Jim's well-earned claim on the vehicle. As Jim slides into the driver's seat, two police *Panda* cars hare round a bend coming into view ahead, speeding with sirens blazing.

"Whoops," says Jim, as he sidles back out of his seat ushering *Crabby* back into place. "Have *they* been watching us?"

"Dunno, Jim. But I did warn you," says *Chirpy*.

"Right, *Crabby*," acknowledges Jim. "You carry on. I can wait a while longer, I guess."

The police cars speed onwards, nearer and nearer, pass them, then appear to hesitate once they've passed, the Doppler of the sirens seeming to audibly dampen the enthusiasm for the chase.

"I wonder where they're off to?" says *Crabby*.

"Wherever it is, they're probably pandering to the criminal fraternity," suggests *Chirpy*, rather proud of his pun.

Neither of his companions notices the quip, or else they don't admit it. *Crabby* re-starts the engine, checks for traffic in the mirrors, slides the coach smoothly back onto the carriageway and heads for *The Sack o' Tatters* at Weppington.

"They do a nice pint there," says Big Jim. "The landlord keeps a real good cellar and his wife cooks a mean steak and kidney pie with new potatoes and delicious gravy. Apparently, she learned the recipe at her *W.I.* meetings. I could kill for that right now."

"Do you think she'll be doin' new potatoes this time of year, Jim? I *love* new potatoes."

"I suppose so, *Chirpy.* But earlier in the year she does it with chips if the new potatoes are old."

They pull into the car park and make their way into the low-beamed old lounge.

"Three pints of the *Fartin' Ferret* please, landlord," says Jim. "My round lads. It's been such a pleasure bobbing around the countryside riding the coach with you both. It's the least I can do."

As the host pulls the pints, his wife drifts in from the smoke room, dusting off a crumpled straw hat.

"It'll never be the same again," she grumbles as she places it delicately on her head.

"Never mind the hat, love… is the steak and kidney pie on?" asks Jim.

"If you opened your nose, you wouldn't really need to ask, sweetheart," she says, brightening up. "I've just brought a batch out of the oven, ready for tonight. I can spare one for someone special. It'll split three ways nicely."

"New potatoes too?"

"Of course. I dug a fresh batch yesterday."

"I'm in heaven," says *Chirpy*, thinking of aunt Nettie.

And so, three-way pie and two pints each later, they're back to the coach, already declaring the test drive an eminent success before they head back for Big Jim's.

-o-o-o-

"I can't believe it's August already," says Harry Fielding to Claude Lord, the day's duty officer at Poxford police station. "It doesn't seem five minutes since we were shivering with cold. And now it'll soon be autumn. I'm sure time speeds up as we get older."

"Ah, now then. *I* have a theory about that, Harry."

"What's that then, Claudie?"

"If you think about it... when you're ten years old, a year's a whopping ten percent of you life up to that point... but when you're fifty it's only a measly two percent, isn't it."

"But surely the ten percent and the two percent are the same aren't they... one year?

"So you'd imagine, but it's just that the first one is a much bigger proportion of your life, so you probably *feel* like you've crammed more into the year."

"Or could it be that later in life you just have more to cram into a year?" suggests Harry.

"But that would make it seem longer, wouldn't it?"

"Only if it was *boring* things you were trying to cram in."

"Thanks a bunch, Harry. You've got me all confused now."

"Don't worry, Claudie. I'm more than confused myself. I never *was* any good at maths."

"Still, you're right about the summer flying by, Harry. I mean it's a whole seven months since that 'Caved-in Skull' investigation started, back in January. It'd all gone very quiet recently hadn't it and now it's rearing its ugly head again, it's bound to come centre stage before too long, don't you reckon?"

"I don't need reminding, thanks a bunch, Claudie. As you know I've been put back on the case now I'm a D.I... well, we've just got back to the station after a wild-goose chase over Weppington way. The landlord of *The Sack o' Tatters* had phoned in to say he'd found what he thought was a Morris man's straw hat stuffed down behind the settle in the smoke room. He'd thought it looked very much like the hats that *The Pockbury Prancers Morris Men* wear and, recalling our appeals for information, reckoned he'd better contact us."

"Yes. I know that's where you've been, Harry. *I took the call, didn't I? I was on the desk.*"

"Sorry, Claudie. Of course you were. My mind's so full of things to remember at the minute, I'd forgotten. Anyway, I thought the hat might give us some much-needed clues, so we dashed there in two *Panda* cars with sirens blazing. But by the time we arrived, the landlord's wife had picked up the hat, inspected it and realized it's her *W.I.* hat from the previous year's harvest festival. 'I've been looking for that all over the place' she said. If only her husband had checked with *her* before he called us out. So then we dashed all the way back with sirens blazing again."

"But why the rush and all the fanfare of sirens, Harry? The straw hat was hardly gonna make a run for it, was it?"

No, Claudie... but it's what policemen *do*. Once you're in a police *Panda* car, you've got to make an impression. I mean it reassures the public that we're on the case. It's the first thing I learned at police cadet school."

"It's back to square one then is it, Harry?"

"Yep. As you know, we got nowhere with the early enquiries. Trouble is, with Parrott putting me in total charge of the *'Caved-in Skull'* along with lots of other unsolved cases, I've had too much on. See, that's what I mean about cramming things in. By the way, he's still in the cooler you know... with the temperature turned right down."

"Who? Parrott?"

"No, the man with the skull. And I hope he's not literally gonna raise his ugly head, Claudie. That *would* give us all a fright, don't you think?"

"Sure would. And *I* hear that Parrott isn't best pleased about the lack of progress, so I imagine Hector will raise *his* head soon and chase your tail again. I shouldn't be surprised anyway," says Claude.

"That'd give us an even bigger fright. What with the

impossibility of identifying him, with no one coming forward to claim what's left of him and a tight budget, I'd be happier if we put the *'Caved-in Skull'* on the back burner for a fair while yet."

"Back burner, eh? That'd soon thaw him out... and then he might *well* raise his head, Harry."

"Doesn't bear thinking about, Claudie."

-o-o-o-

August turns to September and *A.B.V.* have managed to recruit enough of the definite maybes and probables, along with two guest sides, to make their *Fifteen Pub Tour* worthwhile. With some intending to follow on in cars, there are enough to fill a coach comfortably.

"Come on lads. Look lively. All aboard for *The Magical Fifteen Pub Tour*," bawls *Snakey* at the raggle-taggle mob of thirty-five Morris men seeping out into the car park of *The Nautical Maureen*. "We've fourteen more pubs and God only knows how many more villages to get through by tomorrow evening. Those travelling on the coach, make sure you're the ones who should be. And those of you in your own cars, make sure you know the way, or else follow on closely. We're due at *The Pikestaff and Raven* in Great Parva in thirty-minutes, then on to *The Two-and-Twenty Blackbirds* in Little Magna, so look sharp."

"Who's *he* kidding?" says Kit to *Crispy Doc*. "'Look sharp', he says. *You* couldn't look sharp in a boxful of blunt knives, *Crispy*."

"Cheeky bugger," protests the doc. "At least *I've* had a shave this morning. *You* look more stubbly than a stubble field."

"*My* dad's bigger than *your* dad," says Kit, goading *Crispy* on.

"*My* dad's a policeman," replies the doc, determined to give as much as he's getting.

"Get a move on, you pair, or we'll be late," *Snakey* insists.

"Anyway," says Kit, as the pair bustle each other onto the coach, "this tour may be a small one but it looks like being as good as *The Siddlebury Muck Cart Tour* we went on last year."

"I guess so," agrees *Crispy*. "All those bloody Pennine hills... they were too much for my dodgy knees. I'm very delicate you know. Give me the gentle rolling Cotswolds any day."

"And *you're* an expert at gentle rolling, aren't you, *Crispy?*"

"Leave it out, Kit. *You* wait 'til you get to my age."

"Nobody gets to your age... except possibly giant turtles. And even they move faster than you."

"Well, as for all that clog dancing. It does my head in. It's like a demented Dutch army invading the place." adds *Crispy*, determined to have his say and ignoring Kit's slur on his capacity for movement.

"So, what have the Dutch ever done to you, *Doc?*" Kit asks.

And so their banter continues, Kit unwittingly inflicting hurt through his joking and *Crispy* unconvincingly inflicting joking through his hurt.

The hired coach rattles from pub to pub along the Oxfordshire back lanes, navigating gentle bends and gentle inclines less than gently. The happy band of Morris men sways side to side on the bends as one, and lurches back and forwards in unison on the hills; back as the coach hits the uphill stretches, forwards on hitting the downhill stretches. The coach had come at a budget price and the driver is going through the non-syncromeshed gearbox as smoothly as a learner driver with one arm... the *wrong* arm. By the time the travelling bell-endowed Technicolor circus reaches *The Two-and-Twenty Blackbirds*, after much crunching of gears, there's a threat of much Technicolor yawning, despite *A.B.V.* and their merry band of guests having so far consumed, on average, a mere two pints of ale each.

"What *is* that driver playing at?" complains *Pervy* to Gerry on behalf of the assembled company. "Where did you find him and his charming charabanc?"

"What charming carrier bag?"

"Charabanc!… bus…coach."

"Oh, they're in the *Yellow Pages*. Our regular firm was all booked up, but this lot should be reliable enough… they were established in 1895."

"Great! Is that when they acquired this coach? It's probably when they first employed this driver too."

It's half-past noon as they approach pub number four. They're rather well-oiled by now… more so than the gearbox of the coach, which gives up the ghost with a whining, grinding noise, compelling the driver to coast down the slope of a convenient hill. Accompanied by the desperately hopeful crunching of gears and by the separate cars following, they screech into the waiting car park having reached *The Lion and Wardrobe* in Halfway Middling where they're scheduled to have lunch. The mob disembarks merrily, most oblivious to the plight of the driver who, having nonchalantly scratched his head, has already crawled under the coach to investigate the unfathomable assortment of cables, brake pipes, axles, nuts and bolts.

"*The Lion and Wardrobe*, eh?" says one of the guest dancers. "Do you reckon the witch left home?"

"Probably," says his companion. "Or returned home… maybe she caught the last decent coach back up that hill to *Narnia*."

Chapter Fourteen

The Girl I Left Behind Me

A little earlier that same day, approaching noon, *Chirpy* the clippie stands to give oratory to his assembled audience in the sublime lounge-bar of a seventeenth century coaching inn on the back roads of the Oxfordshire Cotswolds. *Crabby* has headed straight for the toilets having driven in some discomfort from the market town of Chipping-on-the-Water some twenty miles away, on this their much-anticipated September excursion.

"Listen here, everyone. Please find a table and take your seats if you haven't already done it. The landlord says lunch will be served for your delight inner minutely... err immer... imminen... soon. Apparently he has another party booked in for lunch, so needs to get ours dished up before they arrive. Now, I hope you've all remembered what you've ordered... *I've* lost me list. Make sure you shout up as soon as the dishes arrive. I gather they'll be bringing out the faggots and gravy first, followed by the ham, egg and chips, then whatever next. Enjoy."

As *Chirpy* moves to the rear of the room to earmark a table for him and *Crabby*, he spies Ida with *Gabby*.

"Dear me, Ida," says *Chirpy*. "I see you're with Bob and not your Albert. Bert's not back in the infirmary is he?"

"No, he's not. He might as well be though. He's just under my feet at home. He really isn't very mobile yet... or says he isn't. He relies on me more than ever before. All he does the whole time is read his *Sportin' Life* and the rest of the time he's watching the racing on the telly."

"Er, where does he find the *rest* of the time if he's watching telly *all* the time, Ida?" says *Chirpy*, rather confused.

"He can read and watch at the same time. He's ambiocular, you know."

"Is he really?"

"I gather that's what it's called anyway, but don't ask *me*. He must find the time from somewhere, cause he always manages to do it. And *I'm* still feeding his canaries. *I'm* still mowing the lawn too. I know the lawn's only four foot by eight foot, but it's another thing to worry about, you know."

"Oh dear, Ida. And is he still on the tablets?"

"Most of 'em, he is. I have to remind him to take them... three times a day. I just hope the district nurse is up to the job."

"You mean she'll be busy mowing the lawn and feeding the canaries?"

"No, Mabel's doin' that."

"Blimey! She's ninety-three isn't she?"

"No, don't be daft. She's ninety-four now. It was her birthday the day before yesterday. Her son arranged for a cake with all them candles on, but before she could blow them out, he tripped on the rug. He's crippled with arthritis you see. He knocked the cake over and set fire to the curtains. Then, quick as a flash, Mabel ran into the kitchen, grabbed the fire extinguisher and put the fire out along with the candles instead of blowing them out."

"*He's* crippled with arthritis?"

"He certainly is. And he's only fifty-five. They took fifteen minutes to clean the foam off him and give him back his walkin' sticks."

"My, my. What a woman Mabel is, Ida. I'm sure Bert'll be looked after well enough."

"Dead right. And when I get back he's gonna start doin' a few things for himself, or else I'll be goin' on a coach trip every week.

"You certainly put the 'ida' in intimidation, Ida."

"And when he *does* get back to doin' some graft, I'm gonna get back to doin' me studies more often."

"Well, what do you study, Ida?"

129

"Not a lot for the last two years. Not since he got to bein' a lazy bugger. But I want to get back to me hobby properly... me astrophysics. I told *N.A.S.A.* I'd let them have me piece on the Andromeda galaxy by the end of last year... and have I completed it?... have I buggery! They'll be gettin' someone else to do it yet."

So Chirpy turns to Gabby thinking *'Did I just hear that right?'*

"So what's your hobby, Bob?" he asks. "Is it brain surgery, or possibly airline pilot?"

"No, mate," says Gabby. "I did once have an urge to paint a few old masters but I changed me mind. I just collect fag packets these days."

That sounds interesting. I bet you've got hundreds of different and exotic packets by now."

"No, not really. They're all Park Drive packs."

"Right," says Chirpy. "I'll just circulate a bit. I haven't spoken with all the others yet."

He sidles away thinking *'Dare I ask the others what they do in their spare time?'*

"Ida, my good woman. May I endow you with a pre-prandial beverage of the alcoholic variety?" asks spotty Romulus Goodbody before making his way to the bar. "And you, Bob? Algy's mater and pater have sent him his monthly allowance, so I'm full of the joys of capitalism at the moment."

"Endow me with a what?" returns Ida, confused by the affectations of the athletically built student.

Bob sits mute in his gabardine mac, bemused by the picture of Romy dressed in a bottle green corduroy jacket, brown corduroy trousers and his lilac and blue university scarf.

"Ida, my dear. He means would you like a drink before lunch?" offers the rotund Algernon Merryweather, interpreting his fellow student's oblique offer. "And since my bank manager here has offered to shell out my coin to cover it, I suppose I can only re-iterate his offer."

"Re-whaterate?" asks Ida, almost losing the thread again.

"Repeat. Confirm, dear Ida," says Algy. "I can only confirm his offer. I'd be glad to buy you both a drink."

"I don't drink much really, but if you're offering... we *are* on holiday after all," decides Ida.

"What will it be then, Ida?" rejoins Romy. "I fear this hostelry has no vintage Bollinger or Moët & Chandon, but they do have an excellent Gewürztraminer."

"A gew-what?" asks Ida.

"It's a white wine, Ida... from Germany," explains Algy, with his rather more accessible vocabulary.

Algy's had the good sense to leave his scarf with his luggage... it *is* a warm September day after all and the only sign that he might be a student are his *Hush Puppies*, which are peeping out timidly at the world from beneath the bottoms of his well-creased but casual trousers.

"Is it like *Libby's Frow Milk*? I had *that* once at a party gathering, when we went to *The Bernie Inn* in town."

"Liebfraumilch? Well, no, Ida. That's from Germany too but I believe you'll find Gewürztraminer a little more refined than that, Ida. I'm sure you'll enjoy it."

"Don't mention the Germans," says *Gabby*, sparking into life at the thought. "I don't want anything involving the Krautes. They gave me sleepless nights when I was in the *Home Guard*. I can still feel the shrapnel they could have given me. I'll 'ave a pint of mild, sonny."

He fires up one of his perpetual chain of *Park Drive* cigarettes, offering Ida one, and descends once more into silence.

"Alright," confirms Ida, leaning in to *Gabby's* match to light the cigarette and taking a deep drag to ensure it's lit. "We'll have a *Gewatsit* and a pint of mild, thank you very much, young man."

"My absolute pleasure," says Romy, as he points Algy at the

bar. "The wine for me, and get yourself one, old chap. You deserve it."

"Fine," says Algy. "I'll treat myself to a glass of the grape too then, shall I?"

He manages to find a spot at the bar as the rush subsides.

"Good Lord!" exclaims Algy. "It's you. The man with the kids at *The Union*. There must have been a dozen or more of them. How come a man as young as you has such a large family?"

"No, they're not mine. I'm a geography teacher," explains John.

"Are you really? How interesting. Did you know that the capital of the Seychelles is S?"

"I believe you'll find it's Victoria actually."

"Is it really?"

"Yes. Anyway I must buy you a drink for your help at *The Union*," says John.

"Later perhaps. I'm getting oodles this time around. Are you on our jaunt with *Chirpy* and *Crabby*? I didn't see you on the coach, did I?

"I *am* on the coach actually. I was sat near the back. I'll get you a drink later on then... maybe in Bamberton?"

"Yes indeed."

John buys himself a pint of *Brigshot Brewery Big Bad Best Bitter* and squeezes himself into a seat at the table where Imi and Gem have huddled close together sat on the wall seat. The couple are perched quietly sipping at large glasses of well-chilled Chardonnay.

"What did *you* order?" Imi asks Gem."

"Chicken. How about *you*?" Gem replies.

"Chicken. It sounds like we might be at the end of the queue then, Gem."

"Maybe, but there's no hurry is there, Imi."

"I'm sure Emma and Celina would have enjoyed it, Gem."

"I doubt it, Imi. They like the blokes too much... all they'd have found here are a happily married man, an old boy with a mac and a pair of college Hooray-Henrys... unless of course they'd have fancied a few days with a dippy-clippie and a manic-depressive driver aboard a vintage coach. Anyway, I prefer it with just the two of us here. We get on okay, don't we?"

"Of course we do, Gem. Of course we do," says Imi.

"Do you mind?" says John, assuming that *he's* the married man referred to. "I might be married, but I'm *not* happy. I'm not happy right *now*, anyway... I only came on this trip on my own because Janet, my wife, said I needed a break from the sprog... our son. She's very understanding like that, but I'm missing the girl I left behind me."

"Oh, you poor man," says Imi, in truth rather teasingly. "But it's only for a few days. Still, I can introduce you to Gemma here if you like. I'm sure she'd appreciate a man of your experience."

John feels the colour rising in his cheeks, coughing nervously. In all honesty, John Barrington *is* happily married, but somehow he's attracted to Imi. He finds her hauntingly beautiful with her high cheekbones, those deep-set green eyes and that rather androgynous frame.

"Maybe not then," says Imi, not in the least aware of the true reason for John's blushing. "So, you have a young son. What's his name? And what's yours?"

"Oxford... Oxford Barrington. That's my son's name. And I'm John."

"Really that's a nice name. Oxford I mean," says Imi, stifling a snigger. "It sounds a bit like the name of a car though, doesn't it?"

"That's what *I* said, but I'm used to it now. Janet chose it. Janet's my wife."

"Yes, so you said, and you're right... a *very* understanding wife she must be, too," says Gem. "And *I'd* say the name sounds very distinguished, John," she adds, subtly apologetic of her friend's barely concealed amusement.

"So that's Gemma, but what's *your* name?" John asks Imi. "And what do you do for a living, girls?" he adds, endeavouring to steer the conversation onto safe ground.

"I'm a medical student," says Gem.

"I'm Imi and *I'm* a prostitute," says Imi, deadpan, then winking at John provocatively.

John coughs into his *Six Bs*, snorting beer up his nose. Gem hands him a tissue. He composes himself and prepares to comment but is unable to bring to mind anything to say.

"No John. I was just joking," says Imi. "*I'm* a medical student too... A trainee doctor actually."

John looks hurt. The girls sip at their Chardonnay.

"I'm sorry John," offers Imi. "I really didn't mean to shock you so."

"That's alright," John assures her, smiling timidly. "*I'd* certainly pay good money for..."

"Don't go there, John," says Gem. "She does karate in her spare time, you know. She's got a pink belt... so watch out."

"Really," says John, not sure if this is another joke at his expense. "I didn't know you could get pink belts."

"Ah, well you see, John," says Gem, "every prostitute needs a pink belt... suspender belt that is... But it's not quite as good as a black belt."

'Oh, dear,' thinks John, blushing pink once more, his thoughts turning to his dear Janet and their sheepskin rug.

"Anyway, John. What do *you* do for a living?" asks Imi with sincere interest. He takes a large draught of his beer.

"I'm a geography teacher. At Saint Jude's primary in Oxford."

"Oh, I know it," says Gem. "A great-uncle of mine went

there. I don't mean he was an uncle who was great... my grandfather's brother you see. He always brought me presents when I was very young, so I suppose he *was* great as well. You wouldn't know him, he's dead now."

"Actually, I do know a few dead people, Gemma. They're not very interesting though."

"Isn't the name Saint Jude an odd choice? I mean thirty pieces of silver and all that?" asks Imi.

"No, no, Imi," says John in earnest. "Lots of people make that mistake. Saint Jude is in celebration of Judas Thaddeus - Not Judas Iscariot... totally different, you see."

"Oh, I see," says Imi, apologetically.

"A geography teacher, eh?" says Gem. "Did you know that the capital of Denmark is D?"

"I believe you'll find it's Copenhagen actually."

"Is it really?"

"The Lion and Wardrobe?" complains *Crabby* to *Chirpy* as he emerges from the door that had led him to the toilets. "I reckon I've just met the witch."

"Which witch is that then, *Crabbs*?"

"You know I told you about that Lewis fella in *The Bird and Baby*... he was Tolkien's mate, remember. Well, Lewis wrote *The Lion, The Witch and The Wardrobe*. You see, he had a witch as well as a lion in his wardrobe."

"That's some wardrobe, *Crabbs*. Good job he didn't have a bird and a baby in there too."

"Actually, he did... an eagle and a child that is... quite a few of each in fact. Anyway, the witch *I've* just seen was coming out of the kitchen with an armful of faggots. Well, an armful of plates of faggots anyway."

"She gets about a bit, doesn't she? What with wardrobes, kitchens and all that?"

"She just scowled at me as if I was about to relieve her of her meatballs at the point of a sword."

"Stand and deliver! Your money or your faggots," jokes *Chirpy*. "Cheer up mate. We're on holiday. The sun is shining, our passengers are happy and the afternoon is stretched before us like a... stretching thing."

"I suppose so, mate. It's a nice pub, ain't it. You could almost imagine *being* a highwayman back in the olden days. I could have been the driver of a mail coach who gave up the drudge of journeying every day and converted to a life of adventure, robbing people of their ill-gotten gains on the highways and byways of good old England and bringing back the spoils here to hide."

"Or, more likely, you could have got caught and hanged for your trouble. Just get back to the reality of the day and enjoy your faggots."

"I ordered the ham."

"In that case, enjoy your *ham*. You're not cut out for adventure, *Crabbs*. Remember, we would have been on a trip to the sea if it weren't for your deciding you didn't like ice cream or sand."

"I thought I might be a highwayman... not a pirate."

"But, you're not cut out for either, mate. Stick to sitting behind the wheel of a bus. You know you prefer traffic lights to turnpikes."

Crabby has a flashback to his dream of walking the high street traffic lights down the aisle.

"Don't remind me. Traffic lights! Ugh!"

"At least there aren't any traffic lights out here in the quiet lanes of England. Just don't let your imagination run away with you, *Crabbs*."

"I suppose you're right."

"You know, seriously *Crabbs*, we could do better for ourselves than the council buses. I mean, I do love the heady heights of the upper-deck, but I think I could get used to this coach idea. You know, we could do worse than dump the council and set up our own pleasure trip company. I can see it now... *'Crabby and Chirpy's Cheerful Charabanc Tours'*, and it needn't just be here in England. If only you could shake off you fear of ice creams, we could go abroad and tour the seaside towns *there*... say to the Isle of Wight, or maybe France or Spain or even further. It seems to be all the rage lately. Just imagine the demand."

"But what about me mum and dad. They'd never cope without *me* around."

"Of course they would. They're resilient old buggers from what I've heard you say. And if they needed any vehicle and machinery repairs, cousin Jim... *Big* Jim that is, not *Little* Jim... would help out. As you know, he's like you... always grovelling around on the floor. He spends more time horizontal than upright."

"I don't know. I'd really have to think about it, but I'm sure I couldn't manage without me routine, you know."

"Sure you could. You know, we could specialize in places that don't have many traffic lights."

Of a sudden, *Chirpy* and his happy assemblage of revellers make out the crunching of gears and the screeching of brakes, as a coach turns into the car park, followed by a gaggle of cars. In moments, the pub is overwhelmed by a surfeit of Morris dancers, streaming into the lounge-bar like a swarm of bees around the honey pot of hand-pumps. Unlike bees, they don't buzz. Rather, they bump and jostle in a cacophony of voices, bells and shouts of 'Two pints of *Fartin' Ferret* if you please, my good lady', and the like.

"Oh no! Please God. Not Morris men," cries John Barrington. "They seem to follow me everywhere I go. I bumped into thousands of them dancing in Oxford back in April when we were on a trip with the school kids. It was at *The Oxford Union* and it was almost a catastrophe... not so much the dancing I suppose, but the kids."

"Oh no! Gem," says Imi, echoing John's sentiments. "Morris men! I recognize some of them... from when I did that bit of dancing last year. I don't want them to see me. Bugger! I hate men. They're all the same. I hate them all, I do. Hide me. Hide me," she adds, sinking low into her seat behind Gem.

"Is that why you gave up dancing then, Imi?"

"Pretty much, Gem."

"I can't really believe you're a misandrist, Imi."

"A what?"

"A misandrist. It's the female equivalent of a misogynist... a *man* hater rather than a *woman* hater. I learned it on that optional course I went on last year... for bedside manner and stuff."

"Well, I don't really *hate* them I suppose, Gem. I just don't trust them. Not any more."

"*I'm* the same you know, Imi... not trusting them that is. I can take them or leave them, but I prefer the latter. Mostly they're up their own arses."

"Yeah. And they can stay there for all I care," agrees Imi.

John flushes again, now realising that his attraction to Imi is not only pointless, but also frivolous, flying in the face of his love for Janet. The last thing he'd want is to be up his own arse.

The witch of a waitress materializes from the kitchen loaded once more, this time with the last of the meals for *Chirpy's* party... two vegetarian nut cutlets. She weaves deftly in and out of the plague of voracious Morris men, delivers the two plates hurriedly to two of *Chirpy* and *Crabby's* crowd at table number thirteen, takes a deep breath and re-enters the scrum to be spat out into the kitchen corridor to embark upon round two... the Morris meals.

"Sorry, mate," says the driver of the Morris coach to Gerry. "I'm pretty sure the gearbox is totally seized up. Looks like I've had a major oil leak on me hands. The landlord's let me use his phone and I've been on to the depot. They can't get a replacement coach out to us for at least two or three hours. The only spare is just on its way back to the depot from Northamptonshire."

"Hell's teeth," says Gerry, in a panic. "We've got thirty-five Morris men to shift after lunch, haven't we. We can't wait *that* long. We're due on our way to Bamthorpe-in-the-Bush in just over an hour and then straight after that we're in Bamthorpe-on-the-Hill. The whole thing's turning into a disaster."

"Sorry, that's the best we can do. The boss says we could try some other companies, but they won't send anything without cash up front, and the boss won't do that."

Crabby overhears them and offers to have a look at the coach. Even here in his best togs, he can't resist the urge to get down and dirty.

After attempting to put the coach into gear and then wriggling under the coach and squirming out again, *Crabby* reports back.

"I'm afraid you're right mate. That's a gone-gearbox if ever I saw one."

And *Chirpy* realizes that by some, arguably happy, coincidence they're heading for the same villages as the Morris tour. Not one to miss an opportunity, he chips in.

"I say, chaps. *We're* heading in your direction. We're intending to pay a visit to those two charming little places ourselves on the way to our digs in Bamberton. We've got half a coach free. Well, not free... I reckon we could cover our added costs for a fiver a head."

"And I could get the boss to send the replacement coach to Bamberton if you want," says the Morris coach driver.

"It'd be a bit of a squeeze, but maybe we can fit the surplus into following cars," ponders Gerry, "but it's your boss who'll have to pick up the extra costs."

"Oh, I wouldn't know about that," says the driver. "You'd have to take it up with *him.*"

"Right. It looks like Hobson's choice," says Gerry, with resignation. "We'll do it. But I want to speak with your boss on the phone."

Before long, places are found in following cars for about half of the Morris men off the coach. The rest file onto the *Chirpy* and *Crabby* coach, full of real ale and renewed mirth. Much sundry baggage belonging to the travellers on both coaches is now stowed in the overhead racks to make room for more bums on seats. *Crabby* slides the gearbox into action as smoothly as butter sliding into the hot orifices of a toasted crumpet, and off they go.

"Any more fares now, please?" jokes *Chirpy*, as he paces the aisle surveying his expanded flock. "We'll be in the bushes of Bamthorpe before you know it."

"Chance'd be fine thing," says Robbie Watts to *Figgy* Figgis.

They've parked themselves on a seat near the back of the coach. Behind them, on the back seat, sit Imi and Gem. Imi has taken off her jacket and is cowering hidden behind it, not wanting to have anything to do with the uncouth mob now descended on them. John, keeping a discreet distance from the girls sits on the far side of the back seat gazing out of the opposite window. In front of Robbie and *Figgy* sit Fred and Kit. Ida and *Gabby* sit near the front, behind the driver, in a confusion of enthralment and bemusement... Ida the more enthralled and *Gabby* the more bemused. Romy and Algy are away with the fairies, in a cloud of alcoholic giggling and raucous singing. Ballads and shanties issue forth in a chain worthy of Bob's *Park Drive* cigarettes. Malodorous Morris musicians, led by *Quacker*, are fingering melodeons menacingly with the consequential demented wall of sound worthy of a rock band on a mission promoting deaf aids. Dan the Fool stands in the aisle conducting the music, waving his bladder aloft, occasionally thwacking anyone who sings out of tune, which much of the time includes everyone.

For the moment, although Imi recognizes several of the Morris men, none of *them* have recognized *her*, either in the pub or on the coach, from their previous Morris encounter. She conveniently has the disguise of being dressed today in what might be loosely considered as female clothes; a white cotton summer coat, a cream blouse with a modicum of a frill and denim jeans that are usefully ambivalent as to sex. *Snakey, Pervy* and Gerry are sat at the front, on the opposite side to the driver, somewhat po-faced, wondering what spawn of the devil they, as the principal officers of *A.B.V.'s* committee, have generated. For once *Snakey* is speechless and grits his teeth in hope of the whole Morris tour not falling to pieces. *Crispy* is not discernable among the mayhem, hidden more comprehensively than Imi, under a pile of *other Morris men's'* clobber which had fallen from the rack on the last bend.

"Hi, girls," says Robbie, turning to face Gem and her semi-hidden friend. Hope you're enjoying yourselves. It's not often you get the chance to share a coach with a band of virile young Morris men. Anyway, what's with hiding under the jacket, darling? Anybody would think you don't like men."

Robbie can usually spot a female at two hundred paces, even if camouflaged by a strategically placed coat, so Imi has no easy chance of escaping detection, hemmed in as she is under her cotton coat.

"Jesus, Imi. What did you ever see in Morris dancing?" Gem whispers to her friend behind a raised hand.

Imi returns the whisper, "Not a lot. I only did it for a few weeks, Gem. It seemed like a laugh at the time."

"Sod off," shouts Gem at Robbie, protective of her partner.

"Anyway, it's *you* that's sharing *our* coach, so behave."

"Yeah. Sod off, you twat," says Imi, unable to resist a comment and exposing two eyes and a nose from under the jacket to facilitate her rebuke.

"Ooh, get you," says Robbie, in truth taken aback by the venomous outburst from the pair. "Sorry I spoke."

"So am I," says Imi as she makes to shrink back into hiding.

"Cool it Robbie," says *Figgy*, looking to de-fuse the atmosphere "You're obsessive, you are. Leave the poor girls alone."

Kit, having turned around in his seat at the confrontation, darts a glance at the pair of wide eyes, vulnerable yet somehow flaunting, disappearing under the jacket. He senses a faint hint of recognition, as if he's seen a long-lost girlfriend. A déjà vu *'I'm sure I know those eyes,'* he thinks.

Chapter Fifteen

The Willow Tree

"Look," says the promoted D.I. Harry Fielding, as he addresses his new team who have been assigned to the *'Caved-in Skull'* investigation, "we're still getting nowhere with this case and Hector Parrott is giving me grief, because the Chief Superintendent is giving *him* grief. And apparently, to make things worse, there's to be no more overtime payment."

Disgruntled murmuring rises from the assembled team.

"But, I'm sure you'll agree," continues Harry, ignoring the mumbling and muttering, "the search for *justice* is our motivation."

"Perhaps we should go door-to-door again in Pockbury then, Mr. Fielding, sir?" asks the bright young W.P.C. in the team.

"I can't really see the point, Sharpe. There aren't that many doors in Pockbury and I'm sure we've exhausted all possibilities there. A few of the residents have sold up and left the area because of the affair, but we spoke with them before they left."

"So, you don't think the murderer could be one of the people who moved away then, sir?"

"No, I don't, Sharpe. And I prefer not to use the term 'murderer'. I'm convinced that the *killer* is far more likely to be from outside the Pockbury area."

"So what do we do for now, then, sir?" asks another, not so bright young thing.

"I dunno, P.C. Blunt. But whatever we do, it's to be done in normal working hours."

"We could have a reconstruction, couldn't we, sir?" Cedric Blunt suggests.

"Not really, Blunt. We haven't any idea how it happened, so how can we re-construct it? In any case I can't imagine hoards of local people were walking through Pockbury woods at the time of the incident. I'm convinced that the presence of Eric Stotesbury and Twinkle was quite the exception."

"It could have been suicide," suggests P.C. Blunt.

"Blunt... how could he stove-in his own head? Are you sure this is the right job for you, lad? Look, I *had* thought maybe we should put out another T.V. appeal, but on balance it would be a waste of time without more background evidence. If my judgement can be relied on, I reckon it could be more productive if we do a more thorough trawl of the woods around the scene. We could possibly find the murderer's weapon."

"I thought you preferred not to use the term 'murderer', sir," says W.P.C. Sharpe.

"Well spotted, Sharpe. You'll go far with initiative like that."

Blunt looks dejected. *'Why didn't I think of that?'* he ponders.

D.I. Fielding, having out-flanked his only rival in the promotion stakes, is ready to encourage her, though one day he may regret it. He still has far to go and she's only a step or two behind.

Christine Sharpe dresses as sharply as her name might suggest. She habitually wears her black stockings and her neatly pressed regulation black skirt and fresh-every-day white blouse. Her shoes are always as highly polished as any in the station and in the high-gloss reflection her fellow officers are forever attempting a glimpse of the *'Persil*-white' knickers they imagine she wears. So far, she's displayed just the right balance between initiative and subservience to place her highly in the regard of D.C.I. Parrott. However, she draws the line at wearing the skirt when out in the field, and who can blame her with all those nettles. So her superior officers have compromised and allowed trousers... less flattering but avoiding the need for dock leaves.

-o-o-o-

The coach passengers, conjoined as they are by fate, reach Bamthorpe-in-the-Bush, welcomed by a small crowd of Morris admirers basking in the early autumn afternoon sunshine outside *The Bush Inn*.

The coach ejects its human cargo onto the front entrance path, then makes it's way around to the car park, but Imi and Gem stay on board.

"Come on Imi. We ought to go in and get a drink. You'll feel much better if we do."

"No, Gem," says Imi, quaking at the thought. "I can't face it. Morris men... I hate them even more than men."

"But Morris men *are* men."

"Are you sure about that? Once I'd tried dancing Morris, I soon found out what a strange breed they are. Men are chauvinistic enough... but Morris men? They should all be tipped off a cliff, as far as I'm concerned... bells and all. They get everywhere and they're just spoiling our day together. At least ordinary men don't go around seeking attention quite so conspicuously."

"I suppose not, but wasn't that Sid a man?"

"I told you not to mention *him*, Gem," snaps Imi, eyes wild and nostrils flared. "Anyway, he was a man but he wasn't a Morris dancer... that fat git couldn't dance if you wired him to the mains. I'd still tip him over that cliff though."

"Sorry. Sorry, but I just wondered. You seem to hate him with a vengeance."

"So would you, the way he behaved towards me. Anyway, I don't want to talk about him. I'd rather be with you. We don't need *him* or any of these Morris jokers."

"Okay. I shan't mention him again, but for the moment we're stuck with the bells brigade, at least 'til Bamberton when they get their other coach."

"Roll on."

Here in Bamthorpe-in-the-Bush, *A.B.V.* are in fine fettle and offer a spirited performance on the spacious, parched lawn. The small crowd grows as the air fills with the less than mellifluous mix of sticks clashing, melodeons wailing, pipe trilling and tabor beating. The jingle of bells competes with the jangle of collection boxes. The crowds are in and out of the bar topping up with ale, their thirsts heightened in sympathy with the sweaty shirts and dripping brows of the dancers.

The coach journey from 'Bush' to 'Hill', two miles at most, seems like twenty miles in the company of Beelzebub... all sweat and stale beer, all fire and farts, a Hell on wheels for *Chirpy's* holiday makers now paired with the Morris revellers. John has developed a headache and sits in his corner at the back of the coach. Imi and Gem are doing their best to ignore the mayhem that's taken over the whole coach and Ida and Bob are all but oblivious to the raucous mêlée around them. As for Romy and Algy, they're still in their element. *Chirpy* is full of cheerful apologies to his ticket holders, not sure after all if he's made the right decision to share the coach with the revellers and he's more than a little anxious for Big Jim's upholstery.

At Bamthorpe-on-the-Hill the merry throng of dancers is ejaculated from the coach like a bursting boil... an assortment of infected matter spewing out into the lane that houses *The Hilltop Arms*. Algy and Romy lead the holidaying contingent out into the now noisy hamlet hot on the heels of the rabble that is *A.B.V.* and guests. Gasping for fresh air, Gem and Imi head straight for the toilets... Gem to freshen up and Imi to be physically sick after her claustrophobic ordeal. They slip inconspicuously by the twenty-yard queue for the gents and are fortunate to be into the ladies' loo ahead of the few other women on the scene. Recovering from her puking in one of the cubicles, Imi freshens her mouth and washes her hands at one of the two basins.

"Thank the Lord I escaped from that cult of madness before

it drew me in deeper, Gem," declares Imi, frenetically.

Gem looks down suspiciously at her own basin, raising an eyebrow at gurgling noises as the waste trap protests and a surfeit of urine makes its way by from the adjoining male toilets and swills along in the waste pipe on its journey to the main sewers. She pictures Morris men being washed away on a flood of used beer all the way to the local treatment plant.

"Hold on tight, Imi," says Gem, attempting to calm her friend. "Only this last village, then we're on our way to Bamberton and that replacement coach for the Morris mob."

"I'm not gonna make it, Gem. It's all too much to bear," says Imi. "Why me? Why us? Is it the god of men getting his own back on me for being so anti?"

"Probably," agrees Gem, placing her arm around Imi's shoulder. "But hey, come on now. I'll look after you like I always do. You do know I've kept an eye out for you ever since we met, don't you, and that won't change."

"Oh, Gem. What would I do without you?" says Imi, submitting to a brief warm embrace, before they each take a deep breath, grit their teeth and head out for the final leg of their road back to sanity.

"Are you sure this was such a good idea, *Chips*?" says *Crabby*, as they finally reach the bar.

"Of course it was, *Crabbs*," replies *Chirpy*. "We should do it again sometime. Look how everybody's enjoying it."

"I don't mean our outing itself. I mean giving this lot a lift."

"Maybe next time I wouldn't offer, but it *has* paid towards our drinks. So what'll you have?"

"Just half o' bitter, *Chips*. I *am* driving you know, and I've had a couple of pints already. And that's another thing... how come you never share the driving?"

"That's because I can't drive a bus, can I. I haven't got a licence."

"Perhaps you should get one then. That way you'd know what a responsibility it is."

"Come on mate. Things could be worse. We could be at the seaside with all that ice cream."

"Very funny, *Chips*. To be honest, I could get to like ice cream as long as it didn't come with Morris men thrown in."

"Right it's a deal. Next year we'll go to the seaside and *I'll* buy the ice creams. South coast, I'd say... Devon maybe. You'll just love it. They don't have too many traffic lights down there either, though I can't guarantee there'll be no Morris men."

"We'll see."

Now when *Chirpy* says 'look how everybody's enjoying it', he's not perceiving how much agony Imi is in. Nor indeed is he aware how withdrawn John is, sat at a corner table alone in a sea of dancers like an *Earthling* at an *'Aliens* Rule' convention. Instead, he's focussing on Algy and Romy who are soaking up the pints like the most seasoned of *A.B.V.* men, boisterous as the mob itself. Algy has overlooked the fact that beer has a major component in water and he appears to be free of his aqua-aversion syndrome for the day.

"Come on, Algy, Romy," says *Crispy* Morgan. "You could both do a simple Bampton dance as well as *I* can."

"That's not saying much, *Crispy*," butts in Dan Copley, whacking the doc playfully on his head with his profligate bladder. "My cat could do a better job of single stepping than you."

"Get stuffed, Copley," says *Crispy Doc*, in playful protest. "There's only one thing more annoying than you and that's your bladder. Put it away, why don't you? Before I take my penknife to it."

"But surely, *Crispy*, you wouldn't harm a poor defenceless bladder would you?" Algy protests on the Fool's behalf, after quaffing a good third-of-a-pint in one hit. "And anyway, I'm not cut out for dancing. I'd need to lose some weight before I could even contemplate it," he adds in unthinking disregard of *Crispy's* own bulk.

"It's alright for you, Algy, my friend," explains *Crispy*, defending his bladder-stabbing comment. "*You* don't have to put up with this fool's misplaced inflated appendage, week after week, do you. Most men have a sports car for a penis extension... he relies on his massive, disembodied bladder."

"*I'm* game for a go at dancing," says Romy, diverting the conversation. "This Morris lark can't be that difficult."

"Great," says *Crispy*. "All you need to remember is that the 'single stepping' in the dance goes...one, two, three, hop... one, two, three, hop... in time with the music. Easy peasy."

"Actually, *Crispy*," laughs Dan, "that's '*double* stepping'. And I thought *I* was supposed to be the Fool here."

"Oh, yes. Sorry, Romy," admits *Crispy*. "I meant one hop, two hop, three hop, four hop..."

"No probs, my dear boy," says Romy, rather drunkenly slurring his response. "If I can mashter Latin declensions, I can mashter thish... one hop, two hip, hip-hop, tip-top... what, what?"

And he collapses in a fit of giggles.

"I really don't think this is a good idea, *Crispy*," says Dan. "And anyway *Snakey* would never allow it."

"Well, it's not up to *Snakey*, *is* it. It's up to *Pervy*."

"Like I said... *Snakey* would never allow it. Anyway, if you're insisting that this streaky lump of scholastic inebriation can do a dance at the drop of a hat, you'd better explain that the Bampton dance we're doing today is a corner dance."

"Yes, Dan. I know. I was coming to that," insists *Crispy*.

"Good."

"You see, Romy, the Bampton dance we're doing today is a corner dance," echoes *Crispy*. "Between the distinctive figures, we dance corners... number one and number six dance the corner together, then numbers two and five, then numbers three and four."

"I shee," says Romy... but of course he doesn't, "so if there's three corners it musht be a tri... a triangular danshe, right?"

"No. it's a rectangular dance."

"Sho why aren't there four corners?"

"No. Like I said, there are three corners, but towards the end we do a hey which is two figures of eight and sometimes we do rounds which is circular."

"Thish is doing my head in," says Romy. "And *I* thought I was *good* at germometry in school. I'd better give it a mish after all."

He slumps back in his chair, all but unconscious from the drink, burping profusely.

"I can shmell alcohol," Algy slurs, rather worse for the demon drink himself.

"I can shmell it too," chirps up Romy, "A-L-C-H-L..., I mean A-L-C-O-L-O-L, err A-L-C-O... oh, forget it. It all goes down the same way whichever way you spell it."

"That'sh right," agrees Algy. "Whichever way you spill it, it always goes down. It never goes up, does it... except occa... occas... sometimes after you've topped it off with a curry, that is."

Pervy Peverill calls the dancers to order, "Outside, you slovenly lot. We're dancing out front in three minutes. *A.B.V.* are first on."

So Dan jumps to attention while *Crispy* girds his loins lethargically. They leave the university students where they are, semi-comatose.

John makes his way quietly outside, still nursing his headache and, with the aid of an overhanging willow tree, hoists himself onto the garden wall of the house on the opposite side of the lane, facing the pub. He tries to enter into the spirit of things, but sidles along the wall on his backside as far away from the music as he can in deference to his aching temple. He's remorseful, thinking of Janet and their young sprog, Oxford.

'Why oh why did I let Janet persuade me to come on this trip alone? Why couldn't the pair of them have come along with me? Sprog would have really enjoyed this music and the waving hankies. And, as for me, I was sure I could get along with the rest of the trippers, but everyone seems to be ignoring me or else patronising me. Mind you, I suppose it's my own fault. And anyway, I'm probably better off sitting quietly on my own for now, what with this headache and all.'

And in anguish, he tips back his head, looking to the blue skies, loses his balance and topples over the wall into the well-tended vegetable patch behind him, his fall terminating abruptly with a rather pronounced 'squelch'.

"Oi! You bloody idiot!" comes a call, founded more in distress than anger, from a rather rustic old boy who John mistakes at first glance for an oversized garden gnome wending his way towards him.

"I'm *so* sorry," offers John, struggling to his feet in a daze, nursing a bruised shoulder and doing his best to clean off fragments of pumpkin from his jacket.

"You bloody, stupid idiot! That was my prize pumpkin. I was gonna win the produce show with that next month. It was the best one I've ever grown. My poor baby."

"I'm so *very* sorry," emphasizes John. "I'll buy you another one," he adds in desperation, now nursing two headaches... one in his head and the other in a vegetable patch."

"No, it's alright. Really," says the gnome fellow. "I always grow a couple of spares and luckily you've landed on one of *them*. My pride and joy is the next one along... so, it's lucky for you... I can put *this* away now."

And John swiftly becomes aware of how lucky he really is as the old boy retreats to his shed with a double-barrelled shotgun under his arm. Forlorn once more, John returns to his thoughts of Janet and of his son. Taken by veritable shaking, brought on by his vegetable adventure, he makes his way to the refuge of the coach to recover from his ordeal. *Crabby* has ensconced himself in the driver's seat, knowing that *A.B.V.'s* Squire, *Pervy* Peverill, will soon be rounding up his heaving flock for the journey onward to Bamberton and hopefully to the rendezvous with their replacement coach. *Chirpy* is looking to gather up his merry band of charabancers too.

"What is it with these people, mate?" asks *Crabby*. "Why do they have to be so wild and raucous?"

"I don't really know," says John. "Though I *can* see the skill of the dancers and the complexity of the dances now I've watched it a bit. There's obviously a devotion to the tradition, something medieval or even primeval about the whole idea. Perhaps it comes from the days when cavemen used to club their women and drag them off by the hair to set up family."

"I can't see that with this lot. Medieval? It's bleddy-evil more like. They won't even let women near enough to be clubbed if they can help it."

"Perhaps that's a redeeming aspect of it all then. At least it spares the women a headache," decides John. "*I* feel as if I've been clubbed right here and now. In fact I was nearly *shot* by a gnome a few minutes ago, just for falling into his pumpkin... his reserve pumpkin at that. Would I really miss the countryside or what? It's all a bit too much for me, but I suppose it's their way of letting off steam. I mean some people achieve serenity with stamp collecting or fishing or building elaborate electric train sets with all the scenery... or even, heaven forfend, with yoga."

"It's John isn't it?" says *Crabby*.

"Yes, *Crabby*. That's right."

"I can see your point, John," says *Crabby*. "*I* like train sets myself, though I'm not too keen on stamps. I *did* used to do train-spotting once, but I gave it up when all the steam trains went to the scrapyards. That was a sad time, that was... what a waste of good engines. Mind you, I *was* getting a bit old for train spotting anyway. I prefer messing with real engines and anything mechanical these days."

"That's very interesting, *Crabby*," says John.

"Talking of hobbies," the bus driver continues, "*Chirpy's* cousin Big Jim, spends a lot of his time doing up old coaches and tractors and things. He did this one you know... he can even do signwriting. He's far better at mechanicals than me. And this coach... now that's a *real* hobby... salvationizing works of art. He's self-taught, he is... you don't need teachers if you've got the passion. To tell the truth, I imagine I'd have been happier as a Victorian meself, working with beam engines... all brass and oil cans and stuff."

"*I'm* a teacher actually," says John, rather defensively. "I teach geography. But I *do* agree that this *is* a lovely coach. I just hope the mob doesn't do it too much damage."

"So do I. I mean, I don't know what Big Jim will say if it goes back to him all messed up."

And as John talks with *Crabby* in this brief sanctuary away from the clatter and whirlwind of their temporary companions, his headache melts away, the serenity of the moment drifting over him, enveloping him in a fluffy cloud of enlightenment.

"You know what, *Crabby*? *I* should become a Buddhist. I'll live in a temple to soothe my temple. Then again, I couldn't leave my lovely wife, Janet. And there's my new son, Oxford. I couldn't let *him* down. When he's growing up, I'll make sure he gets train sets and fishing rods and all those kinds of things. I just hope he doesn't decide to be a Morris man. I mean I do admire it as a tradition, but I just couldn't stand all the noise."

On the journey onwards from Bamthorpe-on-the-Hill to Bamberton, Imi stares out of the window, lost in thought.

Gem sits transfixed by the sea of singing Morris men's backs seated there in front of her, struggling to fathom why so many, supposedly sensible, men would get so carried away over bells and ribbons and jumping up and down, athletic though it no doubt is.

'I suppose it's a bit like football really,' she thinks. *'But at least football involves a goal... the goal of goals that is. Perhaps it's more for the aesthetic aspects of it... more like needlepoint embroidery or possibly flower arranging with beer attached for good measure. I have to agree with Imi though... all men must be mad.'*

Imi, attempts to trace the contours of the slowly changing landscape on the window with her finger... the beautiful rolling hills in the distance, the magnificent hedges, peppered with tall ash and oak trees, the farm gates all drooping on their hinges like all good farmers' gates do, if they're not entirely unhinged... the gates that is, not the farmers. And the sheep roaming on the distant slopes, suspended like white clouds in a green sky, float by as if being transported back to Bamthorpe.

'Sheep,' she ponders, *'We're all like sheep really, aren't we... seemingly wandering free, going where it pleases us, yet in truth following the crowd, frightened if we get separated from the flock. And in sticking together, all the more likely to face the chop... the universal lamb chop.'*

"At last, Imi! Bamberton!" declares Gem, nudging her partner from her sheepish daydreaming as the battle-bus reaches the destination for their overnight accommodation.

The George and Worm Inn sits in the town hall square facing the rich, amber stone façade of the imposing eighteenth century municipal building. The town hall clock strikes five, but reads ten-past-one.

"Yep. Bamberton," says Imi. "It looks really sleepy for such a large town."

"I know, but wait 'til this lot wake it up. At least it's big enough for us to sneak away somewhere quiet, away from the smell of beer."

Gerry checks and confirms that the Morris tour's replacement transport is waiting for *A.B.V.* and their guests around the corner from the town hall square, at the coach station.

"Right, you motley bunch," calls *Snakey*. "Make sure you bring all your stuff. Get what you don't need for the dancing loaded onto the new coach. It's only fifty yards away. Then back here for our first spot. The pubs here in the square will be open at six, so we can just about fit in an hour's dancing before then."

Those who've travelled in their cars are already parked up in the square and their extra passengers are unloading kit to get *it* onto the new coach too.

"Oh, fig," says Dan. "Not more bloody dancing?"

He's as deflated as his bladder, which has somehow developed a slow leak. The whole gaggle of dancers and musicians has gradually become more subdued on the journey from Bamthorpe-on-the-Hill. After numerous dance spots, a large pub lunch and an average intake of alcohol that would last any sane person a month, they've slowed down to the speed of *Crispy*. Two spots here in Bamberton and they'll all be off home after an eight-spot day leaving seven performances for tomorrow, hopefully with a more reliable coach.

"You've not been at my bladder have you, *Crispy*?" asks Dan.

"As if. It's the beer that's been at your bladder, mate. Time you learned to control it."

With great effort, the Fool raises his stick on high and brings down its deflated attachment on the Doc's head with the force of a wet flannel and the sound of a wet haddock.

"Gerroff, you prannie," protests *Crispy*.

"Just look at that pair," says Kit Harbury to Fred Moulton. "Anyone would think they were brother and sister."

"Ugh! What a thought. Which one's the sister?" says Fred.

Chapter Sixteen

Mine's a Double

"Come on folks," announces *Chirpy*, as bright as ever, to his own charges. "Time to worm our way into *The Worm*, so form an orderly queue. They *are* expecting us. *Crabbs* will help you with your cases."

Ida and Bob, who'd been sitting near the front of the coach, are first in line for checking in at reception.

"Good evening madam, Good evening sir," offers the treacly young man behind the desk.

"Classy here, ain't it, Bob," whispers Ida.

"Yeah. It looks posh, don't it," he replies, stubbing out a *Park Drive* in the pristine crystal ashtray that's perched on the end of the counter and hitting the plunger of the beautifully polished brass bell sat next to it.

"That's nice," says Ida.

"Actually, sir, that's for your use if I'm not here," offers the receptionist, brushing back his *Brylcreemed* quiff with his left hand.

"Sorry," says Bob. "What's the point of ringing it if you're not here? You won't hear it will you?"

"I shan't be far away, sir. Now then, I assume you're together. What name is it? Mine is Wesley," he says, wiping his quiff hand discreetly on his waistcoat and picking up his clipboarded list with the other.

"Well, Wesley, *I'm* Ida. And *this* is Bob."

"And the surname?"

"Mine's Hall. What's yours, Bob? You never *did* tell me."

"It's Smith, Ida... Bob Smith," says *Gabby*.

"Oh dear, madam," says Wesley, nervously tweaking his defiant quiff, and wiping his fingers once more. "Oh dear."

"What?" says Ida.

"We've got you listed as Mr. and Mrs. Hall, madam."

156

"Ah, well, don't worry. You see my husband, Albert... Albert Hall that is... he's at home with his leg. He isn't really up to travelling yet, so we agreed I'd come with Bob here."

"Oh dear, oh dear," says the treacly, panicking young Wesley. "We've booked you into a double room."

"Don't worry about it," says *Gabby*. "We always sit next to each other on the bus. And we share our fags, so I don't see why we can't share a bed."

"Ooh, Bob. Fancy that. But no hanky-panky mind."

"Of course not, Ida."

"Oh dear, oh dear," repeats the young receptionist. And carefully placing his clipboard on the counter, he turns to the cabinet on the wall behind him, saying. "Very well then. Here is your room key. It's number seven... on the first floor... the second one along from the landing, on the left. Oh dear, oh dear."

"Come along my good chap," says Romy Goodbody, some way recovered from his alcoholic binge. "My friend and I are whacked. We've had a very long day you know...we've been Morris dancing."

"I see, sir. My apologies."

"No need to apologize, my man. It was an enlightening experience," says Algy, "but we're certainly ready for our room now."

"No, sir. I meant apologies for the brief delay in dealing with you, sir. And which name am I looking for?" says Wesley, slicking back his hair once more and picking up his clipboard.

"Romulus Goodbody and Algernon Merryweather."

"Oh dear, oh dear."

So more of *Chirpy* and *Crabby's* entourage is booked into the inn... John, followed by Imi and Gem ('Oh dear, oh dear') then *Chirpy* and *Crabby* themselves. The Clippie and the driver are sharing a room too, so that's five rooms for the nine of them; a double for Ida and Bob, a single for John and twin rooms for each of the other three 'pairs'. And following them, the rest of *Chirpy's* travellers.

"Look, Ida," says Gem, when she and Imi learn of the unlikely pairing of Ida and *Gabby* in a double room. Swap with us if you want. We don't mind a double and you can have our twin. That way, at least you can have a separate bed from Bob, if not a separate room."

Imi nudges Gem, tittering with a frisson of excitement.

"That's very kind of you, me dear, but it's no trouble really," Ida answers.

"I insist Ida," says Gem, in truth more than eager to get Imi into the double bed, all the more to enjoy their brief holiday together.

"Right. If you insist, then how could we refuse? That alright with you, Bob?"

"Sure, Ida, anything you say, luv," replies *Gabby*, lighting up another *Park Drive*. He offers them round but no one takes a cigarette."

Gem and Imi, after spending an hour or so chilling out on their double bed and cleansing themselves of Morris man madness, decide to venture forth into Bamberton to seek quiet refuge in a welcome glass or two of wine and something to eat.

Treading the narrow back streets, they come across a tiny bistro and peeking in through the invitingly bucolic window, they can see a scattering of small tables draped with green and white gingham tablecloths. The candle-sconced walls are adorned with images, strangely ethereal in the candle light... pictures of famous French characters; Molière, Edith Piaf, Jacques Brel, Claude Monet, Pierre-August Renoir, and more, all framed it seems to live an eternally enthralled existence. Strangely, the very Spanish Salvador Dali also features in the eclectic mix of celebrity.

"Perhaps the owner's part French and part Spanish?" says Imi. "Let's go in. It looks so quiet and peaceful."

"We'd better check out the menu though, and stay if it suits," suggests Gem. "What do you say?"

"I'm happy with that," agrees Imi, "but first and foremost, I need a nice glass of wine."

And in they go, accompanied by the tinkling of the traditional little doorbell, "Ugh! Morris men!" exclaims Imi, shuddering at the reminder of bells.

"Hi girls, Welcome to *Chez Miguel*," says the eponymous owner of the bistro, greeting them with a broad moustachioed smile. "What would you like, my pretty ladies?"

Imi offers a guarded smile in return, still mesmerized by the little Aladdin's cave of Frenchness, but wondering if she can cope with a chauvinist Miguel. They both ponder the menu and the wine list.

It turns out that the owner, Miguel, is in fact a rather charming Nepalese-Mexican. He has a French grandmother, Magdalena, who at the age of eighty-one still cooks and serves in the bistro.

While the wine list suggests that Miguel has a masterly knowledge of French wines, his knowledge of wider French culture is perhaps rather scatological.

"We love your beautiful French pictures," says Gem, approvingly, "but, Salvador Dali? Isn't he Spanish?"

"Salvador Dali?" says Miguel, thoughtfully. "I must speak with granny Magda. She told me that he's French. She is not always reliable in this way... she even tried to tell me that Jacques Brel was from Belgium."

Never mind," says Gem. "This is a lovely place. I'm Gemma, and this is my lovely friend Imi... Imelda."

"Imelda," says Miguel. "I believe that means you are a fighter of great power."

"You're certainly right there," says Gem.

"And what about Gemma's name?" asks Imi.

"Gemma? I am not so sure what this means. I think perhaps it is Italian and means precious when stoned."

"I believe you mean precious stone," Miguel, says Gem.

"I think you are right," Miguel apologizes.

The girls order frogs' leg fajitas and settle for a bottle of the house wine, which turns out to be a perfectly acceptable Beaujolais Vieux... in fact the Beaujolais Nouveau from the previous November.

"Can I get *Mary Jane* for you?" Miguel enquires, with a cautious glance around him, making sure the nearby tables are unoccupied.

"Mary Jane? Who's *she*? What does she do," asks Gem.

"I mean grass. *You* know, girls... weed."

His voice falls to a whisper as he utters these words, nervously checking the adjoining tables again.

Imi nudges her companion, giggling. "He means pot, Gem... marijuana."

Gem coughs, "Thank you Miguel, but we'll stick with the frogs' legs if you don't mind," she suggests.

"You are lovely ladies. I have no girlfriend at the moment. Perhaps..."

Imi, now a little agitated, glances daggers at the gregarious Nepalese-Mexican.

"No, Miguel. The frogs' legs will be fine, thank you."

Before long, Magda brings their fajitas. They're delicious and are soon devoured, accompanied by the uncorking of a second bottle of the Beau-vieux.

After chatting for a while, quaffing the remains of that second bottle, they pay their bill and bid farewell to the amorous, yet somehow benign drug-pusher.

"Goodbye, lovely ladies. Be good now."

Imi and Gem make their way back into the streets of Bamberton, arm in arm and as high as if they'd accepted the offer of *Mary Jane*.

"I love you *so* much Gem. Let's not go back to the inn yet," Imi whispers in her companion's ear.

They take a turn that leads them away from the centre of the town and they soon come across the cleanly manicured municipal park. Its close-clipped lawns and late summer flowerbeds are seductive beneath the promise of a lapis twilight. A fountain sits enticingly under the eaves of an intimate arbour, deploying Eros to shoot a crystal jet of water from his bow. The jet arcs lazily into a waiting pool of diamond-dancing water, and the chatter of the falling droplets is like summer rain on the sea.

"Look, there at the back of the arbour, Gem. What's through that kissing gate do you reckon?" says Imi, now gazing close into her companion's deep, almond eyes.

"Let's see," says Gem, returning the gaze, floundering in those dazzling green eyes of Imi's.

They part grip for a moment or two and, gently waving the overhanging shrubbery aside, they slide through the narrow Victorian wrought iron gate, swinging it first to and then fro on squeaking hinges. Clasping each other afresh beyond the gate, a rough-hewn neglected path entices them on through the backwoods of untamed trees and bushes. The sounds of the fountain fade. Down, down the path slopes to a clearing, a dell letting in a last piercing shaft of light from the setting sun. The shafts fall revelatory on a bed of lush grass under the canopy of an ancient hornbeam, and down they lay, stretched out to the sky, taking in the precious interlude while the twilight turns towards dusk.

"Hola, bellas damas," hollers Miguel from somewhere in the depths of his bistro as Gem and Imi pass by, returning to the town ... "Hello, lovely ladies," he obligingly translates.

They titter and walk on by and, approaching the main street

that leads on to the town hall square, they hear the steadily growing sound of Morris music. Then up springs the frantic wailing of an ambulance siren. As they reach the main street, the ambulance speeds on by them on its way to Bamberton Community Hospital. They reach the square, clinging close to the walls of buildings, hoping to slip by the marauding mass of the Morris and back into the refuge of *The Worm Inn.*

Fred Moulton is sitting on the steps of the town library, looking a little shaken. Gem can't resist asking about the ambulance.

"Oh, it's you again. I'd have thought you'd had enough of Morris dancing for one day."

"More like for a thousand days, actually" suggests Imi, coming out of her man-hating mode a little.

"Well, it was like this... Err, did you know you've got grass marks on the shoulder of your blouse, by the way? There look," says Fred, pointing, distracted for a moment.

Gem strains to see the telltale marks, then the pair look at each other and giggle.

"Yes, we know," says Gem, " but do go on."

"Oh yeah... It was like this... You know my mate Kit?... He's dancing in this Adderbury stick dance... the sticking can get a bit fraught and erratic at the best of times, but more especially when everyone's tired. Our Fool, Dan Copley, is doing his fooling... he's managed to re-inflate his bladder in *The Lighthouse Inn...* don't ask... I know we're a hundred miles from the sea. Anyway, damned fool Dan the Fool decides he can weave in and out between the sticks in the chorus. He gets his timing all wrong and Kit fells him with a cracker. Breaks open his skull, he does. Blood everywhere. I reckon Dan'll be okay though... there's not much inside his head to damage. Well, the ambulance gets here in minutes and, after the ambulance men have wrapped his bonce in a temporary bandage... or was it vinegar and brown paper?... off it speeds to the local hospital."

"And you're all carrying on dancing?"

"Of course we are. It's traditional. Once, a bloke dancing for *The Pockbury Prancers* fainted in the middle of a hand-clapping dance and they finished the dance with five men stepping round him and over him *before* they called for help."

Imi shudders, not so much at the thought of the man who'd passed out, but at the mention of Pockbury.

"Oh, dear," offers Gem. "I do hope he's alright."

"Not really," says Fred. "He's been told not to dance any more after passing out like that."

"No... your *Fool*, you fool."

"Oh, I see what you mean. Yeah, *he'll* be alright. He's tough as old boots really."

The next morning dawns fair. *Crabby* and *Chirpy's* excursion is poised to get back on its own track, and after breakfast they'll be on their way exploring the Cotswolds again in the depths of wildest Oxfordshire.

"Hello, is that you, Jan? How are you, love? And how's Oxford? Is he behaving? Are you sleeping well? I'm really missing you, love," John rattles off his questions over the payphone in the foyer of *The George and Worm Inn*.

"Yes, John... Okay... Fine... Yes, but crying a lot... No, he's *crying* a lot!" she replies to each of his questions, and adds. "I'm really missing *you* too, love."

"I'm sorry, Janet. I should be there with you."

"No, John. I'm glad that he's crying. It shows he's got good lungs. And *he's* probably missing you as well, John. You needed a break, so you enjoy it while you can. You'll be back in geography classes next week."

"Don't remind me, Jan."

"Are you still having the nightmares, John?"

"No, Jan. Not last night anyway. I dreamed a lot, but not

nightmares."

"Good, because if they don't go, I'm definitely expecting you to revisit that yoga therapy."

"In fact last night I dreamed of you and me, Jan. We were much older and you were serving coffees in your coffee shop... beautiful coffees... and I was grinding beans," he tells her over-excitedly. "There were Arabicas... Sidikalang from Indonesia and Gesha from Panama, and there was Robusta from Vietnam and loads more. I knew all the names, Janet... I must have been listening to you and your coffee shop meanderings more than I realized."

"Steady on, John. You sound like you've been *on* the coffee since dawn. All that caffeine... you'll be hyper. Your chakras will be even more out of balance. And anyway... be careful, John Barrington. That's *my* dream, not yours."

"I don't care, Jan. It's a revelation. We must make it happen. I want to be free of the geography treadmill. And I want to be part of your dream. Barista Barrington, that's me."

"I'm so pleased, John. We must start making some positive plans as soon as we can."

"Oh, and Jan. I forgot to mention our little Oxford was in the dream as well. But he wasn't little. He was grown up, and very beautiful he was too. He was in the shop with us, tidying the books after customers... dozens of customers. And he was married with a beautiful wife and they had two kids, a boy and a girl. Our grandkids, Jan. And they were named Burford Barrington and Witney Barrington."

"Oh, John. I'm missing you even more now."

"I know. Me you too. I'll soon be home Jan."

And with that, they say their emotional farewells, as if they were to be apart for years, not days. John hangs up the phone and wanders into the dining room for breakfast, the fresh aroma of instant *Nescafé* in his nostrils.

Two nights in *The Worm* and touring the area free of the Morris men turns out to be a tonic for everyone on the *Chirpy* and *Crabby* trip and when they return home there's nothing but praise for the pair. The madness of the brief collaboration with the dancers had set the bar a little lower for the remainder of the trip and everyone, including John, now felt it had been a worthwhile adventure. The only lasting downside is the superficial spoiling of Big Jim's upholstery… mostly beer stains and a surreptitious vomit stain found on the back seat, left by an anonymous donor. Whether this was a benevolent gesture by a Morris man or one of their own company was debateable, but *Chirpy* squared it with Big Jim when the coach was returned, and all was well.

Chapter Seventeen

Happy Man

Towards the end of September, the weather is on the turn. When the skies are clear, the evenings are now bringing with them a chill mist and in the mornings the greenswards over in Pockbury are dew-ridden. The swallows are looking urgently in their diaries and reminding themselves of their appointment with South Africa, the young of the summer season flexing their wings to strengthen them for the first of their annual long-distance flights.

It's eight-thirty in the morning and D.I. Fielding is busy organising his re-trawl of the woods in the vicinity of the crime scene. It's a good time of year and with the sun cooling a little from its August intensity, the physical exertion of the search will create less sweat than it might have done, even though most members of his team are not as fit as they should be.

"Boss, couldn't we wait a bit longer... 'til the dew's gone?" enquires P.C. Blunt. "My trouser bottoms are already soaked through."

"I'll be blunt, Blunt. I don't want namby-pambies in my team. If you want to be a wimp, you should have joined the fire brigade. Why didn't you stop and roll up your trousers, or tuck them into your socks like W.P.C. Sharpe here."

"Sorry, boss."

"Right. Now this is where the remains of the victim were found. If we fan out from here, we can cover the old ground and then go beyond the perimeter of the first search."

W.P.C. Sharpe steps forward, "But, sir? If we fan out, then by the time we reach the limits of the old search, the gaps between us will be getting too wide won't they?"

"Sharp thinking, Sharpe. And just what I was thinking myself... So, what do you propose?"

"I reckon if we put down markers, we could join up at the

old limits and explore further a segment at a time."

"Just what *I* was thinking. Right get to it every one. I'll leave you in the capable hands of Sharpe here. You all know what we're looking for. I'm off to make further enquiries at *The Bogtrotters' Arms*... if I can wake the landlord, that is."

P.C. Blunt, feeling rather inadequate, tucks his trouser bottoms belatedly into his socks. *'Sodden trousers! Why can't we wear shorts, like the police in Bermuda do?'* he thinks, morosely.

-o-o-o-

By nine o'clock Kit is preparing his kit for the last of *A.B.V.'s* summer outings. The pubs will soon all be dispensing with their summer ales and instead dispensing their winter warmers; *Harvest Mash* will give way to *Santa's Sack, Thresher's Firkin* to *Wee Threeking Gold*.

"I can't say I've missed the 'mellow fruitfulness' much," Kit says to himself as he loads his car with hatbox, rag coat and bell-pads. "Another season over. Practice in the village hall from next week. Hey ho."

He eases himself into his clapped out, pale green Volvo Estate and heads off to pick up Fred Moulton. They're driving over to *The Nautical Maureen* to meet the rest of the side.

"Chuck your stuff in the boot, Fred. We'd better be moving. We don't want the wrath of *The Third Reich* falling on us."

"Jawohl, meine Herr! We don't want nightmares do we?"

"Certainly don't," says Kit as he eases the car into the traffic. "Mind you, I *have* been suffering with nightmares just lately... For a month or two now."

"Oh, yeah? What are they about... Morris dancing? Did you go the wrong way in the Adderbury hey? Remember last year, when *I* did that, *Pervy* gave me a red card and he wouldn't let me in Adderbury dances for a month."

"No, nothing like that. They *are* sort of Morris related

though," says Kit, hesitantly. "It's nothing really."

He indicates to turn right as they approach the busy junction with the town by-pass.

"Come on, Kit. You *have* to tell me now. Are they about dancing mixed Morris... men and women together? You know how much the thought of women in bell-pads turns you on. Does one of 'em turn you on, then turn you down, night after night?" persists Fred, laughing at the idea.

Kit, persuaded by his mate's probing, opens his thoughts further, "No, not women, Fred. Remember last September, when we went to Pockbury for *The Prancers' Ale* meeting."

"No. I didn't go to that. I thought I told you. I was at a big rock concert over in Birmingham. What a night *that* was. Head-banging, stage-diving, crowd-surfing... the lot."

"Yeah? How come your brain isn't more scrambled than it is, Fred? Anyway... a big night for you and me both... there was head-banging at Pockbury too."

"Blimey. I know Morris can get a bit heavy, but head-banging?" says Fred, wondering whether or not he'd chosen the better gig.

"It's just... that business a couple of months ago on the T.V. news when we were at the *Bottom and Barnacle*... about the dead body they found. They said they thought it had happened around July time *last* year, but maybe it could have been in September. Well, It's been playing on my mind ever since. You see, I can recall this weedy bloke who was at the *Prancers' Ale*. I think that he said he came from Midwinter Regis way... I fetched him a right clout as he was turning into the hey in *Happy Man*. I ended up with blood on me hankies, but he didn't flinch at all... just finished the dance and disappeared. I never saw him again."

"It happens. A blood sport... that's what Morris is."

"It was all a bit ghostly, Fred... as if he hadn't really existed at all. And every time we dance that dance since then, my anxiety goes through the roof. Now I've been having these nightmares."

"Why now? It's all in the past mate. Forget it," says Fred, trying to help, but still sniggering at the thought of Morris head-banging.

"But I just *can't* forget it, Fred."

"So you think you might've killed a Morris man?" says Fred, now realising how worried Kit is about it, "Blimey, Kit. I could tell you weren't yourself lately... I guess it's no wonder. What're you gonna do?"

"I dunno, Fred. I've been turning it over and over in my mind. I can't really believe I've killed anyone, but you never know... a blow on the head could have had a delayed effect. Maybe he just staggered off into the woods and died."

"Do you think you should go to the police, then?"

"That's what I've been mulling over. But it *was* an accident after all, wasn't it?"

"Well, you're never gonna be at peace unless you *do* go. *You* know that much."

"I suppose you're right."

So Kit does his best to get through the day's dancing, becoming more and more sullen as the outing wears on. Then *Pervy* announces 'Happy Man, Adderbury' and Kit can't face dancing it. He resolves to go to the police station the following morning to try and explain what he believes has happened.

"Good morning, sir. Can I be of assistance?" asks P.C. Blunt, who happens to be on desk duty at the police station. "It's a nice day, to be sure," he adds cheerily.

"Morning," replies Kit, dejectedly. "But I can't really see what's good about it."

"I'm sorry about that, sir," says Blunt, rather regretting that he'd tried to be quite so cheery first thing in the morning. "Perhaps we can help to make it better."

"I doubt it, constable. Things couldn't be worse really, but I don't imagine they could be *better*."

"We'll have to see, won't, we... to make things better, not worse."

"You see, I think I've killed a man," says Kit.

"What? When? How?" says Blunt, looking nervously over his shoulder for support, anxious that he might need to make an arrest.

"That thing over in Pockbury. I'm sure I know what happened."

"Very good, sir. I'll just get someone to assist."

P.C. Blunt edges his way to the office door behind the counter, keeping an uneasy eye on the man on the other side of the desk, half expecting him to hightail it out of the station. He pushes the door ajar and shouts.

"Mr. Fielding, sir. There's someone here wants to see you."

"I thought you were out searching the woods again, Blunt. Sharpe left *you* in charge, didn't she?" comes the reply.

"The team know what they're doing now sir. I left Cyril Treadwell in charge."

"Just *tell* me next time. I shan't have insubordination. Anyway, now you're here can't you deal with this, Blunt?"

"Not really, sir. I thought I'd better tell you. It's a bit important. It's about Pockbury."

D.I. Fielding puts down his pen, raises his arms in frustration, makes his way over to the door and squeezes through it, Blunt still impeding it from opening adequately.

"He says he might have killed a man, sir," says Blunt. "The *'Caved-in Skull'* man, sir."

Harry Fielding tenses at this announcement. "Perhaps you'd better come this way, sir. What name is it?"

Err, Kit. Kit Harbury."

"Blunt... get some tea organized, will you, and send W.P.C. Sharpe along to interview room 1."

"Do you want some of those chocolate digestives as well, sir?" asks Blunt, trying to be helpful.

"No thank you, Blunt," says Fielding, exasperated at Blunt's poor grasp of the true seriousness of the situation and wondering if the staff has a secret stash of biscuits he doesn't know about. "We're not having a picnic, *are* we?"

"No, sir. Sorry, sir," says Blunt, sheepishly, wishing he hadn't asked. And off he goes through the door at the far side of the office to find Sharpe and the kettle. *'So, Harry didn't know about the chocolate digestives... damn,'* he thinks.

Harry Fielding raises the counter flap and beckons Kit to join him, raising an eyebrow as he follows him through a separate door and down the adjoining corridor to the interview room. Kit is wondering now whether he should have come here at all.

"Start the tape running if you will, Sharpe," Fielding instructs his colleague, and he speaks the formalities into the microphone before commencing his interrogation... date, and time, parties present etc. "Now Mr. Harbury, I understand you may have some information for us regarding the Pockbury killing. However, before we start in earnest, I have to tell you that you have the right to remain silent and to appoint a solicitor if you so wish. Nevertheless, since you've volunteered your presence here, I assume you may be happy for us to proceeded as we are."

"Yes, I guess so," says Kit, timidly.

"Tell me then, Mr. Harbury, what's it all about?"

Kit is taken aback somewhat. Shaking nervously, he's hit by a sudden wave of realisation that he's kicked off a formal investigation into the circumstances of his possible involvement in the fatal skull cracking. After much anxious heart searching he'd all but convinced himself that, since the wounds inflicted on the Morris man at Pockbury had been accidental, it wouldn't be taken this seriously.

P.C. Blunt arrives delivering tea for three... with no chocolate digestive biscuits and leaves the room. Then the distraught Morris man spills his story, explaining how back in September he'd struck the mystery dancer a heavy blow to the head in the village hall, albeit accidentally.

"It all sounds very plausible, Mr. Harbury," declares Fielding, "except that our corpse had been lying there since July according to our pathologist, though he could have been wrong, I suppose. And the poor victim has some pretty horrendous damage to his skull... If you're the killer, then the legality of Morris dancing should be reviewed."

"Perhaps Oliver Cromwell had the right idea, sir," says W.P.C. Sharpe. "I mean banning that kind of thing."

"Indeed, Sharpe. Perhaps Charles II is culpable in all this for bringing it back. I've always been sceptical about the monarchy."

Fielding says this rather inadvertently forgetting that the ubiquitous portrait of Her Majesty the Queen is displayed, as in Hector Parrott's office, on the wall behind his desk. Unlike Parrott, he doesn't live with the expectation of a knighthood.

"On a more serious note, I'm afraid we shall have to keep you here while we carry out a few immediate investigations. This may put a whole new perspective on things, Mr. Harbury." continues Fielding. "I take it you have no dependants or pets at home requiring your immediate attention," he adds with a compassion that shows his human side.

"No. I live alone in my flat. I *did* have a goldfish that I won at the fair on the air rifles, but that died last week."

"Good. Now, we shall need to take a blood sample."

"Actually, I flushed the dead goldfish down the loo. And anyway, goldfish don't have any blood, do they?"

"Well, sir... they are *cold* blooded, I believe. But I meant *your* blood, actually. It may be that your blood type matches the traces found on the corpse."

"Oh, of course. Sorry, officer."

'But it wasn't me, I tell you,' Kit thinks, tempted for a moment to contradict his confession.

"In the meantime, we'll need your address and other details. And a key to your flat if you please. We need to take a look around. We can obtain a search warrant if you insist, but all that will do is extend your stay here... and I have to say that P.C. Blunt's tea would perhaps persuade you against that."

Kit fishes in his pocket for a key. W.P.C. Sharpe turns off the tape recorder and commences to take down further particulars.

"Very well, sir. We shall be as quick as we can. Meanwhile, the W.P.C. will escort you to a cell. If you're hungry, we'll send out for fish and chips. I could do with something myself, though I do prefer a pie with *my* chips... chicken and mushroom would be nice. We'll make arrangements now for taking the blood sample and you should be free to go home before too long, hopefully by sometime early tomorrow... we can't afford to keep feeding you. Our residual budget for fish and chips this financial year isn't too healthy. It's going the way of D.C.I. Parrott's cigars."

Fielding dispatches W.P.C. Sharpe and P.C. Blunt to expedite the search of Kit's flat, instructing it as a matter of protocol, since he isn't entirely convinced that Kit is implicated in the killing. After all, the body certainly wasn't dressed in Morris kit, though the remnants of his coat and trousers *had* been somewhat ragged. And it seemed that he was far larger than Kit's description of the Morris phantom. So Fielding dispenses with the thought of forensics being involved for the time being.

The flat is rather disorganized and Kit is certainly not fastidious in the way he keeps things. The sofa is replete with cushions and coats and other garments, laid there in disarrayed layers, like some sedimentary archaeological record of the aeons. The pantry is not inviting either... stale bread and a half-eaten tin of baked beans sporting a long-handled spoon being the main attractions. Perhaps P.C. Blunt's tea might after all be an attraction to Kit, rather that a put-off. The cupboards are no better, with all and sundry stuffed in them… and in among the disarray of contents, there is discovered a pair of scrunched-up handkerchiefs, and on them are telltale dark brown bloodstains.

"We'd better bag them up for *Grisly*," says Sharpe to Blunt.

"Now then, Fielding, are we making progress on the '*Caved-in Skull*' investigation?" asks Chief Inspector Parrott.

"Er, yes… *and* no, sir," says Fielding to Parrott. "You see, this character Harbury says he may have killed the bloke when he hit him in a Morris dance in the village hall at Pockbury back in September. But *our* chap doesn't seem to have been a Morris dancer… his clothes were more those of a traveller, a vagabond. Besides, from what *Grisly* tells us, he would probably have weighed about fourteen stone and Harbury reckons the mysterious disappearing dancer that he hit was skinny. Not only that, the bloke's head was pretty well smashed in, so I'm pretty convinced he'd never have made it out of the village hall with injuries like that, It just doesn't add up."

"Even so, Fielding, you'd better wait on those blood sample results you tell me you're pursuing before you release him, just to be sure. You never know, there might just be a match."

"Yes, sir. We're expecting them back this afternoon, though *Grisly* says it'll be quite difficult to establish any match, given the advanced deterioration of the body."

-o-o-o-

"Right, Mr. Harbury," announces Fielding, the following morning, "you can go now. You can collect your key and your other effects from the desk."

"You mean, it *was* an accident? Thank God for that."

Happy Man

Kit feels a great flood of relief rush over him.

"No, not exactly, Mr. Harbury. Whoever you hit *may* have been hit accidentally, but it wasn't *our* man... for a start, no way was he 'weedy' and fortunately for you, your blood doesn't match the rather rare strain we found on the victim of the Pockbury killing. Furthermore, whilst the blood on hankies we've found at your flat doesn't match your own, neither does *it* match either of the two types found on the body. With all the other factors taken into account, I'm minded to believe that there's a Morris man running around the country somewhere, with the memory of a sore head and, like you, terrorising other dancers and the public with his stick and bells."

"Thank God for that!" repeats Kit. He pays a cursory backwards glance at the cell he's been kept in overnight, walks the corridor and picks up his belongings from the desk. He thanks P.C. Blunt for his admirable tea making and congratulates him on the excellent choice of fish and chip shop. He walks out, a happy man, into bright September sunshine and thinking, *I'm so relieved. The skinny bloke isn't the dead bloke and the blood on my hankies is just from an injury to the mystery Midwinter dancer.'*

'What now, then?' ponders Harry, sitting baffled in his office.

Chapter Eighteen

Bubonic Fairies

"Sir! sir!" calls out Blunt.

"What is it now, Blunt?"

"The team has found something in the woods, Mr. Fielding, sir."

"Are *they* still out there?

"It's a big area, sir."

"I suppose so."

"They suspended the search over the weekend, what with the overtime ban. But they've been back on it today," explains Blunt.

"They've not found a gingerbread house, have they?"

"No. It's a bag of Morris kit."

"Well done, Blunt. Is it with *Grisly* yet?"

"Just on its way now, sir."

"Right. You'd better congratulate the search team."

"Thank you very much, sir. I will," says Blunt, not sure if this compliment includes him, as part of the team.

"And Blunt."

"Yes, sir?"

"Hightail it and get that Harbury character back in here, will you."

"Yes, sir. Right away, sir."

'*A please would be nice,*' thinks P.C. Blunt as he makes for the door.

-o-o-o-

Fred rings the doorbell of Kit's flat. Kit puts down his late morning bowl of cornflakes and makes to answer the door.

"Hi ya, Fred, I didn't expect *you* today."

"No. We're between jobs this week, so I've got some time off.

You told me *you* had the day off, and seeing as how you were a bit down the other day, I just wondered how you're feeling now. Have you got over the Pockbury thing?"

"That's good of you, Fred. Actually, I *did* go to the police. I *really* thought I'd killed that bloke in the woods. But they did tests and everything, and it wasn't me."

Kit makes his way back down the hallway to re-join his cornflakes. Fred follows him.

"Are you looking for condensation, Kit?"

"No, I'm looking for my cornflakes."

"No. I mean *compensation*."

"Oh, right," says Kit, chuckling at Fred's malapropism. "Why would I be looking for compensation? They only kept me in for one night and that was because I handed myself in. I'm just relieved to be clear of all that worry. I honestly thought the world was about to end. Anyway, *I'm* free this morning too. Let's go into town and see what's cooking."

"Yeah. I was going in anyway later, to buy the latest album by *The Bubonic Fairies*."

"Good luck with that one. You let me listen to them once and I'll stick with *Monsters of Folk - Volume II* if you don't mind."

Kit finishes his cornflakes, dumps the dish and the spoon in the kitchen sink and puts on his jacket. They head back through the hallway for the front door just as the obscure-glazed panel is overshadowed by two blurred figures. Kit opens the door. It's P.C. Blunt and another, rather burly, constable.

"Good morning, sir. I'm glad we caught you in. I trust it's convenient for you to come down to the station again."

"What if it's not?" says Fred, protectively.

The burly P.C. fidgets, subtly swaying from one foot to the other, and places a cautious hand on his pocketed truncheon. Kit's newfound smile drops from his face like a lead Zeppelin. The air falls silent for what seems like an eternity.

"I suppose that's okay, P.C. Blunt," says Kit at last, gritting his teeth resignedly, "but what for?"

"There've been developments. That's all I can say for the moment."

"I'm coming *too*," declares Fred. "It's not fair th…" he falls silent as 'P.C. *Burly*' fondles his truncheon once more.

"No problem, sir," says Blunt. "You can wait in reception."

And so, Kit finds himself in interview room 1 again. Fred sits in the reception area under the watchful eye of P.C. Blunt.

Inspector Fielding drops a bagged bundle of clothing on the interview desk and W.P.C. Sharpe activates the tape recorder. Fielding again confirms the date and time and parties present. There's no offer of tea this time.

"Now then, laddie. How do you explain these?"

"What?"

Fielding tips out the dishevelled collection of clothes from the plastic bag. There's a barely perceivable tinkling of bells as they fall onto the *Formica* surface.

"Morris clothes. That's what. These were found yesterday in Pockbury woods, not a hundred yards from the scene of our little crime."

Kit's jaw drops. He recognizes the colours.

"They were what that mysterious disappearing Morris man was wearing… *you* know… the bloke that vanished from the village hall that night. Like I told you, he said he came from Midwinter Regis way."

"Did he now? Well, we've checked that out and the last report of anyone missing from that area was back in the war, when an Italian prisoner went a.w.o.l. In the meantime, luckily for you, we've been able to rush through an analysis of bloodstains found on these clothes and the only match is with those on *your* handkerchiefs. The clothes *do* look as if they belonged to your skinny chappie, so it seems to corroborate your little tale. But I really believe we must locate your dancing spectre to find out why he disappeared so mysteriously and without his clothes. What's more, I can feel a glut of interviews with Morris men coming on ... now *there's* something to look forward to. We'll be starting by contacting *The Pockbury Prancers* as soon as we can. You don't happen to have their phone number do you?"

"No, but I know a man who *will* have contact details. Gerry Newman, our Bagman."

W.P.C. Sharpe switches off the tape recorder and Kit heaves a sigh of relief. He rejoins Fred in reception and makes to thank P.C. Blunt again, only this time sarcastically, saying...

"Thanks. Thanks for nothing, mate."

"Yeah. Thanks for nothing, mate," echoes Fred, defiantly.

"I'm only doing me job," says Blunt, somewhat hurt by this dual rebuke, but Kit and Fred are already out of the door.

Kit has had a restless night and half wakes in a start, dreaming. He's onboard a coach, much like the one that rescued *A.B.V.* on their interrupted tour of fifteen pubs. *This* coach though is painted in bright primary colours of red, blue and yellow, infused with fluorescent pinks and greens. Psychedelic images of Morris dancers and their musicians leer out at him menacingly. A swirling brew of imps and devils, of witches and wizards, of woods and battered skulls and bloodied handkerchiefs weaves in and out of the windows of the coach. A music swells... a discordant mix of *Bubonic Fairies* and melodeons, with the incessant wailing of a pipe and the driving beat of a tabor. For one moment he's *outside* the coach, suspended in air, a helpless and remote witness to this mayhem and the next he is sucked in through the very windows and is plonked on the seat he'd occupied on the Cotswold Morris tour. He's looking back over his seat at Robbie and *Figgy*. And beyond them are those two girls, one half hidden behind her coat... but those eyes. Those haunting, flaunting eyes.

'What were their names?' Kit thinks, scratching his head... *'Gemma and Imelda? that's it... Gem and Imi.'* And now, consumed by a tumult of confusion and with a cold sweat rising, in a flash he realizes. *'Those eyes! Surely not?... 'Boy-girl? Man-woman? It was! It was her! She was the vanishing dancer. Hers were the eyes of the Morris man at Pockbury.'*

Wide awake now, the dream receding, he snatches a further thought, *'What if she's the killer?'*

"If you're sure, you'd better go back to the police," advises Fred, when Kit tells him of his dream that evening.

"I'm not sure if I *am* sure, Fred. I don't want to set another hare running on a goose chase."

"I suppose in the end it's up to you, but how will you ever live with it if you don't? Hare today, goose tomorrow is what I always say."

"I guess you're right, Fred," says Kit, not quite fathoming Fred's maxim.

-o-o-o-

"Morning, Mr, Harbury," offers W.P.C. Sharpe, who happens to be on the desk at the station. "Have you brought your bed with you? The rent here isn't cheap you know."

"No," says Kit, shrugging off the well-intended levity, "I haven't brought a bed, but I need to see D.C.I. Parrott."

"Sorry, he's not in at present. Will D.I. Fielding do?"

"I suppose so, but it's *really* important."

"Sorry. He's not in either for the moment. Will *I* do?"

"I suppose so, but it's *quite* important."

"Well, I *have* been known to deal with *quite* important things."

"Right," says Kit. "I think I know who the Pockbury killer is."

180

"Ah... perhaps that *is* really important. We'd better wait for D.I. Fielding, Mr. Harbury. Oh, here he is now. Harry... sir, Mr. Harbury's back."

"So I see... and?"

"He says it's *quite* important. He thinks he knows who the Pockbury killer is."

"It's *really* important, actually," suggests Kit.

"Should we wait for Chief Inspector Parrott, sir... if it's *really* important?"

"No need for that, Sharpe. I'm quite used to dealing with *really* important things. Can you get us tea please, Sharpe. And, by the way, we need a new tape in the interview room."

"Yes, sir. I'll find P.C. Blunt."

"He's not here at the moment, Sharpe."

"Bugger," she curses under her breath and, louder now. "Chocolate digestives?"

"No, I don't think so, Sharpe. Remember the budget, woman," says Fielding. *'Where are these bloody chocolate digestive biscuits everybody seems to know about?'* he ponders.

Fielding escorts Kit to interview room 1. Soon tea arrives and W.P.C. Sharpe inserts the new tape, pressing the record buttons. The formalities are repeated.

"Just for the record, you understand, Mr. Harbury," says Fielding, reassuringly. "By the way, sir, you can call me Harry. May I call you Kit?"

"Yes, of course."

"Now," continues Fielding, "before we start in earnest, we've had very little success with the bag of Morris kit, Kit. Your so-called Bagman, Gerry Newman recognized the kit as similar to that worn by this mysterious Morris man of yours, but he has no idea where the dancer came from or indeed where he went to. As for Midwinter Regis. We've asked every soul who lives there and none of them seem to know any Morris men."

"There's the thing, Harry. I don't reckon it *was* a man. I believe it was a *woman*."

"Are you kidding me, Kit? A woman could never have caused that much damage with a wooden implement."

"Don't you be so sure, sir," says W.P.C. Sharpe. "You should see what *I* can do with a rolling pin. Even with a spatula I could lay you out with a single blow between stirs of the saucepan. Women are more powerful than you imagine, in so many ways."

"Right. I suggest we don't dwell on that thought, Sharpe. Just you keep the safety catch on your spatula."

The W.P.C. feels she's scored a point for female equality here and D.I. Fielding feels more than a little uneasy at the threat to the glass ceiling that is his masculinity.

"So, Kit. What makes you believe we should be looking for a woman?"

And Kit relates the story of his accidental crossing of paths with the enigmatic girl on the holiday coach, and his dreamed eureka moment that seems to point to his brief encounter with the ghost-dancer.

Fielding raises an eyebrow at the psychedelic aspects of Kit's dream, but continues, "So where does this Imelda girl come from?"

"I've no idea, unless it really *was* Midwinter Regis. But I did overhear the pleasure trip conductor talking to his driver on the rescue coach and they called each other *Crabb* and *Chips* or some such, and I recall hearing them say they normally work on the council buses in Oxford. *They* may know something about her."

"Crab and chips, eh? Sounds delicious. I must see if our chip shop does that. Anyway, we'll make enquiries at the council about the conductor and driver. That should give us a lead. Leave it with us, Kit. We'll let you know how we get on."

Enquiries at the council and at the bus depot bring results and Harry Fielding gets to speak with *Chirpy*.

"And where might we find this Imelda woman, then, Mr. Chips?"

"*Chirpy* to you, guv. I can't be absolutely sure, guv. I remember her mentioning a bloke called Roderick when she bought her tickets, but then she turned up to the coach with a woman. Now, what was *her* name? Gina... no Gemma. That's it... Gemma."

"Yes, Gemma it is, Mr. *Chirpy*," says Harry.

"*Chirpy*... just plain *Chirpy*, officer. I don't really know any more than that, officer. Imelda's not really a regular customer, not as regular as some of the others. I've only seen her once or twice on the council bus. I could keep an eye out for you, though. Anyway, what's this all about?"

"I can't really elaborate right now, sir," says Harry, not wishing to overtly suggest a link between Imelda and the case in hand. "All I can say is that we're pursuing a serious enquiry."

"Right then, officer."

"So that's all you know about her, is it?"

"Afraid so, officer. Hang on though, guv. Now I come to think of it... on the coach trip one of our regular customers Ida, Ida Hall that is, spoke with this Imelda and her mate Gemma quite a lot." And here, *Chirpy* begins to ramble, as he is inclined to do with his everyday passengers. "The two girls were a bit close, but they seemed to get on well enough with Ida and *her* companion *Gabby the Mac*... Bob that is. I don't see anything of Ida's husband, Bert... Albert that is... Albert Hall... that always makes me laugh, that does. He'd been in the infirmary with his leg. Now Ida *is* a regular... if you get on our 9.30 bus into town on a Wednesday or Friday morning, you're pretty sure to catch her."

"Thanks, Mr. *Chirpy*. We'll look into it."

"*Chirpy*, guv… just plain *Chirpy*."

Chapter Nineteen

Lollipops

On the following Wednesday, Harry Fielding and W.P.C. Sharpe find themselves sitting side by side on *Chirpy's* council bus, looking conspicuous in their uniforms waiting for Ida, who's sitting alone on the seat in front of them, to finish her *Woodbine*. There's just the three of them on the upper deck of the bus, so Fielding decides to try a few questions there and then. There's no record button for W.P.C. Sharpe to activate.

"It's Mrs. Hall isn't it?" asks Harry, waving his warrant card at her as she turns in some surprise.

"Yes. Who wants to know?" says Ida, having failed to fathom the declaration on the card.

"D.I. Harry Fielding, madam," confirms Harry, waving the card vigorously at Ida.

"Right," says Ida, "Only I really can't read your name when it's upside down."

"Oh, sorry, Mrs Hall," says Harry, inspecting his inverted card as he withdraws it and puts it away.

"I wonder, can you tell us anything about a woman called Imelda?" he asks. "She was on the coach outing you went on recently, I believe."

"Imelda? No, not a lot really. She seemed very nice on the outing. A bit shy, though she seemed to speak to the women more than the men. She and her friend Gemma didn't seem to be keen on men very much at all. They were just like sisters... always cuddling each other. They even slept in our double bed."

"What? You mean there were four of you?"

"No, of course not. I mean they slept in our double *room*."

"So where did you and your husband sleep?"

"In *their* twin room. But it wasn't my husband. It was Bob... *Gabby*, that is. Albert, my husband, was at home with Mabel

185

and his leg."

"Right. I won't ask. But you must have learned a little more about them than that?"

"I do recall seeing her, Imelda that is, on the rounds in the infirmary when Bert was in with his..."

"Yes, with his leg. Please go on, Mrs. Hall."

"She's a student there. And I heard her talking to Mr. McMorran, Roderick McMorran, Bert's surgeon. I think *her* name is Chester... something. That's right, Imelda Chesterton. Her and the surgeon seemed to have a thing going when they were on the wards. There was this Seth Perkins in for a hernia operation after his *Tango* dancing and *he* reckoned Imelda and Mr. McMorran were both Morris dancers."

"I see. Morris dancers, eh? Thank, you, Mrs. Hall. That's very helpful. If we can just note your address in case we need to speak with you again."

"Of course you can. Anyway, what's this all about?"

"I can't really say right now, madam."

"Right you are, but give that Imelda my regards... and that nice Mr. McMorran too, if you see him," says Ida.

"Of course we will," says Fielding as he and Sharpe get up and make there way to the stairs to alight at the next stop. "We should have brought the tape machine with us, Sharpe."

"But there's nowhere to plug it in, sir."

"I know, Sharpe. Just a figure of speech, you understand."

"Yes, of course, sir."

On the rear platform, W.P.C. Sharpe says quietly, "Next stop please," and presses the stop button herself, normally the domain of *Chirpy*, who's distracted from his duties for a moment by a woman misguidedly wanting to know how much a ticket to London would cost. Sharpe seems to be good with buttons, what with tape recorders and now bell-pushes on the bus... another figurative feather in her burgeoning peacock of a hat.

"At last, we seem to be getting somewhere, Sharpe."

"Yes, sir. And now we need to get somewhere else. How do we get back to the station, sir?"

"Ah. Yes, Right... a nice brisk walk would be agreeable. It's a distance, but the exercise will do us both good. Did I tell you about the time when I was on the beat?"

"Yes, sir. Just a few times, sir."

"You see, back in the day, being on the beat meant walking for miles and miles, not driving around in *Panda* cars. We didn't even..."

"...have bicycles, sir. I know, sir. You told me all about it."

"And one time, I saw this naked man in Nottingham with what looked like a parakeet of all things on his shoulder and..."

"I know sir. It turned out to be a parrot, Mr. Fielding. You told me that too, remember? You said the man thought he was a pirate and that he'd buried his clothes at some forgotten spot marked X. It seems that parrots play a large part in your life, don't they, what with the D.C.I. and all... perhaps Mr. Parrott's a reincarnation of the parrot, though I can hardly imagine him climbing onto the shoulder of a naked man."

And with this, W.P.C. Sharpe breaks into a trot down the high street, making a beeline for Poxford and the station, looking to outrun her superior officer. D.I. Fielding, unfit from too much desk-flying, hobbles along in an endeavour to keep up, but is soon left a hundred yards behind.

By the time Fielding reaches the station, Sharpe is telephoning the Infirmary and the General Hospital, enquiring after Imelda Chesterton and Roderick McMorran.

Before long, despite his protestations at the interruption to his busy diary, the surgeon is sitting in interview room 2. Room 1 is currently occupied by a mini-conference aimed at solving a recent spate of surreptitious thefts of lollipops from crossing wardens in the area. Imi is also at the station, held for the moment in one of the cells.

"Roderick McMorran," says Harry Fielding...

Tempted for a moment to bypass the usual formalities, he thinks better of his brief cavalier lapse of protocol and asks Sharpe to do the necessary once more.

"Now then, Mr. McMorran, you may be able to help us with our enquiries. We have reason to believe that you're a Morris man."

"Don't be absurd, man. Who in their right mind would want to be a Morris dancer? Anyway, it might be a bonkers activity, but it's not illegal, is it?"

"Well, no, sir but perhaps it *should* be. Quite frankly, it's giving me headaches at the moment. Tell me, Mr. McMorran. Do you *know* any Morris men?"

"Of course not. The only time I've even heard Morris dancing mentioned was by one of our student doctors, young Imelda Chesterton. I looked at her thigh for her."

"Oh, did you now?"

"Yes. Apparently she'd injured it whilst dancing, but she said she'd given it up almost as quickly as she'd started. You know, we seem to specialize these days in dancing injuries. I'm sure it's one of the main reasons the *N.H.S.* is so overstretched... from people overstretching themselves that is."

"That's as may be, sir, but we have more pressing matters to attend to if you don't mind. I believe you had a thing going with Miss Chesterton, didn't you?"

"Only briefly. I went out for meals with her a couple of times, but she broke it off. Silly woman bought us some tickets for a coach trip, but there was no way I could have found time for that in *my* busy schedule. And I wouldn't want to sit on a blesséd coach mixing with the hoi polloi, even if I *could* find the time. I mean could you really see *me* sitting on a coach?"

"Very interesting, I'm sure," says Fielding, "No I couldn't really see you sitting on a coach, sir. And even if I could find the time, I probably wouldn't *want* to see you."

"May I get back to work now?" sighs the surgeon," I have a very busy diary you know. I've a lollipop lady to attend to this afternoon... the operation is scheduled for two o'clock, straight after my golf session. She was injured in a fight with a balaclava-wearing thief who stole her lollipop. That's the sort of thing you should be investigating, not Morris men."

"Believe you me, sir, we're doing all we can on both fronts. And for that reason, I must ask you to bear with us. We may have more questions for you later. We can find a spare cell for you whilst we ask your colleague Imelda a few questions. Tea?"

"But... protests Roderick, what about my lollipop lady? And my golf? Wait until my solicitor hears about this."

"I'm afraid she'll just have to wait, while we try and get this thing licked. We'll contact the infirmary straightaway for you so they can put the lollipop warden on hold. And after all, postponing operations is par for the course these days, isn't it? As for solicitors, you can bring one in if we decide to question you further. If you bring one in *now*, just remember that they probably charge more by the hour than surgeons do."

W.P.C. Sharpe escorts the surgeon down the corridor to a cell. She shouts to Blunt for tea, and then collects Imi to take her to the interview room. The ritual starting of the tape and the rote of noting introductory details is performed as always.

"May I ask you, young lady? What's all this about you being a Morris dancer?" asks Fielding.

Imi seethes at the patronising tone in his question, "And why would you be asking me about that? Surely you don't want to take it up do you?"

"Of course not, petal. But we have a serious matter to get to the bottom of. So I'd be grateful for your answer."

"*Petal!* For pity's sake, don't call me *petal*, you sexist plod.

189

Anyway, what about a solicitor?"

"No, it's definitely a Morris man we're looking for."

"No. I mean for me."

"I wouldn't advise it for the moment, missy. They *are* very expensive you know."

"*Missy!* It gets worse. Look, I only did the Morris for a few months if you must know. I wasn't very good at it. It can take hours of practise, all the moves, all the steps and all the different village traditions. And apart from all that, it's ruined by men. You men are chauvinistic at the best of times. But Morris men, and now policemen too, seem to make a career of it. Anyway, what's Morris dancing got to do with the price of fish? It's not illegal is it?"

"Would that it were, miss. Would that it were. We're looking into what seems to be a Morris dancing related incident. You must have heard about the Pockbury *'Caved-in Skull'* case. It's been in the papers and on the T.V."

"Sorry, I don't watch the news *or* read newspapers. News just depresses me. I used to take it in when I lived with my parents, but it was doing my head in so I gave it up. No news is good news, I say."

"I'm afraid the news is that someone's head *has* been 'done in' as you put it. Anyway, so what made you take up the dancing in the first place?"

"I dunno really. I saw a team of women dancing when I was on holiday in Dorset. *'That looks good'* I thought, especially the stick dances. They were asking the audience to take part and I did. After that I had the idea of taking up the dancing myself. I was considering joining a team, but the nearest women's side was miles away, so I decided not to bother. Then I found some videotapes of lots of Morris dances. They were in the music shop on the high street and I practised for a while in secret back in the flat."

"Do you live in the flat on your own?"

"No I've got three flat mates, but two of them are out every night picking up blokes. The other one's Gem. She's my soul mate, though she often tagged along with *them* and that's when I got the tapes out... when I was in on my own. The neighbours came round to complain a couple of times, so I turned the volume down to a whisper."

"Then it *was* you at Pockbury Village Hall, was it? The mysterious disappearing dancer?"

"Sure. I was there. I thumbed a lift to the village, changed in the toilets and joined in the dancing. I may be a woman, but I passed myself off as a man. They probably would have burned me as a witch if I'd dressed as a woman dancer. Anyway, it's always a bit of a free-for-all at these gatherings. They invite guest sides and a few 'odds and sods' dancers turn up, so I sneaked in okay. With all that beer flowing, some of the blokes can hardly recognize the men in their own side, let alone the guests. But some of them noticed my kit wasn't from a side they knew. I'd designed and made it myself secretly. I didn't even tell the girls at the flat about my weird, newfound hobby, though Gem knows a bit about it now. One or two of the dancers asked where I was from so I just said Midwinter Regis. Other than that I jumped in a few dances and hid behind my tankard between times. One bloke, Kit his name was, took a bit of a shine and talked me through some of the dances. Then, like a fool, I got up for an Adderbury stick dance..."

"An Adderbury dance?"

"Yes, a dance from Adderbury, All the Cotswold villages have there own distinctive dances. I went and pulled a thigh muscle, but with adrenaline kicking in, I carried on. Then to crown it all, this Kit fellow crowned me with his stick just as I was turning into the hey. It was a real swipe on the head... look here's the scar. A few inches lower and I could have been blinded."

And she parts her neat-cut hair to reveal a discreet inch-long

191

scar on her scalp.

"You know, Adderbury sticking can be really dangerous. *I* ended up with blood on my hankies and shirt. *He* got blood on *his* hankies too, but he was pissed by then, so he hardly noticed. I went to the bog to clean myself up and decided I'd had enough, so I changed back into my jeans, bundled up my kit and slipped away. I don't think he, or anyone else, missed me in their fog of bells and alcohol."

"Fascinating. Then what happened?"

"I decided to give up the idea of Morris dancing there and then. The head wound was shallow enough not to need stitches and thankfully soon healed, but my bloody thigh still pains me sometimes now, despite the attentions of *Slasher* McMorran... fat lot of good *he* was in the end because when I do anything athletic it hurts like Hell... Gem would certainly tell you that. Anyway, back at Pockbury, I dumped my bag of kit, bells and all, in some bushes in the woods and took what looked like a rough path through the trees. Then the fields led to the far end of the village and on to the main road. From there I hitched a lift back into Oxford, and now here I am, innocent of any crime except having associated overmuch with men."

Imi shrinks back into her chair and she weeps, emotionally overwhelmed by the ordeal of all the questioning. Sharpe offers her a tissue and she takes it, burying her face deep in its comforting softness.

"I see," says D.I. Fielding. "Innocent you may be, but *we* believe it might be otherwise. Our pathologist's July date definitely looks like it could be wrong."

Imi looks up from her paper hanky, her eyes appealing to her questioner for mercy.

Fielding coughs uncomfortably, "So, you didn't come across our portly gentleman on your way back to the road and bludgeon him to death then?" he says, deliberately and cruelly trying to catch the lapsed Morris dancer off her guard.

"No! No! Of course not," she protests, another flood of tears welling up.

"I'm afraid we'll need a blood sample and we'll need to search your flat," insists Fielding, "so let W.P.C. Sharpe here have your address and other details, and a key to your flat if you please. We can obtain a search warrant if you insist, but all that will do is extend your stay here... and I have to say that P.C. Blunt's tea would perhaps persuade you against that."

Imi wipes her eyes, and delves in her pocket for a key. W.P.C. Sharpe turns off the tape and again commences to take down further particulars... She's almost as good with a pen and notepad as she is with electrical buttons.

"Blunt," says D.I. Fielding. "When W.P.C. Sharpe has parked Miss Chesterton in the cells, I want you to accompany her to her flat."

"What? P.C. Sharpe's flat?"

"No, Blunt. Miss Chesterton's flat."

"Oh, right you are, sir."

"The pair of you did alright searching Mr. Harbury's gaff. See if you can find any more bloody handkerchiefs."

"What about Mr. McMorran, sir?"

"Leave him to cool off for a bit. I don't much like his attitude. He's up his own bum, is that one, pardon my French."

"Wow! The things surgeons can to do nowadays, Mr. Fielding, sir."

D.I. Fielding smiles. He's starting to take to Blunt.

"Can I get you a cup of tea, P.C. Blunt? Before you get off to that flat? You deserve one, my lad."

When Sharpe and Blunt arrive at Imi's flat, they've no need of the key. They find Emma and Celina there. W.P.C. Sharpe waves her warrant card at them and explains as prudently as possible that they need to search the place with a view to eliminating their friend from the police enquiries. The potential need to obtain a search warrant is dispensed with using the usual implied threat of a protracted visit to Poxford for the pair.

"Perhaps you'd both like to go for a walk whilst we do the necessary?"

"That's a bit rich," says Emma. "We'd rather stay and watch if you don't mind. Who do you damned well think you are, barging in here without a by-your-leave?" she adds, folding her arms in defiant stance.

"We're not going *anywhere*," agrees Celina, folding *her* arms in like manner.

"That's fine," says the W.P.C., in truth taking exception to the attitude of Imi's flat mates.

So Sharpe and her accompanying police officer commence the necessary business of turning the place inside out. Before they start, the rooms are in a perfect, neat and tidy state, unlike Kit's flat. By the time they're finished they aren't.

"Celina," whispers Emma, as P.C. Blunt rummages in a set of low-level drawers, "look at that lovely arse. I could fancy a man in uniform, couldn't you?"

"I could fancy a man out of his uniform too, as long as he let me hold onto his helmet," Celina whispers in return.

Blunt turns to see what they're up to as the pair fall to flirtatious sniggering.

"I trust we can leave you two girls to tidy up," suggests W.P.C. Sharpe when the search is complete. *'These two sound like they could do with a bit of discipline,'* she decides. "But before we go, girls, I'd like to ask you a few questions. Better here than down at the station, would you say?"

"I suppose so," they each say in turn, Celina echoing Emma, each relinquishing their resistant stance and opening up to questioning.

"That's good, girls. Now from what we can see, Imelda doesn't much get on with men, does she?"

"You can say that again."

"Does she have any boyfriends? We know she gave up Morris dancing, as soon as she found it dominated by men."

"Morris dancing?" says Emma, laughing out loud. Celina nearly pees herself as they both fall to the floor in fits of giggles.

"Yes, Morris dancing. Didn't either of you know about it?"

"Look, you *are* kidding aren't you? She's not sent you round here for a joke has she?"

"No joke I'm afraid, girls."

"In the last year, the only bloke I know that she's been out with," says Emma, "is a surgeon called McMorran from work. But that lasted about as long as a chocolate fireguard... and seemed just as messy."

"Yes, we know about *him*," says P.C. Blunt.

"Oh, and a while before that, there was some mysterious bloke called Sid," says Celina. "That didn't last long either, though we don't know quite why she ditched *him*. Apparently, they did have a blazing row after a few months together and that was it. If his name was ever mentioned afterwards she'd fly into deep fits of irritation, even anger, calling him 'that fat git' and worse."

"To tell the truth," says Emma, "we reckon Imi and Gemma, our other flat mate are an item. You can't prize them apart lately."

"Is this Gemma a Morris dancer?" asks Blunt.

More fits of laughter.

"No way. Imi's the flighty one. She comes up with all the mad ideas. Gem's a calming influence. She'd never be so bonkers."

"You've both been very helpful," says Sharpe, rather disingenuously. "We'll be on our way. Sorry about the mess."

"Isn't it about time you let me out of this place?" complains Imi to P.C. Blunt as he opens the cell door and asks her to escort him to interview room 2.

"Sorry, Miss, but Mr. Fielding wishes to speak with you again," replies Blunt.

Interview room 1 is occupied, this time by W.P.C. Sharpe with a young trainee police constable. Sharpe is questioning a man accused of stealing the crossing wardens' lollipops. He's a local teacher who turns out to be innocent of any wrongdoing. It seems he's fed up with the queues of traffic holding up his homeward journeys after school each day and so is sympathetic to the thief, but the teacher proves to have an alibi for the key dates and times in question.

Harry Fielding is already in room 2, sitting behind the interview desk, drumming his fingers pensively.

"Right. Sit yourself down, Miss Chesterton. P.C. Blunt... you know how to switch that tape machine on, don't you?"

"Yes, sir. Right away, sir."

The usual formalities are performed.

"Now, my dear," says Fielding, rather less patronisingly, not wanting another flood of tears. "We've rushed the blood results through faster than usual and it has to be said that we've drawn yet another a blank. We don't intend to hold you further."

In fact Imi's blood matches that found on Kit's hankies and on the Morris kit recovered from the woods, which only serves to strengthen Harry's conclusion that neither Kit nor Imi had anything to do with the *'Cave-in Skull'* man.

"Oh, thank God," cries Imi, in a flood of relief.

W.P.C. Sharpe offers another paper tissue.

Imi takes the tissue, wipes her eyes once again, and in her relief says, "I should have mentioned before, but I did see a fat bloke in the woods. He came at me in the dark... confronted me, he did."

Fielding pricks up his ears, on the scent afresh.

"It was Sid!" says Imi, her relief now subsiding with the

realisation that D.I. Fielding's investigative flame has been is rekindled.

"You mean the fat git?" says Harry. According to your friend Celina, you had a *boyfriend* called Sid, didn't you?"

"Yes. That's him. He wasn't exactly a *boyfriend*, but he *was* a fat git."

"So what happened in the woods?"

"Nothing. I didn't recognize him at first. He'd really let himself go since I'd last seen him. He looked like he hadn't shaved for days, weeks even, and his clothes were grubby and falling to pieces. I guess he must have been stalking me, found out somehow that I was going to Pockbury and then followed me there. 'Hello, Imi,' he said in a creepy whisper. 'It's been a while hasn't it.' I screamed at him, pushed him out of my path and ran. I thought he was following me at first, but when I looked back in the gloom, he'd stopped in his tracks and just stood still, seeming to be in a trance, staring after me."

"Well, it looks like this Sid is our corpse, but if *you* didn't kill him then we still have a big mystery on our hands."

Fielding takes a deep breath and adds, "Now, Miss Chesterton. I'm inclined to believe you. And with no positive evidence, I'll be looking to let you go. But mark my words... we'll be keeping an eye on you and if you're leading us a merry dance, we'll pounce on you before you know it."

Blunt switches off the tape machine, realising he'd simply pressed the play button, and says nothing.

"Let that bloody surgeon go, will you Blunt," instructs Harry.

Harry Fielding is now getting rather overwhelmed with his responsibilities. Claude Lord's prediction that Parrott would raise his head at the frustrating lack of progress on the '*Skull*' case proves to have been insightful. Harry is no longer *Harry* to the D.C.I.

"Get it sorted Fielding, or heads will roll. And my head's going nowhere, understand?"

"Yes, sir. I'll step up the investigations even more."

And within days, the team is addressing a list provided by *The Pockbury Prancers* of their dancers and those of visiting Morris sides. Harry had placed the list in his drawer and hadn't got around to acting on it due to the pressures of all the other serious crime erupting around him.

Harry decides after all to revisit the contact details of all the residents of Pockbury itself. Now possessing two lists, he has a hundred and twenty-seven prospective suspects, including Morris men from far and wide but excluding children and the residents of a nearby elderly persons' home.

The blood sampling service is overwhelmed by long queues forming for several days at the clinic... what seems like a never-ending succession of addicts awaiting their fixes.

And for all that, when the queues are finally dealt with, and the testing laboratory has caught up with the flood of blood, not *one* match for the blood traces on the '*Skull man*' comes to light.

Two of the Morris men who had been at the village hall on that September night have since gone to live in Europe and prove difficult to find. But those blood results turn out to be irrelevant to Harry's quest too, as do all those for the Pockbury residents.

The desperate D.I. Fielding is now wondering if the village hall dancing took place on the same night as the killing after all and if there may be no link whatsoever between the two.

But then a further, final search of the woods comes up with another find... what looks to be the killer's weapon... a solid ash stick, thirty-three inches long with square cut ends, but splintered and with bloodstains proving to match both strains on the body. The stick, found in a location remote from both the body and the discarded Morris kit, is confirmed to be indeed...

a Morris stick.

"Oh, no," cries Harry in anguish. Surely I don't actually have to *interview* all those bloody Morris men now... and think of all those solicitors turning up at the station."

The intrepid Harry falls to reflecting morosely on his stalling career, wondering what more he can do to re-assert what detecting clout he may have had.

'I bet that ancestor of mine who Parrott referred to would have solved this case by now,' he concludes.

Chapter Twenty

Old Busty

It's five-thirty in the morning, with the promise of a clear September sky and an Indian-summer day. But in the gloom of the council bus depot it's all headlights and diesel fumes as ever when *Chirpy* clocks on after the all-too-brief holiday jaunt.

"Good mornin', *Crabbs*," say *Chirpy*, brighter than ever, as he straps himself afresh into his ticket machine.

"What's good about it, *Chips*?"

"Everything. Our excursion turned out to be brilliant, wouldn't you say? Different to what we expected, but brilliant all the same."

"I dunno about that. It was pretty good I suppose but give me the depot any day. You know where you stand with the depot and our good old council bus. I wouldn't part with her if they paid me."

"But they *do* pay you, *Crabbs*."

"Exactly. That's why I wouldn't part with her."

"Her? You'll be giving her... it, a name next."

"I already have. I've called her *Busty* for years...*Busty the Bus*. That's what I call her. Didn't I ever tell you?"

"No, you didn't. You kept that one quiet. When are you getting married? You'll have to let the traffic lights down gently, you know. Like I said before, Proceed with caution... that's the motto. Don't treat it... her, lightly, mate."

"I wish you wouldn't go on. I just like buses, that's all, and this one in particular. We've been together for so many years, me and *Busty*."

"An' it don't seem a day too long..." sings *Chirpy*. "Anyway, look here. There was a note on my ticket machine from the manager. Here, look... *Jacko* wants to see us in the office, straightaway."

"I hope he don't delay us. We're due on the road in ten

minutes."

"That's as may be, but he said it was important. Could be that they're gonna sack us. Mind you, I don't really care. If they do, then we'll definitely set up on our own. *'Crabby and Chirpy's Cheerful Charabanc Tours'* could definitely become a permanent feature. The name has a ring to it, don't you think? I'd still put *your* name first… after all, it is *me* who's the cheerful one, or so they tell me. *You* can't come between me and *cheerful.*"

"Now then. I'm afraid I have some unfortunate news for you both," says *Jacko*.

"What did I tell you, *Crabbs?*" says *Chirpy* from the corner of his mouth.

"I don't really know how to break this to you," continues *Jacko*, "but your bus has been written off while you were away."

Crabby's jaw drops, incredulous. *'What?'* he mouths silently.

"You see, we had a relief driver in as usual to take over for a few days 'til you returned. Only the agency sent us some duffer and it turned out he had hardly any double-decker experience, especially of city driving. I'm afraid he wasn't up to the job. He didn't know Oxford at all, so he got lost on his first run out and the flaming idiot turned down Rogues' Lane and…"

"Don't tell us," says *Chirpy*, rather un-chirpily. "The low bridge!"

"Oh no! Not the low bridge?" cries *Crabby* in distress. "No, not my precious bus?"

"I'm afraid so. You'll be driving a different bus from now on. At least it's nice and new… well only a month old. In fact it's the only one like it in our fleet. We didn't know, but headquarters have been checking this model out at our supplier's place down in London and apparently they were pretty impressed. We've arranged for them to send us this one as a replacement for that old wreck you've been running, so in a way the agency driver did us all a favour. You should see what it can do... automated this, mechanized that and intuitive the other... It's even got a facility for the driver to collect the fares, but that's for the future. Right now, I'm trusting it to you pair as our most valued and experienced team. The insurers said we can take the old bus to the knacker's yard, next week hopefully, as soon as their assessor has done a proper inspection for the insurance claim. Needless to say, the council's legal team will be pursuing the agency for negligence. The police have interviewed the driver and he's being charged with reckless driving or something like that. When they first got to the scene, they thought it might be manslaughter... they found a severed head that had rolled down the stairs and out onto the pavement. Then they discovered that the only passenger on the upper deck had been a bloke travelling at the front. And would you believe it... he's a ventriloquist. His dummy warned him just in time and he'd managed to duck, but the dummy wasn't so agile and the bridge made short work of it, launching the head like a golf ball down a fairway."

"Blimey, what a turn up," says *Chirpy*.

"But I can't drive it without some training, boss," says *Crabby*. "What with automated, mechanized intui-thingys, I'll be all at sea."

"I hope not. It's not fitted with *lifeboats*, you know," says *Jacko*, trying to make light of the situation, at last realising how upset *Crabby* is. "But anyway, we've rescheduled the timetable this morning so that you can have a crash course on the new bus beforehand. An experienced driver like you will soon get used to it."

"'Crash course? I'd use a different turn of phrase if I were you, Mr. Jackson," says *Chirpy*.

"But where's old *Busty*?" protests *Crabby*.

"Old *who*?" says *Jacko*.

"He means the old bus, Mr. Jackson," explains *Chirpy*.

"Oh, right. It's down the bottom of the yard. You should see what a mess it is. Half the upper deck's ripped off... peeled back like a sardine tin."

And with this, *Crabby* and *Chirpy* make their way out of the building and trudge over to the old bus to pay their last respects, both dejected but *Crabby* the more down in the mouth.

"What am I gonna do, *Chips*?" says *Crabby*. "I can't bear it. I thought I was fed up with drivin' the streets all day, but now I realize all the more that I was born to drive old *Busty*. This heap of modern technology won't be for me, will it. It sounds too sophisticated. I bet it almost drives itself. It's like whoever designed it is cuttin' me balls off."

"It won't be long before buses *can* drive themselves, *Crabbs*. At least for the moment they can't, but they *can* already operate without a conductor, so where does that leave *me* in a few months' time? They're already sharpening the knife for *my* bollocks."

A minute's silence, and they both trudge back into the depot building. The instructor, up with the bus from London, hands *Crabby* the ignition key and shows him the controls. *Crabby* climbs sombrely into the driver's seat. There's not even a separate cab now, and the instructor stands beside him on the front mounting platform. *Chirpy* stands behind the instructor feeling like a spare part at a wedding... or is it a baptism? *Crabby* fires up the new vehicle and prepares for a practice drive around the block. The scrolling information panels on the front and rear of the bus spell out rather prophetically *'Not in Service'*.

Not a happy day for the valiant pair. *'Heads will roll,'* imagines *Chirpy*.

-o-o-o-

"Oh, Gem," bursts out Imi. "It was awful. It looks like that body they found in the woods was Sid and I'm sure they still believe *I* killed him."

"So why do they think it's Sid?"

"I told them I saw him in the woods at Pockbury one night... when I went Morris dancing."

"You went to Pockbury to Morris dance?

"Don't think I told you *everything* about my Morris adventures, Gem."

And so she tells her friend all about her secret stash of videotapes, her trip to Pockbury Village Hall and everything she's told the police about her flirtation with the Morris. Gem listens intently and sympathetically, but she already knows a little more about her companion's brief communion with the dark arts of the Morris than Imi realizes... the secret stash of videotapes weren't as secret as Imi thought.

"But, you *hate* men, Imi. You dump Sid and *Slasher* and between times you think to hook up seriously with the most staunchly 'men' men you can find."

"No. I did hate Sid then I explored the Morris before I went out with *Slasher*. I suppose I was on the rebound after Sid. I went dressed as a man just to try and be 'one of the boys' I suppose. And what a mistake that was. As for McMorran, I don't know why I even thought about going out with him. He's more chauvinistic that a whole clutch of Morris men."

"Well, it's all over now," offers Gem, sympathetically. "The Morris men have gone, *Slasher's* gone and Sid too it seems."

"Sid's gone, alright. I might have hated him, but I wouldn't have wished him dead really, even though I said I'd happily tip him over a cliff. And *Slasher?*... he's still got his bollocks. I do bump into him from time to time when I'm on training sessions at the infirmary. He just stands and gawks at me and then I have flashbacks of Sid in the woods, staring after me."

And with this, Imi breaks down in tears again. Gem puts a loving arm around her and comforts her with a reassuring kiss, as they melt into the sofa together.

"Don't worry, whispers Gem. "I'll look after you. We'll find a new way into the future. Believe me. We can change things for the better... together."

They talk for a while then fall asleep, to be woken at two in the morning by Emma and Celina trundling in from a night on the tiles with their latest choice of Oxford dongs.

The following night, Imi and Gem are together alone again.

"No, I really mean it, Imi," insists Gem.

"But, Gem. We're in the middle of our training. We can't just up sticks and go and live abroad... not for a couple of years at least. We can't just toss away our futures like that."

"So, you'd rather put up with the likes of *Slasher* McMorran would you? If you do, you'll be throwing away your life to save it. What kind of sense does that make?"

"I dunno, Gem. I really don't know."

"Look, Imi. South America is a great opportunity... Brazil for instance. It's a country that's starting to catch up with the world and I've heard that there're new openings for all kinds of medical careers over there. And just picture all that sunshine."

"I know. I can understand all that, but *Brazil*? Going to live in *Blackpool* would be exotic and daunting for me. Especially right now, with all this blokey business."

"But don't you see. All the more reason to go *now*... whilst you need a new direction. I've already made enquiries and it's not as complicated as it sounds. And we could always come back if we didn't like it."

"Look, Gem. I shan't say no, but I'll have to give it some serious thought. Give me a week or two at least."

"Just don't take too long, Imi. The opportunity won't be there forever. The more you get embroiled in this place, the harder you'll find it to break free."

-o-o-o-

Chirpy is standing in the queue for a lunch break meal in the bus depot canteen. It's nearly a week since he and *Crabby* took over the new *'Monster-bus'* as they've come to call it.

"Two portions of shepherd pie with chips and two cups of tea Agnes, please me dear... one's for me and one's for *Crabbs*... he's just parking the bus."

"Right you are, luv. Bread and butter?"

"Oh, yes please, Agnes me dear. I nearly forgot. Got to keep up the energy you know. I'm fair whacked... up and down stairs all morning. I'm not getting any younger you know."

"Tell me about it, luv. I'm glad Seth and me moved into the bungalow earlier in the year. It was after he did himself a permanent in the *Tango*... down at the local *Palais* you know. His hernia's been mended but he daren't strain himself no more. I used to love me dancin' and now all we do of an evenin' is watch telly. He *will* keep sayin' 'I'm just off upstairs to get me pipe' then he gets to the far end of the hall and realizes we ain't got any stairs no more. And I play along with him... it's the only way he'll learn, you know."

"Come along Mrs. Perkins," complains *Jacko* Jackson who's next in line after *Chirpy* in the queue. We've *all* got jobs to go to."

"Look, Mr. Jackson, it may have escaped your notice but *I'm* already *at* my job, so be patient if you don't mind. I'm doin' me best, aren't I. You'll put me in more of a spin than I used to be in on the dance floor with Seth."

"*You* tell him, Agnes old gal," says *Chirpy*, in support of the endearing canteen lady.

She reminds him of his favourite dinner lady from his school days... *she* was always being harangued by the deputy headmaster, old *'Big Bonce Bazza from Bromsgrove'*.

"You deserve a medal for working here, Agnes," says *Chirpy*. "I know *I've* had enough of the place. It's not like the old days any more. We used to have a bit of a laugh, before they thought about bringing in new-fangled buses. And then there's the tighter timetable and new shifts and what have you. These days it's all 'do this and do that and do it now'… nothing but hassle. You can only put the blame on the management, I reckon."

Jacko looks at *Chirpy*, astonished at this uncharacteristic outburst.

"You just be careful, mate. If you don't watch your step you'll be out of here in a flash."

The manager seems to have forgotten that *Chirpy* is one half of 'our most valued and experienced team'.

"To be honest, *Jacko*, I don't give a fig. If I left here tomorrow, the only people I'd miss are my pal *Crabbs* and Agnes here. And me best passengers of course."

"Aah, that's nice, ain't it Mr. Jackson," says Agnes. "Don't you think he's a lovely man?"

"No he bloody well isn't. Talking like that about senior management."

"Actually, *Jacko*, I was talking about junior management, and you know just who *that* means."

"Well, just watch it. If you're looking to be free from all this hassle, it can be arranged you know."

"Piffle," says *Chirpy* as he picks up his heavy tray of meals and turning his back on the manager, heads for the table at the far side of the canteen where *Crabby* has just plonked himself.

"What was all *that* about, *Chirpy*?" asks the driver.

"I was givin' *Jacko* a piece of my mind. He can go and walk on the moon for all I care."

"Hey. Go easy, *Chips*. You might end up out on your ear. *Then* what would you do? In fact what would *I* do? We're an inseparable team aren't we?"

"Indeed we *are*, my dear *Crab-apple*. But you see I have a crafty plan. The way I see it, *I'm* on the way out. We're only gonna get more of these new-fangled buses and they won't need bus conductors will they. So if I can get them to sack me now, I can claim it was constructive. That way I could get redundancy money *and* extra compensation too. I'd be able to claim that they've left me traumatized and unable to work, don't you see? I'm sure I can construct that constructive dismissal."

"But what about *me*, *Chips*? I mean *I* hate the new bus too, but I need the job."

"Ah, well that's where you're wrong. You see, I've had a quiet word with Big Jim and he's agreed to buy the old bus, then *I* can buy it off *him* when I get me redundancy money."

"But it's a wreck,"

"But it ain't, see. Jim reckons he'll be able to buy it for peanuts and he can modify it to convert it to an open-top bus."

"What good is that? It's always chuckin' it down in England. It's all a bit seasonal ain't it?"

"Ah... not everywhere in England's wet you know. From what I can make out, Kent is really quite dry compared with Oxfordshire, especially in the summer. There's lots of tourists come over from France and such like to Kent because it's on the doorstep. I mean, give 'em a Lilo and they'd float across on the tide. And in the winter, we can still use the lower deck... take out and store the upper seats and close off the stairwell and it'd be just like a coach. And *you* could get a taxi for the winter months... *Crabby the Cabby* sounds catchy don't it. And remember I said that '*Crabby and Chirpy's Cheerful Charabanc Tours*' could operate on the continent... well if you think about it, France could come to *us*. And if we *really* wanted to, we could take the bus over on the ferry and do pleasure trips over there too. I mean we're experienced holiday tour operators now aren't we."

"Are there any Morris men living in France?"

"I doubt it… probably no more than there are onion sellers in hooped sweaters and berets riding around England on bicycles. I mean the French don't like the English very much do they, except when we're visiting on holiday and buying stuff off them, but we could win them over with our wonderful holiday tours. I reckon that now we're in the *Common Market* the sky's the limit."

"But the council wouldn't give *me* any redundancy money or compensation. I mean to say, they still need bus drivers, don't they?"

"Well, yes… for the time being, but I can see those driverless buses turning up in the not too distant future."

"Don't be absurd, *Chips*."

"But *I'd* put in all the money, *Crabbs*. And I'd give you an equal share in the business. All *you'd* need to do is drive."

"But what about me old ma and pa. They need me."

"No they don't, mate. The older generation is hard as nails. I mean, *we* grew up through the war, but we were sheltered from it. *They* had to survive it… and that war was a worse conflict than the most conflict-ridden Morris tour. And with all that rationing too, they're used to hardship. Your parents will go on longer than you or me, *Crabbs*. You've got to make your own life in this life, or life ain't worth living."

"I suppose it's tempting, especially if I could be re-united with old *Busty Bus*… well, half of her anyway."
"That's my boy. I'll buy the bus anyway. You can call her *Busted* instead of *Busty* for now."

Chapter Twenty-one

I Did It My Way

When Ida had returned home from the 'Grand Tour' of the Cotswolds, she'd wondered how Bert has been getting on. The district nurse seemed nice enough, but she's young and attractive. In the depths of Ida's mind she'd imagined Bert sweeping the nurse off her *National Health* shoes and dancing her into the sunset to Frank Sinatra singing *I Did It My Way*. She hadn't really thought for a minute that the district nurse might prefer some of her more age-compatible patients. So Ida now has a few regrets about gallivanting around the Cotswolds with *Gabby*. Of course it never enters her head that Albert might be feeling similar anxieties about *Gabby* and *her*.

Mabel next door had promised to pop in occasionally when the nurse wasn't there, and Ida was happier with *her* helping out a bit. The nonagenarian neighbour isn't thought of by Ida as a serious marital threat to Bert and her, and she'd have brought in the coal ready for winter... she's good like that. So, Ida casts her mind back to the day she'd come home from the Cotswolds...

"Cooee. Bert. I'm home. It's me," calls out Ida as she opens the front door.

She extracts her key from the *Yale* and closes the door behind her with her foot. She cocks an ear towards the lounge door at the end of the hall, perceiving the melodic tones of Glenn Miller's *In the Mood*. Placing her small but heavy travelling case in the open space under the stairs, she opens the lounge door, calling as she does.

"I'm back from me holiday. I hope you've been looking after yourself and eating w..."

And there's Bert dancing energetically, in full swing, not with the district nurse but with the landlady from *The Hat and*

Beaver. Realizing Ida is home already he hides cowering behind the ample landlady.

"You little bugger, Bert Hall! What did I tell you about her? Turn that bloody racket off. Now!"

"But I thought you liked Glenn Miller, Ida."

"I do. But I don't want to share him with *her*. And as for *you* madam... sling yer hook. And be quick about it!"

Bert shimmies over to the record player and turns off the music. The landlady grabs her coat from the back of the sofa, picks up her handbag that she'd placed by the fireside scuttle, and scuttling by Ida cautiously, she makes for the front door.

"How *could* you, Bert? I've only been gone a few days and here's you havin' it away with the bane of my life. And I don't even know her name, you little shit."

"But Ida... *I* don't know her name either."

"A likely story."

"I can explain, Ida."

"It'd better be good, Bert."

"Look, Ida. Me leg's behind me now and..."

"Is it, my lad? It's behind you, eh?" Ida scowls impatiently.

"No. No, Ida. I mean it's gone. I feel so much fitter now and I asked her to come round to teach me some new dances. She's really good you know. It was so I could take you to the *Palais* for a special night out. Honest, love. You have to believe me. It's true."

"Let me warn you, Bert. From now on, *my* leg'll be behind you and it'll kick you up the backside if there's any hanky-panky goin' on," snaps Ida. "I suppose you've been goin' up *The Beaver* too, haven't you?"

"Only the once Ida... so that I could persuade her to come and help me."

"Right, then," Ida says, calmer now, thinking maybe she's jumping to conclusions. "I'm sorry I snapped at you, luv, but I *did* warn you about seein' *her*, didn't I. We'll forget it this time, but no more landlady, understand, or I'll be straight round to *Gabby's* for a night of passion. And since you're so fit, go and put the kettle on. I'm parched."

"I will, pet. Straightaway. Then you can tell me all about your little holiday," says Bert, relieved to think that Ida believes his explanation, yet a little put out that she doesn't seem to trust him.

"Oh, by the way, some chap called while you were away, Ida. from *'NASTY'* or whatever place he said it was. He sounded American to me... his accent was just the same as that John Wayne on the pictures."

"Oh no! *N.A.S.A.*, Bert... it was *N.A.S.A.* But hang on a minute?... we haven't got a phone."

"No, Ida. He called at the door. He had a uniform on and he said it was something about chocolate. *Galaxy*... that's it. And he said he was waitin' for someone called Anne. Anne Dromeda... that's who it was. Well, I told him we didn't want any chocolate, but he was very persistent. 'No' he said... 'it's Messier.' 'Well it would be,' I said, 'It's been very warm lately. It *is* chocolate you know.' I couldn't really understand what the heck he was on about."

"Oh no, Bert! He meant Messier 31... The Andromeda galaxy, you idiot. They're finally running out of patience. You really are gonna have to start doin' things again, Bert, so I can get on with my thesis. If you can dance, then you can mow so get your arse into gear... from tomorrow morning."

"Yes, Ida."

"If not, I'm sure I can persuade *N.A.S.A.* to send another man to the moon you know. Anyway, I've got to get cracking on my research piece. I'm off down the central library as soon as can be."

"Yes, Ida."

-o-o-o-

Algernon and Romulus have sobered up after their arduous jaunt and are preparing to part company for the imminent start of their respective Michaelmas terms… Algy staying in Oxford and Romy roaming back to Cambridge.

"Algy, old bean. How, under the stars of Zeus, shall we cope with a whole two months at college before we break up for Christmas? You know, I still can't believe this further education lark needs as much as six months every year. It's no wonder, after the rowing, that there's never any time for shooting and fishing and seeking out girls."

"My, my. I don't know what *your* college is like, Romy, but there's plenty of totty around at Wadham. Quite a relief, literally, after boarding at Winchester, don't you know."

In fact, Algy is having no real success at all in his quest for female companionship.

"Lucky you, Algy. Magdalene still doesn't have women in the place and, after seven years at an all boys' grammar school, it's unfair… indeed it's unbearable. Aphrodite just doesn't get a look in. If I'd have known how much I'd crave women, I'd have gone to a different college."

"You mean *you* had a choice, Romy? *My* A level results meant I only just scraped in, even with a bit of help from pater… he went to Wadham too you see and he's a personal friend of the Senior Assistant Vice-principal. Anyway, surely there must be plenty of girlies at the other Cambridge colleges."

"True, but just try getting them into your room after gates. I had this fling a while back with a girl called Angela who was in the *Footlights*. But that fizzled out before it had started. She was all over me 'til she found that 'back to mine' was an impossibility. I reckon Hephaestus must have fashioned those gates in the fires of Hades to keep his missus Aphrodite safe. Sort of like a cumbersome chastity belt."

"I wish you wouldn't go all Greek on me, Romy. And anyway, I'd have thought with a name like yours you'd have a preference for ancient Rome over ancient Greece."

"I just prefer the Greeks, that's all... far less decadent if you ask me, Algy. Mind you, come to think of it, I could try my hand in the *Footlights* again if they'll have me... plenty of the fairer sex there."

"Wouldn't you be better to put your *feet* in the *foot*lights?" says Algy.

"Very funny, you old teaser. What about you, Algy? What're you gonna fill all your time with for two months?"

"Oh, me? Girls and more girls. Wine and more wine. You name it."

"For myself, I'm into the rowing pretty much now, Algy," continues Romy. "So maybe girls should continue to occupy the back seat... not literally you understand... no female cox for us, thank you. If I apply myself, I imagine I'll be in the eight for the boat race next year, depending on how training goes this winter. Look out Oxford, here I come."

"Like I told you before," says Algy, "water doesn't interest me... unless it has whisky in it, of course. 'Take more double malt with it' is my motto."

"But tell me, what are you actually studying, Algy?"

"*Economics* with elements of *Accountancy*. But I hate it. I would have preferred *Oriental Studies* to tell the truth," says Algy. "Either way, old bean, I could do with more than two months' term time to fit it all in."

"*Oriental Studies* eh?" replies Romy. "So your education is going west rather than to the east."

"Very funny, my man. You must have thought of that by *occident*," quips Algy.

"Oh yes. So *very* funny, Algy. Isn't university education wonderful?"

"Yes. I suppose it is, Romy. Everyone should do it."

Chapter Twenty-two

Fat Tuesday

ALGY & ROMY: In truth, Algernon is sinking into oblivion and his place at college truly *is* 'going west'. Studying is almost non-existent. He attends hardly any lectures and is in grave danger of being sent down. He's not enjoying university life and is on the verge of giving it all up anyway. But if he does he knows his parents will likely disown him and cut off his allowance into the bargain. Despite avoiding water at every opportunity, dear Algy is fated to sink without trace, disinherited by his *Merryweather Towers* parents, dross in the eyes of an unsympathetic world, unwanted like the dead-yeast dregs of discarded wine bottles.

Romy however is going from strength to strength. Before long, his place in the Cambridge rowing eight is secured and he's found succour at last with the principal rower in the women's team who's turned out to be the best female stroke Cambridge, or indeed Romy, has ever known. He's destined for a first-class honours degree and will re-enter the real world to become a well-respected paragon in politics or banking or some such venerated institution, all stemming from his grammar school education.

-o-o-o-

IDA, BERT & BOB: Ida is waiting at her usual bus stop when along comes the new bus driven unenthusiastically by *Crabby*. The bus glides to a stop, but Ida is confused. There's no platform to mount at the back of the bus. *Crabby* hasn't quite got the hang of the entry to the bus being at the front near the driver and has overshot the queue of passengers. Ida follows the rest of the queue for the ten-yard trek to climb aboard.

"Good morning, young man," she says to *Crabby* when all the others have got their tickets and she reaches the driver, "I take it that *Chirpy* is upstairs, is he?"

"No, me dear. He doesn't work here anymore. It's me who you pay now."

"Now that's a real shame. He's such a *nice* man. Arranging that outing too."

"I know," says *Crabby*, more dejected than ever. "I'll be joining him soon, the way things are going. We're sorting out the old bus and we're gonna do holiday trips in Kent, with rides along the coast roads too."

"Well, I never. It'd be nice to work *there*. You know when I was younger, we lived near London for a while and me mum and dad used to take us down to Kent for hop picking in August every year. It was beautiful… the weather was always warm and dry and we used to picnic in the hop gardens. I'd love to visit again one day, so let me know if you have any tickets, won't you. I'll tell me mate *Gabby*. He might be interested to know, too. He'll be sittin' upstairs."

"That's right. He got on at his usual stop. I'll let *Chirpy* know that you're interested when I next see him and he'll put you on our list. You'd better let me have your address for him."

Crabby's mood lightens at this entrepreneurial encounter. He takes the fare from Ida and 'ding-ding' goes the old bell in his mind.

"Mornin' Bob. Dear me, what *is* the world coming to? No back entrance and no conductor," says Ida, after working out the logistics of the upper deck.

"Mornin' Ida," replies *Gabby*. "I know, old gal. I mean, look up there… notices sayin' 'It is preferred that you do not smoke, for the comfort of fellow passengers.' I mean bugger me, Ida."

"But *I'm* not a 'fella' passenger, *Gabby* so you can light up for all *I* care. A man's got to have his pleasures in life, you know."

"To tell the truth, I've been contemplatin' pleasures lately,

Ida and I've joined a paintin' club at the college. Not paintin' and decoratin' mind you. It's one of them proper art class courses."

"What, you mean with nudes and that sort of thing?"

"No, nothin' like that. It's landscapes and still life and respectable portraits. I prefer oils meself, or acrylic. Acrylic is much the same as oil only it's faster dryin'.

"Good for you, *Gabby*."

"I've always wanted to paint a few old masters."

"What? You mean school teachers?"

"No Ida. I mean paintings like that Rembrandt chap did. I've been to the first class and the tutor says I've got it in me. But anyway, how are you gettin' on with your physics thing?"

"I'm starting to get back into it. Apparently *N.A.S.A.* called round while we were on the outing, but Bert didn't understand. Can't blame him really though... I've never told him much about me passion for it. I'm trying to track down the *N.A.S.A.* man because I've come up with a few new ideas. Ideas that could change the way we see the universe."

"That's interestin', Ida, but in the meantime here's a fag."

"Thanks, Bob."

"And how's Bert getting on now, Ida? Is he a bit more mobile?"

"When I got home from our trip, I found him with that woman from *The Hat and Beaver*, I did. He said it was only so she could teach 'im some new dances to enjoy with *me*. But I'm not keen on that sort of thing to tell the truth, so it's alright with me really if he gets his thrills with the landlady from the fiery furnaces of Hell... as long as he gets back to the fiery furnace at the foundry now, to bring in the pennies again."

"Good for you, girl. *You* concentrate on your galaxy thing."

"I will, Bob. Believe you me, I will."

When Ida eventually meets up with the *N.A.S.A.* man, he

introduces himself as the Deputy Assistant Vice-head Commander... almost the head honcho of the whole agency, "You see, ma'am, I've been sent over from Cape Canaveral to explain that we need your Andromeda thesis more urgently now for a space mission that's in an advanced stage of development. There's a conundrum that's baffling all our top scientists and we believe your work will lead them to an answer. We want you to join us in Florida for the foreseeable future."

Now Ida has been hiding her light under a bushel and quite apart from being an accomplished astrophysicist she's a shrewd negotiator. Before long she's landed a long-term position in the *N.A.S.A.* team and three weeks later she's on her way to Florida, all expenses paid. And she never *does* get to visit *Chirpy* and *Crabby* in Hastings.

"Look, Bert. I can't miss out on this opportunity. All my life I've been reaching for the stars and now's my chance to shine. If she'll have your canaries you'll just have to shack up with your landlady, whatever her name is. I'm sure you'll enjoy that. You can be up *The Beaver* permanently, and if she's not exhausted looking after your every terpsichorean need, she can get your *Sportin' Life* for you too."

"But, Ida. You seem a little upset, me dear," says Bert, feigning sad protestation. "I wish there was something I could say to make you change your mind, but I know you have to follow your passion."

He says this with enough conviction for Ida to feel a pang of guilt, but not enough to give her second thoughts. Inside, Bert is high-kicking his heels with the pub prospect and landlady delight before him. He soon finds himself settled into the pub and although he never goes back to the foundry, his landlady insists that he get the coal in as a trade-off for the on-going dancing lessons.

And when Ida's divorce papers come through a couple of

years later, she marries a retired astronaut in Florida and they spend their honeymoon at *Disney World*. At *N.A.S.A.* she's now developing her post-Einsteinian theory that E doesn't $=mc^2$ on Sundays or bank holidays... a potential weft against the warp of time. Her only regret is that she finds it almost impossible to get her hands on a pack of *Woodbines* without importing them to order.

Over time, Ida's friend *Gabby* becomes renowned for his artistic skills, so much so that more than once he's visited by the police investigating some very convincing new 'old masters' that have been reported as forgeries. However, the authorities never manage to pin them on *Gabby*, thanks to an intricate web of deception involving several shadowy fences and an offshore account. In time he's made enough money to buy himself a whole warehouse full of macs, but prefers to stick with just the one he's got, belt and all. He even continues to add to his prolific collection of *Park Drive* cigarette packets.

-o-o-o-

FIELDING, SHARPE & BLUNT: Harry Fielding sits in tears in the restroom sipping hot tea that W.P.C. Sharpe has brought him.

"Tell me all about it, Harry," she says.

"You know, Christine, it's just all so disappointing. Parrott helped me get my promotion and now I'm in the thick of it nothing seems to be going right. The *'Caved-in Skull'* thing is still getting nowhere. The lollipop thefts have started up again and I can't see us ever catching the sneaky felon. And on top of that there's now a spate of thefts of young men's underpants from washing lines in the area."

Harry's sinking fast, likely to go the way of Sergeant Bumble who's still on extended stress-related sick leave.

"I'm never going to get promoted above D.I."

"Don't be daft, Harry. It'll all come good in the end. It always does."

"I'm not so sure. I've just run out of ideas."

"Perhaps I could help a bit more, Harry. *I've* got a few ideas. Not sure if they'll turn anything up, but you never know."

While the W.P.C. has some sympathy with Harry's plight, she's hopeful of promotion herself to D.I. status and so she's being a little devious. It's more likely that anything her ideas turn up will be to the benefit of *her* career, rather than Harry's. But he's naïve enough to give her rein.

Harry Fielding never does solve the case of the 'Caved-in Skull'. In fact, the entire team at Poxford police station are baffled despite their best efforts. Even when *C.I.D.* and *The Home Office* are brought in to review the case, no one can pin it down. The line is drawn at involving *Interpol* and so in due course the degraded corpse is put to rest unceremoniously to make way for a new occupant at the mortuary. The case, like the body, is put to bed, archived to add to the dubious annals of Poxford law and order. Harry never climbs above the rank of D.I. His colleague W.P.C. Sharpe however, rises to become D.C.I. when Parrott retires. P.C. Blunt leaves the force and sets up a security firm that goes on to preside over the most ridiculous lapses in security the banking industry has ever known.

o-o-o-

JANET & JOHN: "I don't believe it, John," says Janet. "How can they pass you over for the deputy headship, now that old Humphrey Harrison's died?"

"I've always said that I wouldn't stand a chance when the old boy retired or fell off his perch, Jan. As I keep telling you, there's a big queue for the head posts and I'm not as far up it as the headmistress is up her own backside."

"She still does yoga then, John? I mean she's well into her sixties... *she* must be up for retirement any time soon, surely?"

"That's not the way it works at the school, Jan. You see she's very flexible."

"Ah, right... I said that you should have taken the yoga more seriously, seeing as how flexibility seems to be the key."

"You know very well what I mean, Janet."

"I do. And I know what *I* mean, John. I'm telling you straight. I won't have our Oxford going to school there. On a matter of principle, I won't. I'd rather he went to Saint Lucifer's than Saint Jude's."

"But there's no such place, Jan."

"Not in Oxford, John. But I'm sure there must be one somewhere. Look, the point I'm trying to make is that life would be unbearable for him at St. Jude's with an emasculated geography teacher of a father in the same building."

"Okay. That's it then, Jan. You're right of course. Enough is enough. We're gonna get that coffee shop of yours and I'm swapping my chalkboard for an apron and a coffee roaster. We'll set things in motion tomorrow. First stop the bank manager. But let's make it somewhere in the villages. Say out Burford way."

Janet smiles. Her dream is about to get a kick-start. She turns to their young son who's playing contentedly on the rug with his building blocks.

"Now then my boy, she says. I have a very important question for you. Would you prefer to go to school in the countryside or in Oxford, Oxford?"

The boy giggles, utters a simple gurgle that Janet and John interpret as 'country slide', and he adds another block to the wobbly edifice he's busy assembling... a construction John now perceives as a coffee shop.

Before the following year is out, the pair are established in their new shop, *Barista Barrington*, which is replete with comfortable arm chairs and a selection of books... some for browsing over extended coffee sessions and others for sale to add to their revenue from the affluent tourist classes. And Oxford is attending a local school... Saint Lucia's."

-o-o-o-

CHIRPY, CRABBY & JIM: By the time the new year comes in, Big Jim has worked wonders on the old bus and she's undergone her re-spray. *Crabby* couldn't wait to get his hands on *Busty* and now there'd be no need for him to call her *Busted*. The paint job is almost complete. The intrepid pair had agreed on a green and cream livery. *'Crabby and Chirpy's Cheerful Charabanc Tours'* is now being emblazoned on the full length of each flank in a shade of orange complemented by gold highlights, all befitting the classic vehicle she's become.

"She'll be ready in good time for the summer, then, Jim?" asks *Chirpy*.

"Of course she will, *Chirpy*. She'll be ready for next week, mate."

"Brilliant, Jim. We shan't need her in earnest 'til the new season in May, but we can tout her around town to drum up bookings. We're looking to operate mainly in the Hastings area. I can see it now... in a few years we'll have a whole fleet of buses. I've managed to get me compensation for unfair dismissal agreed, so we can afford to commit now. Anyway, we *have* to, now that I haven't got a job... The council showed me the door straightaway when I told 'em I'd take them to the European Court for discrimination against bus conductors if I didn't get the terms I'd demanded. I had to sign a gagging order though."

"But you've told *me* now, *Chirpy*."

"That's different... I've had to tell *Crabby*... haven't I, *Crabbs*.

222

And you're family, aren't you. I mean, let's face it... you wouldn't spill the beans on you beloved cousin, would you?"

"Of course I wouldn't, *Chirpy.*"

"And if you did, the first thing I'd do would be to take *you* to the European Court."

"Don't worry, *Chirpy.* I couldn't face the European Court... I've got a morbid fear of foreigners... I mean some of 'em are women."

"Don't let *them* hear you say that, mate."

"What, Europeans or women, *Chirpy?*"

"Both, I suppose... especially European women."

"Right. By the way, how's your application for an operating licence in Hastings going?"

"It's being given final consideration by the council committee later this month, but we've been told unofficially that it's a formality really," explains *Chirpy,* chirpily. "Anyway if *they* refuse us, we'll just set up in Sussex next door to 'em. They wouldn't like that would they... could bring their tourist trade to its knees."

"So how's *Crabby* taking all this?"

"Well, Jim, he's been put on a conductor-less service since I hung up me ticket machine. But he's ready to give in his notice as soon as we've got the permit. He realizes now how much hard work it is collecting fares."

"In some ways, I envy you both, mate," says Jim, wiping his oily hands on an oily rag. "All that Mediterranean sunshine."

"Hang on, Jim... we're only goin' to Kent, mate."

"But it'll be *like* the Mediterranean compared to here, *Chirpy.*"

"I suppose so. Kent, Sussex, even Dorset or Devon... they'd all be warmer than *here,* Jim."

"It all sounds pretty brilliant, *Chirpy.*"

You really *could* join us, you know."

"I know," says Big Jim. "And there's always lots of attractive French girls on holiday in Kent, France bein' just across the

Channel. How cool is that?

"But I thought you said you've got a morbid fear of foreigners, Jim."

"Yeah, but I've been thinkin' about what you've been sayin'. I'd just have to try and get used to 'em."

"Right, Big Jim. I'd say that once me and *Crabby* get established you could bring down the old cream and red coach... it went like a dream on our excursion. I intend for us to expand and we'll need a good mechanic too... *Crabby* knows plenty about the everyday stuff, but not the real nitty-gritty stuff like you do."

"Sounds good to me, *Chirpy*. I really would like that, and my driving ban's finished too. I can see it now... *'Crabby, Chirpy and Big Jim's Cheerful Charabanc Tours'*.

"Hang on, mate. *I'm* supposed to be the cheerful one. *You* can't come between me and *cheerful*."

"Just a figure of speech, *Chirpy*."

"Anyway, Jim... *Busty Bus* isn't long enough for *'Crabby, Chirpy and Big Jim's Cheerful Charabanc Tours'*.

"But I've been worrying about me mum and dad?" *Crabby* chimes in anxiously. "I was relying on *you* to keep an eye on them, Big Jim. Who's gonna help them if you come down south?"

"There's always *Little* Jim, mate. He's still up to it you know," says Big Jim, reassuringly.

And come the end of the month, Hastings council has approved their operation, so final preparations get underway. *Chirpy* gets the bank to look further at his business plan and they approve a supportive loan to add to *Chirpy's* compensation money. The bank manager says he'd be keen to be one of the first to book a trip with *'Crabby and Chirpy's Cheerful Charabanc Tours'*. This enthusiasm may have been brought about by the offer of a *free* trip for the manager and his family... not strictly ethical to accept, but that's some bankers for you.

That following summer proves to be a hot one and the charabanc trips are subscribed to the hilt. In their first year the three valiant bus-keteers are so busy on every day of the week that Big Jim's coach is soon brought into service alongside *Busty Bus*.

Chirpy is full of beans as always and works through all the shifts. He catches naps when he can, sat in his own monogrammed deckchair on the beach. He's brought his beloved motorcycle combo down and rides it along the coast roads whenever he gets the chance. Occasionally he flaunts authority and rides without a helmet, the sea-salt air wafting in his face. *Crabby* has even got over his fear of ice cream and is virtually cured of his traffic light obsession.

They employ a young, blond French lad who'd been looking for a casual summer job having flunked out of Kent University. His English is better than that of any of the three partners and he proves to be a great magnet for younger foreign tourists... especially the girls, who flock to buy seafront pleasure trip tickets just to spend time in close proximity to this tanned, tousle-haired attraction.

In time, *Chirpy* sells the terrace back in Oxford and invests the proceeds in a tidy, tiny seafront cottage. Not a day goes by when he doesn't think of Nettie and Gregory and his boyhood excursions with them.

The team soon establishes an arrangement with a prestigious hotel in the town that offers special deals on bed and board to those clients who also sign up for the longer distance day-tours that take them variously to Canterbury or to Royal Tunbridge Wells or along the coast into Sussex and occasionally into Hampshire.

-o-o-o-

IMI & GEM: At Heathrow airport, the two star-struck lovers sit drinking coffees on the concourse. Over the last few months, Gem has been delving deeper into the whys and wherefores of making the break to South America. It turns out that the Brazilian authorities are looking for medical staff with the particular nascent skills that the two girls are developing and there are real training opportunities for them both. Inch by inch, Gem has addressed Imi's ambivalences and at long last Imi has agreed to make the break to be with her only real friend.

"Rio, here we come, Imi."

"Sure. I'm sorry I've been so slow on the uptake, Gem. I'm really looking forward to it now."

"Roll on Fat Tuesday."

"What?"

"Fat Tuesday... *Mardis Gras*... that's what it means. Get stuffed before Lent, that's the idea."

"I didn't know that."

"There's lots of things we don't know about Brazil, Imi. But we're damned well gonna find out soon enough. How's your Portuguese? Look, that's our plane taxiing out right now. See how it's glistening in the rain. We'll soon be leaving the miserable English downpours behind."

"*I* heard that it's as wet in Rio as it is in Manchester."

"That's right. It *is* as wet as England, but it's nice rain... warm and delicious rain like we get here once in a while in our excuse for a summer. And anyway, you dry out quicker on the beach in Rio."

A year passes and *Mardis Gras* comes around again, descending on the city of Rio in a heady whirl of music and colour. The temperature is hot and the sweat flows as freely as the beer. Nobody can resist this Latino dance of life... men dancing with women, men dancing with men, women dancing with women... no one seems to be dancing alone. Given the freedoms of the intoxicating social scene, there's so much more opportunity here for Imi and Gem to fend off male attentions and to do their own thing. Home from long clammy shifts in the city's principal hospital, they share a sensuous shower, foam-sponging each other down with loving caresses. Refreshed, they dress for the weather in breezy cotton and head out for the balmy, barmy carnival.

Gem looks into Imi's eyes as they stroll arm in arm along the late-evening sandy waterfront seeking out the cool Atlantic breeze.

"Are you glad, Imi? Are you *really* glad that we came?"

"Of course I am, Gem. You were so right. You got me out from under a mountain of men and madness. We're so free here, aren't we. Are *you* glad we're here too?"

"Too right, Imi. I'm as relieved as you are to be free of all that crap that was going on," agrees Gem.

Imi turns to face Gem and strokes her hair with deep penetrating fingers.

"Gem? What's this, here underneath your hair? Good Lord! It's a scar. I've got one similar... here, look. I got mine that night at Pockbury thanks to that mad Kit bloke. How did you get *yours*?"

"Oh, I got mine when I was a kid. I fell of a slide. I'm surprised you haven't noticed it before."

And, as they walk along on the beach, Gem thinks:

'Yeah. I am so relieved... relieved to be away with Imi from all that mayhem of Morris dancers and Slasher McMorran.

I'm so glad that I found out about Imi's little 'secret' dancing practises in the flat and her intended excursion to Pockbury.

When Sid turned up at the flat looking for her, I was foolish enough to mention Pockbury to him, but I'm glad that I followed him there.

It was the best thing I ever did to grab that Morris stick from the back of the village hall, tussle with him and smash the fat git's skull in.'

-o-o-o-

KIT & FRED: "I've had enough of this Morris dancing game, Fred," complains Kit Harbury. "What with the police suspecting me of murdering the man in the woods and *Snakey* Snaith suspecting me of murdering dances when they go wrong. There must be safer ways of enjoying yourself, mustn't there?"

"Well, Kit, you could always join the *Bubonic Fairies' Fan Club*," suggests Fred, genuinely trying to help.

"I'll draw the line before that, thanks very much, Fred."

In fact, both of them continue dancing for many years to come, tolerating the oppressive régime that is *A.B.V. Morris*. It seems there's something far too obsessively fascinating about the pastime; the dervish-like whirling of the dance, the incongruous yet infectious sound of the melodeon, the gentle flagellation with handkerchiefs and the maniacal beating of stick on stick.

In later years, they're dancing at a spot in Pockbury and Kit spies an old boy standing at a distance from the rest of the audience. He's holding an exuberant Rottweiler on the leash. Kit ducks out of the next dance for a breather and sidles over cautiously to the pair.

"Enjoying the dancing, mate?"

"Not as much as the dog is."

"What's his name?"

"Diamond. He's called Diamond. *You* know... 'Like a diamond in the sky.' I had another Rottweiler, way back you know. He was the gentlest dog you ever could wish for. *His* name was Twinkle."

'Yes, I know,' thinks Kit. "Diamond's a lovely name for a

dog," he says to Eric Stotesbury. "It's nice talking with you, mate. Still, I must get back for the next dance."

"Sure thing. I've got to get back myself. It's Diamond's dinnertime," says Eric. "Keep on dancing, mate. It's important that the old traditions are kept alive. We'd have no future without a past, would we now."

Eric and Diamond turn away, head down the lane and take a turn at a footpath sign into Pockbury Woods.

- The End? -

The Characters:

The Characters *(continued)*:

The Characters *(continued)*:

The Villages and Towns:

The Inns and Other Watering Holes:

The Beers:

The Morris Sides:

The Morris Dances:

Glossary of Morris dancing terms referred to herein:

Galley: *(p18)*
A manoeuvre in a Morris dance. *(This involves a neat circular movement of the raised foot. Believed to be a corruption of the word 'gaily' as in 'to turn gaily').*

Half-gip: *(p18)*
A manoeuvre in a Morris dance. *(Or Arthritis creeping in... generally affects dancers aged 18 to 30).*

Whole-gip: *(p18)*
A manoeuvre in a Morris dance. *(Or Arthritis crept in... generally affects dancers aged 31 to 105).*

Tankard: *(p22)*
A vessel for containing *(or spilling)* the beer of Morris dancers. *(See also 'Half-gip' and 'Whole-gip' for examples of the cause of spillage).*

Foreman/woman: *(p22)*
The one, usually a dancer, who teaches the dances and sometimes chooses the dances that the Squire thinks *he* chooses. *(A bit like a head teacher dealing with the teachers).*

Molly or Moll: *(p22)*
A Morris man who's supposed to be a woman. *(Apparently?).* Mollycoddle is an extension of the term 'Molly' *(As in: to buy the Molly a beer whenever he (or she?) asks for it. See also 'Rounds').* Molly House *(a brothel)* is also an extension of the term 'Molly' *(Nothing to do with Morris dancing - hopefully).*

Molly dancers: *(p22)*
These perform an unsophisticated form of Morris, usually with handkerchiefs. *(Invariably by unsophisticated dancers).*

Glossary of Morris dancing terms referred to herein *(cont'd)*:

Morris Side: *(p23)*
The formal name for a troupe or team of Morris dancers. *(Not to be confused with a 'set'. Most Cotswold Morris dances involve a 'set' of six or eight men involving two sides, so a 'Side' puts up a 'set' of dancers with a left side and a right side. Simple).*

Squire: *(p23)*
The dancer who is supposed to be in charge of the choice of dances and which dancers are to dance each one. *(Like a football manager controlled by the club owner rather more than he suspects).*

Fool: *(p24)*
A member of some Morris sides who plays frivolous with the audience *(usually the only sane member of the side.)*

Bagman/woman: *(p24)*
The one responsible, especially when things go wrong, for the planning of tours and communications with other Morris sides. *(A bit like a teacher being dealt with by the head teacher. The term 'Bagwoman' should not be confused with the term 'Bag Lady').*

Foot up: *(p26)*
A manoeuvre in a Morris dance. *(Or, when a dance goes wrong).*

Cotswold Morris: *(p27)*
A sophisticated form of Morris dancing with handkerchief, stick and handclapping dances. *(Invariably performed by unsophisticated dancers).*

Glossary of Morris dancing terms referred to herein *(cont'd)*:

Chancellor: *(p31)*
The one who is in charge of the money and deals with the accounts. *(Including the use of the unfathomable category called 'sundries'… a bit like some M.P.s).*

Baldricks: *(p31)*
An item of Morris attire. *(Everyone knows what this means. Sometimes expressed as: %>&*<£^$!).*

Bell-pad: *(p31)*
An item of Morris attire. *(Or a Morris dancer's home where the dining room is given over to making, maintaining and, on rare occasions, ironing kit).*

Sidestepping: *(p33)*
A deft move involving the usual stepping, but with a move to the left, then to the right or vice versa. Particularly useful when avoiding paying at the bar *(see also Rounds).*

The Morris Tradition(s): *(p73)*
The sum total of Morris dances, dance tunes, kit and customs collected through the years and drawn upon, or bastardized, by latter-day Morris sides and their musicians. *(Some would use the word fabricated rather than bastardized).*

Rounds: *(p75)*
A manoeuvre in a Morris dance. *(Occasionally a dancer buys a 'round' at the bar).*

Glossary of Morris dancing terms referred to herein *(cont'd)*:

Hey: *(p76)*

A *whole*-hey is a manoeuvre in a Morris dance. *(Or a cry heard when someone spills the beer of a Morris dancer.)* A half-hey: is also a manoeuvre in a Morris dance. *(Or a cry heard when someone spills half the beer of a Morris dancer).*

Single stepping: *(p148)*

A simple form of stepping. *(Often too complicated for simple Morris dancers).*

Double stepping: *(p149)*

A more complex form of stepping, involving a hop on alternate feet. *(Always too complicated for simple Morris dancers and often too complicated for complex Morris dancers).*

Glossary of Morris dancing terms *not* referred to herein:

Border Morris:
A wild, heathen form of Morris, usually involving the blacking of faces as disguise. *(The disguise being useful should the audience get 'Bored o' Morris'. No one knows whether or not these dancers are sophisticated).*

Clog dancing:
Dancing, mostly from the north-west, *(Not to be confused with clod dancing, which involves dancing in ploughed fields of heavy clay, often by Molly dancers).*

Lally gags:
Molly dancers' ribbons tied around each leg below the knee. *(To stop rats getting at the dancers' higher attributes. See also baldricks).*

Rapper Sword dancing:
Dancing, mostly from the north-east, with flexible double-handled 'sweat-scraper' swords. *(Rapper dances are wrapped in mystery and the audience can sometimes become wrapped in misery).*

Long Sword dancing:
Dancing, also mostly from the north-east, with rigid single-handled swords. *(The dances can also be long, when the audience can sometimes also become wrapped in misery).*

Tanker:
A vessel for containing *(or spilling)* the beer of a whole side of Morris dancers. *(See also Tankard).*

Printed in Great Britain
by Amazon